Family Happiness

Also by Laurie Colwin

Family
Happiness

a novel by

LAURIE COLWIN

Harper & Row, Publishers, New York
Grand Rapids, Philadelphia, St. Louis, San Francisco
London, Singapore, Sydney, Tokyo, Toronto

First PERENNIAL LIBRARY edition published 1990.

Library of Congress Cataloging-in-Publication Data
Colwin, Laurie.
    Family happiness / Laurie Colwin.
      p. cm.
    ISBN 0-06-097272-6
    I. Title.
    PS3553.04783F3   1990   89-45641
    813'.54—dc20

90 91 92 93 94 FG 10 9 8 7 6 5 4 3 2 1

to J. J.

*"God setteth the solitary in families;
He bringeth out those which are bound
with chains; but the rebellious live in
a dry land."*

PSALM 68, VERSE 6

PART ONE

One

Polly Solo-Miller Demarest was the perfect flower of the Solo-Miller family. This family had everything: looks, brains, money, a strong, fortified sense of clan, and branches in Boston, Philadelphia, and New York, as well as London, just like a banking house. The patriarch of the New York gang was Henry Solo-Miller, husband of the former Constanzia Hendricks, nicknamed Wendy. Both were of old, old Jewish families, the sort that are more identifiably old American than Jewish. Solo-Millers and Hendrickses had come from Holland via Spain before the American Revolution, which they had either taken part in or helped to raise money for. Henry and Wendy had three children: Paul, Dora (called Polly by everyone), and Henry, Jr.

Polly was sandwiched between difficult brothers. Paul, a lawyer like his father, had always been mute, preoccupied, and cranky. He was said to be brilliant, but he was so silent that no one had ever really heard him say a brilliant thing. He was forty-three, unmarried, as greatly respected in the legal community as his distinguished father, and a passionate music lover. Henry, Jr., on the other hand, was a lout. He had refused to pursue the normal Solo-Miller and Hendricks occupations—law and banking—and had instead pursued his boyhood adoration of all things aerodynamic and become an aeronautical engineer. He had married Andreya Fillo, a fellow engineer, the daughter of Czech refugees. She and Henry, Jr., behaved more like brother and sister than like a married couple. They wore each other's clothes, did not plan to have children, played with their dog, and dedicated themselves to kite-flying. Henry, Jr.'s large, smelly tickhound, Kirby, was their child substitute and, like his master, he had resisted proper training.

It was Polly who had made grandparents of her parents. She was married to a big, handsome lawyer named Henry Demarest and had produced two nice, sturdy children: Pete, nine, and Dee-Dee, whose real name was Claire, seven and a half. These children were doted on by their grandparents, who never displayed to them the eccentricities they had displayed to their own children.

Henry, Sr., dwelt in what Polly called "the realm of the higher mind." This meant that often he was not fully present. He was a rather silent man who was set in his ways the way Rembrandts are hung on a wall—with great care, correctness, and dignity—but he was funny about food and believed that everything, from vegetables to standing ribs of beef, should be washed with soap and water before cooking, and that all eggs were to be scrubbed before being boiled. For a prank, Polly, as a teen-ager, had once put a chicken into the washing machine.

As a result of these crotchets Henry, Sr., was lied to constantly. He ate happily anything that was put before him as long as someone first assured him that everything had been grown in certifiably organic soil and washed in soap and water. The pollution of the atmosphere was one of his most beloved subjects.

Wendy never got anything right. For years she had called poor Douglas Stern "Derwood," and now everyone, including his own family, called him that. She did not actually refer to Pablo Picasso as Carlos—Polly claimed she did—but she came close. It was a family joke that Polly had married a lawyer named Henry in order not to give her mother anything to screw up.

In general, the Solo-Millers preferred the company of their fellow Solo-Millers to that of other mortals, and they gathered frequently. Every Sunday they appeared at Henry and Wendy's at noon for a meal that some people would call lunch and others brunch. The Solo-Millers called it breakfast.

The household Polly had set up with Henry Demarest was very much like her parents'. This made perfect sense: Henry, who came from a Chicago family rather like the Solo-Millers, shared Polly's feelings about comfort, order, and the way life should be lived. They believed in harmony, generosity, and good works. As a lawyer, Henry was very well respected. He sat on the board of Pete and Dee-Dee's school; he was a Fellow of The American College of Trial Lawyers and a trustee of the school he had gone to as a boy in Chicago.

Polly had a job, too. She was Coordinator of Research in Reading Projects and Methods for the information arm of the Board of Education. That all children learn to read was Polly's cause and it was her job to evaluate the stream of new methods, texts, and tests that poured in to the Board. This job combined some of the things Polly held most dear—service, children, and books—but for all that she was committed to it, she did not talk about it very often. Occasionally a truly crackpot reading manual would cross her desk and she would bring it home to show Henry, but otherwise she left her work at work. She felt that methods of teaching reading were chiefly of interest to other reading technicians, whereas the law was a large subject of general interest.

Polly was good at her job, good at games; and she was also a marvelous cook and housekeeper. She was neither oafish and slobby like her brother Henry, nor finicky and allergic to most common substances like her brother Paul. She had been a remarkably sweet-tempered child and as a girl had mediated any fights between Paul and Henry that had looked as if they might end up in fratricide. Those squabbles had been Paul and Henry, Jr.'s only close contact. Now they met only at family gatherings, although Polly saw both of them frequently.

She had graduated near the top of her class at a fine woman's college (which was Wendy's alma mater), had studied in France for a year, come home and worked as a reading teacher at a private school, married Henry Demarest, gotten a degree in reading education, taught in the public schools, produced Pete and Dee-Dee, and then found herself a high-level job. She was at her office three days a week, and at home on Mondays and Fridays. This, she felt, left her plenty of time for everything—to run the house, to spend time with Pete and Dee-Dee, and to be a helpmeet and sweetheart to her husband.

In addition, she was her mother's favorite lunch companion and a great social asset. Polly was a good listener. She could bring the shy forward or placate the arrogant and hostile. Furthermore, she was always happy to provide something scrumptious for dessert. She had never given anyone the slightest pause. Her family doted on her, but no one felt it was necessary to pay much attention to someone as sturdy, upright, cheerful, and kind as she.

. . .

Sunday mornings always found Henry Demarest lolling in bed, and Polly in the kitchen making pancakes in the shape of spiders, bats, and snakes for her children. Polly loved Sunday mornings. She liked to have everyone at home, and she liked to look out her window and not see traffic on Park Avenue. She liked to watch families come trooping out from under their building marquees and walk off toward Central Park.

Every Sunday morning, more or less at nine-thirty, the telephone rang.

"Hello, darling. It's your poor mother," Wendy would say.

"Hi, Mum," Polly always said. "How many for breakfast?" Because of complicated legal schedules, and because Henry, Jr., and Andreya were sometimes called away to work on special projects, the number of people at Sunday breakfast changed from week to week. "We're all here this morning. Just a second. Pete, you may not use *all* that maple syrup. Sorry, Mum. Who's coming?"

"Your brother Paul is not for breakfast," Wendy said. "He was supposed to be, but he won't be."

"Why won't he?"

"He sent us an express letter," Wendy said. "Emergency meeting in Paris." Paul's field was international taxation, and he was away quite a bit. "Of course Henry and Andreya will come with that ghastly fleabag of theirs. I do wish you could speak to them, Polly. The dog upsets your father so."

"Mother, Daddy hasn't noticed that dog for three years. It's you who can't stand it."

"That isn't true," Wendy, who knew it was true, said in a hurt voice.

"Daddy never notices things like that and you know it," Polly said. She had the telephone crooked under her chin to leave her hands free. On Sunday mornings, Pete and Dee-Dee took turns standing on a chair next to the stove to pour out batter for their father's pancakes. They did not feel it appropriate to give their father bats or snakes or spiders, so they made the ordinary kind, to which Polly always added some chopped pecans. They had finished their pancakes and were taking turns standing at the stove to pour out batter from a small ladle.

"Your father is more sensitive to these things than you imagine," Wendy said.

"I didn't say he was insensitive, Mummy. I said he didn't notice, and he doesn't."

"Well, never mind," Wendy said. "Darling, is that nice bakery near you open on Sunday?" Wendy would ask every week.

"It's open till one," Polly always answered.

"Then would it be too awful for you to stop and get a loaf of that Swiss peasant bread your father is so mad for?"

Polly said it was not a bit of trouble—it was never a bit of trouble. Besides, she had gotten it the day before and wrapped it in a linen towel to keep it fresh. The bakery also made the *pain au chocolat* Wendy adored, and when Polly made her forays to get the Swiss peasant bread, she always got *pain au chocolat* for her mother.

Wendy's telephone call on Sunday was a ritual, like the Swiss peasant bread and the *pain au chocolat*. So were the pancakes, and the pecans in Henry's pancakes, and the fact that the children cooked Henry's pancakes. On Sundays Henry got his breakfast in bed. He worked a tough, hard week, and on Saturdays, if he was not forced to work, he took the children off on expeditions to the zoo, to a museum, or out to a fancy French restaurant for lunch. He said he was training his children to be good luncheon companions for his old age. He and Polly believed that children should learn to dine, which meant tasting new things and behaving at the table. At these lunches they were allowed to have a little wine in their water.

And since every Sunday—if he was not away—found him at the Solo-Millers', Polly felt that his real breakfast should be brought to him, so that he might stay in bed, rest, and read the papers.

Polly did not ever expect to be waited on. She only worked three days a week, and though her job was demanding, too, it was not so demanding as Henry's. She was given breakfast in bed on her birthday, on her wedding anniversary, and on the children's birthdays, since she was their mother.

All the Solo-Millers were big and good-looking. Polly, who had clear gray eyes, thick, ash-colored hair, and creamy shoulders, had married a good-looking man. The sight of him surrounded by bed pillows, warm and sleepy in his striped pajamas, his dark, wavy hair uncombed, and a look of contentment on his face, usually gave Polly heart's ease. Henry Demarest was not unlike members of her family. Like Henry, Sr., and Paul, he was passionately committed to his work. Polly was used to an air of abstraction in men. She had grown up with a father who did not notice a good many things, such as squabbles, sibling rivalry, and teen-age confusion. Paul's means of expressing the higher mind was silence and austerity. His intelligence was legend, so that his mere presence was sufficient and he made few social efforts. As for Henry, Jr., no one else had much interest in aerodynamics, but he talked it at them nonetheless. Henry Demarest, on the other hand, was not austere, was interesting on the subject of his work, and was capable of noticing everything. But when the pressure of his work overtook his spirit and mind, he was not fully present either, and closely resembled Henry Solo-Miller, Sr.

. . .

"Pete and Dee-Dee," Polly said, "set the tray for your daddy. I'm going to take him his pancakes and you two can play till we go to breakfast."

"If we just had breakfast, how come we're going to have more breakfast?" said Pete, who asked this question every week.

"It isn't really breakfast," Polly said. "It's lunch."

"Then how come Nan and Papa call it breakfast?" Dee-Dee said.

"Because they do. It's their first meal of the day, and breakfast means to break the fast." She handed Dee-Dee a napkin and watched her fold it carefully.

"What fast?" Dee-Dee said.

"Fast is what it's called when you don't eat," Polly said. "Bring the plate over here so I can get these pancakes on it. Pete, you pour the coffee and, Dee-Dee, pour the milk *very carefully* into that little jug. Okay, thank you very much. Now, git!"

Henry was asleep when Polly appeared with the tray. She put it on the reading table and closed the window—Henry liked to sleep with the window open all night, and in the morning, once Polly was out of bed and off to make the coffee, he liked to hog all the pillows and take all the bedclothes for himself. It was November and the air was very chill. Polly smoothed the quilt over him and kissed him on the forehead. He had dark, wavy hair and hazel eyes. His features were regular and fine, and somewhat old-fashioned. He opened his eyes and stretched.

"Good morning, darling," Polly said. "Here's your tray. I'll go and see if the paper is here."

The paper had been delivered and was lying in the foyer by the elevator. As Polly walked down the long hallway to the bedroom, she heard Pete and Dee-Dee playing in Pete's room. They had invented an elaborate game called Cows and Hedgehogs which incorporated their favorite animals. Dee-Dee had been brought up on English children's books and craved a live hedgehog more than anything in the world. She felt it unfair that she lived in a country to which they were not native, and to compensate she was given hedgehogs made of every possible material. Many of them had been sent to her by Henry's sister, Eva Demarest Forbes, who was married to an English banker and lived in London. She had been Polly's roommate at college.

Polly felt fortunate in her children. She and Henry actively adored them but they were not spoiled. They fought as siblings will, but they really did love each other. Pete's main goal in life was to scare his little sister, but she was afraid of nothing, while Pete was skittish about a variety of animals and objects. Because Dee-Dee was kind, she often pretended to be scared, since this made Pete feel braver. Never, when the family went to Maine for the summer, did she put snakes or worms or spiders, which she did not mind picking up, down the back of his shirt.

She and Pete were being brought up under the old order, which required that parents inspire all manner of good habits in their children. If parents sat quietly and patiently with children to supervise their play, excellent study habits would flower from the seed of a long attention span. Games that fired their imaginations were encouraged—playing with clay, for instance. Wendy had once given Dee-Dee all her old perfume bottles, and with these Dee-Dee and Pete spent hours making processions. The time you spent with children paid off, Polly knew. It was on this account that her mother was fiercely against her having a job. Wendy, who conveniently forgot all the civic projects she had worked on during Polly's childhood, remembered herself as a sacrificial mother and felt that Polly should do as Wendy misremembered herself doing. The first time Pete had gone to stay overnight at a friend's, Wendy had become alarmed.

"You are farming your children out," she said. "I never did that to you and your brothers. You were not brought up to farm your children out."

Polly had then recounted for her mother the hundreds of times she and Paul and Henry, Jr., had gone to visit friends.

"They came here," Wendy said. "But you never went there."

In her unreconstructed heart of hearts, Wendy did not believe that women should work. When she thought of working women she thought of the lingerie fitters at Saks Fifth Avenue or the heads of large cosmetics companies such as Madame Rubinstein. Among her friends were some quite distinguished women: a prominent pediatrician, the head of the Society for Legal Aid to Orphans. Wendy herself sat on several committees having to do with abandoned, abused, and otherwise homeless children. She believed that a mother's having a paying career harmed young children, but volunteering was quite another thing. You could spend hours at it and harm no one. This, Polly said, was "Wendy's logic." Wendy understood jobs that were glamorous or noble or involved power and intellect, but Coordinator of Research in Reading Projects and Methods—Polly's job—stumped her. And besides, Polly's salary was not crucial: she did not need to work for money, as less fortunate people did.

Polly put the paper down on the bed and riffled through it. She and Henry split the Sunday paper equitably. The sections she liked best were the sections he liked least. They sat reading in silence.

"How were the pancakes?" Polly asked.

"Terrific," said Henry.

"There's one left. Are you going to eat it?"

"No," said Henry. "You eat it." Polly leaned over and speared it with the fork. If she had been alone she would have eaten it with her hands.

"Who's coming today?" Henry asked.

"Paul isn't," said Polly.

"Too bad." Henry liked Paul. "But the astronauts are coming, aren't they?"

Henry did not mind his brother-in-law and sister-in-law, but he did not understand why adults would want to be so underdeveloped. Henry and Andreya, when not wearing each other's clothes, liked to wear clothes that matched. Polly thought they looked like a pair of those ornamental salt and pepper shakers that are made in the shapes of Scottish terriers wearing tams, or of smiling tomatoes with hands and feet.

They seemed happiest in the company of their dog, or with Pete and Dee-Dee, who Henry Demarest felt were their rightful friends. Each Sunday when the weather was good, Henry, Jr., and Andreya took the children kite-flying. This meant that Henry Demarest could read happily under a tree, or talk to his father-in-law, until the children were brought to him.

"They're coming, and they're taking the children kite-flying," Polly said. "They'll bring a kite for you, if you like."

"If they'll take the children, I'll take some work with me," Henry said. "I'm so jammed that anything I get done helps. Any interesting others coming?"

"Mum said yesterday that Henry said something about somebody but she thought she might have gotten it wrong."

"Typical Wendy," Henry said.

Polly and Henry were so right for each other, so unified in their feelings about life, family, and children, and, in addition to loving each other, were so terribly fond of each other that Polly hardly knew when she had first noticed her relief if a conversation with Henry went smoothly. They were not the sort of couple who fought, nor did they bicker or argue. Mostly they discussed things, and there had never been a serious fracture between them. Their few disagreements were the sort well-matched people have.

Henry was having a bad time in his professional life. He loved his work; he was patient and dogged, but he expected results. One big anti-trust case was not going well; another was on appeal. These cases had dragged on and on, and when they came to no satisfactory end, Henry was first furious, then frustrated, and then dark. In the past year Polly had noticed how much oxygen in the atmosphere of home Henry's job used up. Had he always been so moody? So unresponsive? So snappish? So abstracted? So preoccupied?

Polly had grown up in a household in which a father's work was paramount. It was not easy to be the child of a distinguished parent, Polly thought, but it certainly taught a girl her place. In Polly's household, Henry's job was not so much paramount as catered to. Polly had two occupations: her real job and her job of lightening her husband's darkness, if she could. She could not get incompetent judges off the bench, or dig up expert witnesses, or ease the burden of document research, but she could make Henry's home a happy fortress. That, she felt, was her true skill, and if Henry did not particularly notice his well-run and happy fortress these days, he would when the pressure was off him, Polly felt. If he had to be asked whether his pancakes were all right, instead of spontaneously thanking Polly for them, he must at least find consolation in having a loving wife to sweeten his morning. It was hard to be angry at a man as fine as Henry for what Polly considered second-rate complaints. Her goal was to be good and forgiving—that was the mission of people with level and happy temperaments, as her mother had often reminded her. And as the only member of her family who was not moody, quirky, or willful, she had had plenty of practice.

The Solo-Millers dressed for Sunday breakfast. This meant that you could not show up in your old blue jeans, and in the days when Polly had gone for a Sunday-morning ride in Central Park, she was made to change out of her riding clothes and into a skirt. She had spent hours of her adult life wondering what a child could wear that would be formal enough for breakfast and rugged enough to be played in. Polly hated the sight of a child dressed up. She remembered her own childhood clothes as scratchy—Wendy believed that in public a child should look starched. Polly's children were taken to their grandparents' wearing corduroy, and she had insisted that Dee-Dee be permitted to wear trousers.

"Your father will have a fit," said Wendy. Henry, Sr., of course, cared chiefly that his grandchildren did not shout; he hated a shouting child. But on this point Wendy was right: he did not like to see girls in trousers. Andreya was an exception. She did not own a skirt and there was nothing to be done about it.

"I can't think why you want your daughter to look like a hooligan at breakfast," Wendy said.

"I don't want her to have to sit for forty minutes feeling strangled by her clothes," Polly said. "Besides, they're mostly not at the table. They're mostly playing in the park. Why should she have to worry about getting her nice dresses dirty?"

"Modern life!" Wendy said. "I just don't understand it. Everyone wants to look like everyone else. This notion of being *casual*. No sense of decorum or occasion."

Polly favored soft, old, sober clothes. She usually wore to her mother's a cashmere sweater and a tweed skirt. She wore her old blue jeans only in Maine, where that was acceptable dress, and even then, her father flinched a little. "Going around looking like a fright" was his description of the appearance of most young people.

Polly finished browsing through the paper and took Henry's tray into the kitchen. Henry roused himself and went to shower and shave. It was time to get the children dressed and to make sure all their cows and hedgehogs were put away.

"Is Papa going to say about the food?" Dee-Dee asked.

"Yes, darling," said Polly.

"Is he going to say how the eggs are *very, very* old?"

"Yes, darling," Polly said.

"Is Uncle Paul going to be there?" asked Pete.

"No."

"What about Uncle Henry and Andreya?"

"They're coming and they're taking you kite-flying after lunch."

"Goody-goody," said Pete. "Is Kirby coming?"

"Certainly Kirby is coming," said Polly.

"Ma," Dee-Dee said, "will you and Daddy get us a dog?"

"No, for the ten thousandth time," said Polly. "If you get a dog, I will end up having to walk it. You can have a dog when you're sixteen. Now, please go wash your hands and put on your clean corduroy pants."

By eleven-thirty the children were dressed, Henry was shaving, the beds were made, and the Demarests were ready to go. Polly, who was always ready first, sat in the living room, which was speckled with silvery November light.

Her living room resembled her parents', or her Demarest in-laws'. The old Turkish rug was from a Demarest grandmother. The walnut side table had been Wendy's mother's. The two big black vases flanking the fireplace had been made by Henry's sister, Eva, who, in addition to illustrating children's books, was a potter. The sofa was big enough for all four Demarests to plop onto of a winter's night to watch the fire. At each of the three windows was a table that held a flowering orange tree in a big terra-cotta pot. Polly and her mother disagreed about house plants. Wendy hated them and felt only fresh flowers belonged in the house, but Polly loved flowering plants. The children had a hanging pot of jasmine in each of their rooms. In Polly and Henry's bedroom were two pots of sweet bouvardia. In Henry's study was a long copper tray of African violets.

It would have been lovely to stay home, but Polly had never stayed home on a Sunday except when the children had been infants and Sunday breakfast had been briefly transferred to the Demarests'.

Both Polly and Henry had been brought up on tradition. The Solo-Miller family met not only for Sunday breakfast. They observed two Jewish holidays: Passover and Yom Kippur, the latter being the only occasion on which the family made an appearance at synagogue. The ancientness and austereness of this day had a great appeal for Henry, Sr., although Polly could never imagine her father atoning for anything. At Passover they had their own idiosyncratic Seder at which Henry, Sr., delivered himself of a lecture on the meaning of the holiday and its relevance to the American spirit. They celebrated Christmas and Easter as secular holidays, with Christmas trees and Easter baskets. In addition to these and Thanksgiving, they gathered on April Fool's, which was observed by a meal that had almonds in every course for reasons lost in the mists of Solo-Miller history; and on March the twenty-fourth, Henry and Wendy's wedding anniversary, for a simple dinner—soup and Cornish pasties, cake with sugar flowers, champagne, cheek-to-cheek dancing on the living-room rug to the songs of Henry and Wendy's youth. Halloween was always celebrated at the Demarests': Henry, when he was not away, produced a meal of stew served out of a large pumpkin. Nowadays the whole family trooped off to Pete and Dee-Dee's school for their Halloween pageant, and then back to the Demarests' for dinner.

Everyone took part in these occasions. In the summer, Henry and Wendy spent two months at the family house in Maine, on Priory Lagoon—now that Henry, Sr., was a partner emeritus in his firm, he took the entire summer off. Pete and Dee-Dee spent the summers with their grandparents until Henry and Polly, who rented the same house down the road each year for August, arrived. Henry and Andreya liked to hike. They appeared with Kirby and a tent and camped in the woods. Paul came to stay with his parents for a week and swam each morning in the cold, cold water. It was the only time Polly ever saw her older brother wearing anything besides a business suit.

During August, assorted aunts and uncles and cousins showed up. The Philadelphia Solo-Millers, Uncle Billy and Aunt Ada, summered in Priory, too. Henry's sister, Eva, her English husband, Roger Forbes, and their two daughters, Rosie and Theodora, came to America every other summer and accompanied the Demarest seniors to Maine for a week.

Such felicity in family matters is as rare as hen's teeth, as everyone who admired, envied, or disliked the Solo-Millers knew.

Two

Nothing had deviated on the Solo-Miller Sunday breakfast table for as long as anyone could remember. They ate in the dining room, with extra leaves in the table. It was one of Henry, Sr.'s beliefs that a generous amount of elbow room was an aid to digestion and that the American stomach had been wrecked by cramped eating spaces.

At each place was a juice glass, a coffee cup, and one of Wendy's breakfast plates, which were decorated with pheasants and cornflowers. All juice was squeezed fresh: Henry, Sr., believed that harmful metals leached into juice from cans, and also that liquid must never come into contact with paraffin, as in waxed cartons. The whole family backed him on this point, and everyone was happy to take turns squeezing oranges and grapefruits in the old-fashioned squeezer. There were heavy white plates of smoked salmon, silver baskets of toast points, dishes of capers, lemon slices and scallions, and a cobalt-blue dish of niçoise olives. There were covered dishes of poached eggs and sautéed chicken livers. At Wendy's end was the silver coffee service, which fascinated the children because the sugar tongs were in the shape of eagles' claws, and the finials on the coffeepot and sugar bowl were eagles' heads.

The children were briefly settled in the library, while Henry Demarest and Henry, Sr., sat in the living room to chat. Polly followed her mother into the kitchen. Since Polly and Henry were always prompt, and everyone else was always late, this gave Polly time alone with her mother, who was always in somewhat of a fuss. Wendy particularly fussed about the coffee. She was not very good about mechanical things, and thus she had chosen what Polly considered to be the most complicated method of making coffee. Wendy had been using a Silex for years. Its two glass globes confounded her. She did not really understand how the water from the bottom globe was driven up to the coffee in the top globe, and then how it dripped back down, but she stuck by it.

"Darling," said Wendy to Polly, "this damned Silex doesn't work." She stood behind the huge kitchen table wearing a tweed dress with a white apron over it. The kitchen was big and old-fashioned, with glass-fronted cupboards to the ceilings, an old marble sink, and a scullery. Wendy was the shortest member of the family but she presented herself as if she were tall. She had short, thick, curly gray hair, beautifully cut, and Polly's clear gray eyes and beautiful teeth. She wished she were stately-looking but instead she was pretty.

"It never works," Polly said. "It hasn't worked for twenty years. You need an advanced engineering degree to use it. Why don't you get a nice easy pot that uses a filter and filter paper?"

"I can't fiddle with those papers," Wendy said. "They're too confusing."

"They make better coffee," said Polly, sitting down. "They're idiot-proof."

"Well, your poor mother isn't idiot-proof," said Wendy. "I'm very hurt that you think I make terrible coffee."

"I didn't say terrible," said Polly. "Filters are easier, that's all."

"Your father loves his Silex," Wendy said. "*I'm* not hurt that you think the coffee is so awful. If you can't bear it, bring a Thermos. Oh, dear, where did I put that little wooden cutting board? I can't find anything this morning."

Once the cutting board was found, and everything else Wendy had misplaced, Polly and Wendy sat down at the kitchen table to talk. Polly was not allowed to help on Sundays, so she poured herself a little glass of juice and watched Wendy slice a cucumber paper-thin. At this juncture, Wendy launched into one of her favorite subjects.

"Have you been down to Henry and Andreya's loft recently?"

"I was there for dinner last week. I'm sure I told you," Polly said. Henry and Andreya's loft was in a dicey part of town, and Polly was the only family member who ever went to visit, usually when Henry Demarest was away on business.

"I don't understand why he and Andreya want to live in such a dingy place," Wendy said. "Darling, hand me that bunch of dill. It's in the bottom of the icebox wrapped in a napkin. When you went for dinner last time, what did they give you? I think of them as eaters, but not cooks." She chopped the dill on a large cutting board.

"Oh, some sort of vegetable mess," Polly said. "Their loft is really very nice. You and Daddy only went when they were still fixing it up. It's very white and clean."

"Your father doesn't like going into that building through a row of trash cans," Wendy said. "And, to tell you the truth, those awful dirty stairs upset me."

"They're clean now," Polly said. "They washed them down and painted them with mauve deck paint."

"You know, they sold some of Grandpa's furniture," Wendy said. She arranged the cucumber on a heavy white plate. "Those lovely American Empire pieces."

"They got an awfully lovely price," Polly said. The sale of the Empire furniture was a favorite topic. "They bought some gorgeous French chairs made out of metal pipes."

"I just don't understand," Wendy said. "Those wonderful chairs with the rams' heads. For a bunch of metal wires."

"Mum, they hated the rams' heads. They asked us if we wanted them, but we have Grandpa's two chairs, and the desk and the sofa in the study. That's quite enough rams. I told them to sell it. They love their metal chairs, and if you and Daddy weren't so fidgety and went down there, you'd see how chic everything looks."

"They want everything to look like an airplane," Wendy said. "Your brother, I must say, has always been a mystery to me. Sometimes I feel I gave birth to a changeling."

Polly made a mental note to remember this phrase.

Henry, Jr., was the identifiable rebel of the family. He had fought long and hard, with Polly's help, to go to engineering school: the Solo-Millers did not know any engineers and did not know what sort of people they were.

All he had ever wanted in life was to build model airplanes, fly kites, and play baseball. As a child, when not at school, he had worn a baseball cap, blue jeans, a sweat shirt, and a pair of black sneakers that tied up at the ankles. He carried around a slide rule and a pack of baseball cards. Although he was not silent like his older brother, Paul, whom he treated as you might treat the door of your closet if you felt some hostility toward it, no one knew much what he was talking about. His topics were sports, math, and all aspects of flying. Since he was not a little gentleman, he often came home from school with a skinned knee or a black eye. As soon as he was old enough to do without supervision, he began spending all his time in Central Park playing baseball, flying kites, and trying to get into fights.

When angry he liked to sulk, and he spent many hours in his room streamlining kites or annoying everyone by running the motors of his model airplanes.

At engineering school Henry met a girl who might have been his twin, and he married her. His wife, Andreya, looked rather like him. She had red cheeks, blue eyes, and crisp, wavy hair. They had eloped, taking Henry's dog, Kirby, with them. As a child Henry had been deprived of a dog, and Kirby, Polly felt, was his revenge.

It had been unclear to the family for some time just how comfortable with the English language Andreya was. She had come from Czechoslovakia at the age of twelve, and Polly pointed out that she had gone to high school, college, and engineering school in America, but Andreya was quiet, and her bright eyes seemed full of the strain you see in people who are struggling to understand what is said to them.

For instance, Andreya was a vegetarian, but she had never said a word about it. For a long time Wendy had thought there was something wrong with her—for example, a nervous disorder that might cause her to try to starve herself to death. A lovely plate of vegetables could easily have been provided for her, had anyone known. Once the nature of her diet was discovered, a lovely plate of vegetables *was* provided for her and no one felt the slightest alarm when she turned down the roast beef or leg of lamb.

As a couple, Henry and Andreya were of what Polly called "the psychic-twin school." They did not talk much but seemed to understand each other perfectly. Polly felt that algebra or trigonometry was their real means of communication. She knew that Andreya had taught Henry some phrases in her native Czech. He could say, "I worship you," "No, no, little mouse," "Unhand me, viper," "Don't cry, little fish," and a great many oaths and curses, his favorite of which was "Fuck the horse, you dirty bastard." Polly knew that he would eventually teach this phrase to his niece and nephew, although he swore to Polly that he would wait until they were teen-agers.

"I'm sure he and Andreya are perfectly well matched," Wendy went on. "I just wish it was in a way I understood better."

"People aren't always happy in the way that you're happy, Mum."

"I know that," Wendy said. "I just don't see why."

Wendy did not approve of privitistic marriages—partnerships of temperament or ones in which idiosyncratic needs were met. Marriage was social. A family spilled into society. Wendy was dynastic and marriage was a dynastic institution. Andreya and Henry looked more to her like perfect tennis partners than a couple who might present her with a new series of Solo-Millers. She could not incorporate Andreya's family into the family at large. Polly accused Wendy of expecting Andreya's parents to turn up in their national costume, but they were in fact a team of doctors in California, extremely nice and rather formal. At Christmastime they sent a letter to Henry and Wendy, and a basket of red grapefruits. On rare occasions they came to New York and had dinner with the entire family. Wendy was not used to such arrangements. In her day, families merged when a couple got married. A family was expandable, a chain reaction. Polly and Henry Demarest were a perfect example of this, but then Wendy had always considered her reliable Polly a perfect example of a great many things.

As soon as the plates were arranged, the bread cut for

toast, the coffee started, and the table set, the front door opened, and Henry and Andreya appeared with Kirby. This animal was grayish blue with liver-colored spots and short, bristly hair. Henry claimed he was a Bluetick Hound, but actually he was a mix of Springer spaniel, pointer, tickhound, and retriever. Kirby exhibited every trait Wendy found unattractive in dogs. He slurped when he ate and he ate prodigiously. He made awful noises as he drank his water and always spilled it. His attitude at Sunday breakfast was that of an aggressive beggar, doubtless because in his home setting he was denied the sight of human beings eating chicken livers or smoked salmon. He could not be shut up in the kitchen, since he made such heart-piercing whimpers. He made a high screeching noise when he yawned.

He could not be given one of the oversized dog biscuits he loved because he slavered crumbs all over Wendy's rugs, and his cowhide bone made him drool. Henry, Jr., had not trained him to behave in any particular way in a house, although out of doors he obeyed any and every command concerning streets, traffic, and heeling. After an initial period of jumping on Wendy and making himself unpleasant about the scent of the smoked salmon, he generally flopped under the table, rested his head on Andreya's foot, and waited for whatever she might feed him.

Andreya had feelings about dogs. Her vegetarianism was an outgrowth of her belief that all animals had souls. She had confided this to Polly one evening, and when Polly told Henry Demarest he said, "Why doesn't she feel that beets and celery have just as much right to a soul?" Andreya believed that she and Kirby communed in a mystical, inter-species way, and she could deprive him of nothing. It was well known that she fed him salmon on toast points under the table. This made Wendy somewhat frantic but she was forced to keep silent. Andreya could be spoken *about*, but she could not be spoken *to*. Her sweet, slightly bashful European reserve made Wendy nervous.

"Hi, guys," said Henry, Jr., to his family. "Get down, Kirby." Kirby was unaccountably drawn to Wendy and he liked to jump up and try to put his paws on her shoulders. He had just been taken for a run in the park, and his wet, dirty paws were full of shredded leaves. Henry and Andreya never wore coats, no matter how cold it was. They wore wool jackets, and their cheeks were blazing from their walk.

"Make Kenny behave," Wendy said. "Good morning, darling and Andreya." She kissed her son and daughter-in-law. Henry, Sr., clasped his son's shoulder. Their shoulders bumped for an instant. This was their embrace.

Everyone trooped into the dining room. Kirby padded in after them and collapsed under Andreya's chair. As usual, the conversation began with Henry, Sr.'s disapproving of the smoked salmon. Pete and Dee-Dee sat politely still, with evil grins on their faces. Kirby was their lunch entertainment. If they took off their shoes he could be counted on to edge toward them and tickle their feet by sniffing at their socks.

"It is the exact equivalent of cigarette smoking," Henry, Sr., began, referring to the salmon. "Polly, I don't understand how you can let Pete and Dee-Dee near it."

"Daddy, this salmon is very lightly smoked," said Polly. "Mother and I have been all over the city to comparison-shop. This is not only the most lightly smoked, but the most lightly cured. It's barely been smoked at all."

"That's even worse," said Henry, Sr. "Fish flesh is the ideal breeding ground for parasites. At least smoking kills them."

"Yes, Daddy," said Polly. "But this salmon is adequately smoked, although not oversmoked."

"And washed in pure soap and water," mumbled Henry, Jr., but his mouth was already full and no one heard him.

"I, of course, would revise this entire menu," Henry, Sr., said. "I worry about you eating such very old, unfertilized, dead eggs." He had been saying this for years but nothing had ever changed. At *his* place was a little plate of goat's-milk cheese, the kind that is wrapped up in vine leaves. This he spread on toast points, and watched with disapproval while the rest of the family tucked into the smoked salmon and ancient eggs he considered so dangerous.

The big mahogany dining-room table sat twenty with its leaves in. Without, it sat twelve. There was plenty of room for silverware, elbows, and fidgety children. Wendy poured out the coffee, ever mindful that Kirby was being fed under the table. It was hard to dislike Kirby, because he was comical, but Wendy had always felt that dogs belonged in the country, at the homes of others, and should be let free to wander in pastures and fields. In the city they collected fleas and dirt and other unpleasant things on their paws and then brought these paws into contact with one's rugs.

Every Sunday she attempted to catch Henry, Jr.'s eye so that he might somehow discourage Andreya from feeding Kirby under the table, but this never worked. Henry had an enormous appetite and, once eating, concentrated on little else. He would start as soon as he sat down, and he bolted his food. He was now doing something else Wendy found objectionable. He and Polly called it "building a sandwich." They liked to put layer upon layer upon layer of things on a toast point and then eat it in two bites. Wendy, Henry, Sr., and Paul found this disgusting. Polly adored it. In the privacy of her own kitchen she built sandwiches out of the most idiosyncratic ingredients and ate them in two bites, too. Henry Demarest liked a big sandwich, and whole pieces of toast were provided for him. He watched as the sandwich Henry, Jr., was building began to wobble. For an instant it looked as if the whole thing might pitch into his lap. Kirby, ever alert to these potential windfalls, had gotten up under the table. His head rested hopefully on Henry, Jr.'s knee and his tail swished back and forth against Polly's shins.

Now that everyone was seated, the conversation officially began. Usually the table divided into the legal half and the silent half, but Henry Demarest and Henry, Sr., had had their legal discussion, and, of course, Paul was away. The table was quieter without Paul, although he usually got through a meal saying little more than "yes" or "no" or "quite," his favorite expression of noncommittal response. His mere presence gave weight and depth to the legal aspect of the table.

"Where is Paul, anyway?" Henry, Jr., asked.

"He's at the Conference on International Limits," Henry, Sr., said.

"La Conférence des Frontières Internationales," said Wendy, who loved to speak French whenever possible. "I wish Pete and Dee-Dee would start languages."

"They have started," Polly said. "But they barely speak their own language."

"They speak beautifully," Wendy said. "*You* children started languages young."

"I didn't," said Henry, Jr. "Pete and Dee-Dee speak everything better than me."

"Than I," said Polly. She looked at her children, who sat through this conversation trying not to giggle: she correctly suspected that Kirby was trying to lick their ankles.

"I let Andreya do the speaking," said Henry, Jr., of his mostly mute wife. "She speaks every language under the sun." Andreya spoke Czech, German, Russian, and French, but no one had ever heard her say very much of anything in any of these.

"Pol," said Henry, Jr., "pass me the butter. Pass me the toast. Never mind. It's all on your side anyway. Build me a sandwich, will you?"

Polly built his sandwich and then passed the silver toast basket to her children.

"Don't grab, darling," she said to Pete. "When something is passed to you, you take it gently."

"I am a woolly beast," said Pete.

"Even a woolly beast can take a piece of toast without grabbing."

"No, they can't," Pete said. "They have huge, hairy paws." He turned to his sister. "Woolly, woolly, woolly," he growled. Dee-Dee shrieked and gave her brother a soft punch on the side.

"That's enough, you two," said Henry Demarest. "Finish your sandwiches and then off to the library." He turned to Wendy. "Does anything need to be rearranged in there?"

"I cleared away the breakables," Wendy said.

"Woolly, woolly, woolly," growled Pete.

"Enough," said Polly, but she said it sweetly. She could not deny that she loved it when her children got slightly out of hand. They were allowed to bring any toys they liked with them on Sunday and they might take all of the cushions off the chairs and sofas in the library to make forts. Breakfast was rather a bore for them, but it was good training for their later life. They finished their milk and retreated upstairs to the library muttering, "Woolly, woolly, woolly," under their breath.

Meanwhile, a conversation about the future of the aerospace industry had erupted. Henry, Sr., and Henry Demarest pondered the economic issues. Henry, Jr., launched into a speech on a theoretical point. Like most of his speeches—which were not frequent—this one involved the quoting of equations, a signal for Wendy to say, "Darling, no writing on the tablecloth." Henry, Jr., had once actually done this, and Wendy had always been thankful that he had used pencil, not pen.

Henry, Sr., then spoke about the eroding of the ozone layer and the conflict between industrialism and the right of a citizen not to be poisoned by his environment. Polly called this speech and others like it "The History of Pollution," since Henry, Sr., liked to give examples from the past, such as the blighting of the rye crop in medieval France and the spoiling of rural England during the Industrial Revolution. The spoiling of rural England was one of his most cherished topics. He found English agricultural history restful and read in it constantly.

"The common darnel weed was virtually lost in the twelfth century to the fouling of rivers and streams," he said. "It is now extremely rare."

During this recitation, Andreya had arranged her plate of salmon, tomato, onion, toast, and capers as if it were a still life done by a Japanese master. She did not eat salmon herself. She put it on her plate in order to feed it to Kirby. The family was used to her customary silence, but she was so bright-looking, so full of health and sparkle, that she did not look like a quiet or shy person. She smiled when everyone else smiled, and laughed when they all laughed, and no one except Polly felt guilty about not drawing her out.

Polly had tender feelings toward Andreya—the sort of feelings you might have for a woodland creature. Polly wished she could talk to Andreya, but she had no idea what she might say. This confused her, since Polly was generally good with the odd, the shy, and the mute.

This morning Andreya suddenly decided to talk to Polly, next to whom she always sat. She drew her chair a little closer to Polly's.

"Salmon is a pale pink when it is poached," she said. "Why is it so very red when it is smoked? I cannot understand this."

Polly confessed that she had often wondered the same thing and had never been able to figure it out.

"I am noticing these things," said Andreya. "The yolk of an egg is greenish when boiled, while fried they are golden. When green beans are quickly steamed they are very green but too long steamed they become the color of army clothes. What is the name of this color?"

"Olive or drab," said Polly. She was overcome: this was one of the longest sustained conversations she had ever had with Andreya.

"I find that fish is becoming whiter when cooked," Andreya continued. "For this reason I find cooking so interesting."

"I love to cook," said Polly. "But when you cook all the time for four people the object is getting it done. I often forget how beautiful vegetables are. Carrots, for instance."

"Oh, carrots," said Andreya. "They are so beautiful with their leafy tops. And when you cut them they have rings inside like a tree. I am so very fond of root vegetables." She pronounced "vegetables" with a hard *g* and all its syllables. "I when little was taught to make vegetable flowers—roses out of cabbage and so on. Have you ever done this?" Polly shook her head no. "But," Andreya said, "I remember when you made the barnyard lunch for Dee-Dee's birthday. When you had pigs made of eggs dipped in beetroot juice and a pig yard made of spinach and a little fence of fried potatoes. That was an enchantment. It made me feel my girlhood once more." She paused to slip Kirby a piece of toast. "I am always sad that we do not eat the leafy part of the carrot, as the tops are so nice to look at. I often long to see rice growing in its natural state. Have you seen this?"

Polly said she had not, and silence fell between them.

Down at the other end of the table, the three Henrys had returned to their debate about pure air, citizens' rights, and the aerospace industry.

"Citizens," Henry, Jr., said. "They just want to get from place to place fastest, so who cares?"

"The fact is that some people don't want to get from place to place fastest," said Henry Demarest. "And they are worried that what is being ruined can never be reclaimed."

"The idea of balance is an entirely modern one," said Henry, Sr., "based as it is on a confrontation with forces our forebears could not have imagined."

Polly watched as Andreya made herself a sandwich. The result looked like a corner of a Mondrian painting. Andreya was neat as a kitten. She turned to Polly again. Her eyes were brilliantly intense and she spoke as if revealing a secret. "There are blue fruits," she said. "But there are no blue vegetables. Why is this?"

Before Polly could attempt to deal with this question, Wendy, who believed that talk at the table must be shared by all, decided, as she decided every Sunday, to break up the legal half of the table in behalf of general conversation. During baseball season this was not necessary, since all her children, plus Henry Demarest and even Andreya, loved the sport.

"Polly," she said, "when we had lunch last week, didn't we bump into that nice friend of Henry, Jr.'s—Bill Fredrich?"

"Tom," said Polly and Henry, Jr., at the same time. Tom Fredrich had been a friend of Henry, Jr.'s since college.

"I said, 'Tom,' didn't I?" Wendy asked.

"You said 'Bill,'" said Henry, Jr.

"Well, I think of him as Bill but I always mean to say 'Tom.' He's one of your kite-flyers, isn't he?"

Henry, Jr.'s other topics of conversation included kite-flying, where his car had broken down, what was wrong with it, and taking the dog to the vet.

"We don't like Tom anymore," Henry, Jr., said. "We think he's nuts. He took us kite-flying at his parents' house in the country. He bought himself a very expensive kite which wouldn't fly and he got furious because our cheap little kite did. When his kite got caught in a tree, he got his father's twenty-two and shot it."

"My goodness," Wendy said. "Isn't that terribly dangerous?"

"Not unless you happen to be in the tree with the kite," said Henry Demarest.

Wendy also believed that each person must have his or her say. This was difficult in the case of Paul, whose silence was hard and glistening, like chrome. But even Paul made a speech from time to time, and when he did, all at the table sat quietly. Polly said that her hands automatically folded whenever her older brother began to speak.

Polly had always wondered if no one ever asked her anything about herself—she was mostly asked about her children or about Henry when he was away—because she was just a girl, and she had concluded that the answer was no. It was that she was so level, so organized, so normal, so firm in her routine. Besides, her job was not really interesting to anyone at the table. Wendy really could not keep straight what she did. She said she could remember "lawyer" and "professor" and even "aeronautical engineer," but she claimed she should not be expected to remember "Coordinator of Research in Reading Projects and Methods." She referred to Polly's place of work as "your little office," although she was not without pride that Polly worked for the betterment of society through education. And, of course, Polly was knowable—it was one of her charms. She was open and straightforward and generally full of conversation. It was her job to give attention, not to be the center of it. She looked at her mother, who was about to hold forth on foreign-language training for young children. Polly stood up.

"Well, you all," she said, "I've got another of those awful reading seminars downtown and I must dash."

"Oh, darling," Wendy said, "must you? You've barely gotten here."

"I must," said Polly. "I'm seeing you for lunch tomorrow anyway, Mum, so you'll have tons of me. These seminars are boring but invaluable, I'm afraid."

She went around the table kissing everyone good-bye. She loved the way her family smelled, even Henry, Jr., who smelled of baby soap. She kissed her husband on the top of his fragrant head. "Henry, don't let the children eat another thing until I get home except for a glass of milk and a cookie at four. I'll be home by six. At five-thirty take the brown crock out of the fridge and put it into the oven. It's veal stew. The lettuce is washed. All you have to do is make the salad dressing. Good-bye, everybody."

When she went into the library to kiss her children, she found them crumpled in a heap, fast asleep on the couch pillows. The sight of them brought her almost to tears. She was so lucky to have them. That she had actually produced these beings was a constant source of wonderment to her. And they were so *good*, and so kind to each other. They had fallen asleep like a pair of puppies.

Polly felt rather exhausted herself. In the elevator, she was careful not to reveal to the elevator man, who had known her since she was a teen-ager, her intense relief.

Three

At precisely three-thirty Polly stood at a pay telephone several blocks from her parents'. She dialed a number, hung up, and dialed again. It was her signal. The person on the other end picked up instantly.

"Yellow Dog."

"Hello, Linky," said Polly. "It's only me." Link was Lincoln Bennett. He was a painter, and to Polly's initial confusion and constant pain, she found herself in love with him. They had been having a love affair, after negotiating having one, for several months. He was her secret treasure and her secret friend.

"Only you, huh?" Lincoln said. "I kept getting telephone calls all day long, none of which were only you, if only they were. Are you at a pay telephone or is traffic now being routed through your parents' study?"

"Pay phone," said Polly.

"Well, get down here, girl. I can't bear it another minute."

"Okay, Linky. I'm on my way."

"And how did you manage this time, beautiful darling?" Lincoln said.

"I'm afraid I used the fictitious-seminar ploy again."

"It's a good thing no one understands what you do for a living," Lincoln said. "I hope you copped me some leftover salmon."

"I tried."

"Get down here, Dottie. Your poor friend requires you."

Lincoln was the only person who called Polly by her given name of Dora. He called her any number of things as well—he made them up as he went along—all corruptions of Dora: Doe, Dottie, Dorrit, Doreen, and Dot, and on the telephone, Yellow Dog. Lincoln was not given to nicknaming or being nicknamed. No one but Polly had ever called him Linky. He was not particularly whimsical, and this fountain of strange endearments surprised even him. His feelings for Polly brought it out, he knew. Polly was the truest, safest, and most loving person he had ever known, and he felt entirely free to say even the stupidest thing to her.

Lincoln was exactly Polly's age. They had been born in the same hospital a week apart. It was Lincoln's theory that their infant cribs had been side by side and that they had been imprinted on each other.

Paul, Henry, Jr., and Lincoln had all gone to the same school, and the Solo-Millers were not unknown to Lincoln. He had been in their house several times, as a child and as a young man. Now that he was a painter, and generally thought to be a very fine one, attempts had been made by Wendy to collect Lincoln: he himself was very collectible and Wendy knew that he came from such a nice family. But Lincoln was not much of a fan of families in general, and in specific he found the Solo-Millers rather antipathetic. He disliked the idea of a family front. He found the Solo-Millers, with the exception of his beloved one, smug, thrilled with themselves, self-enclosed, and so secure in the superiority they radiated that it was hard not to feel that their goal was to make other people feel inferior, less handsome, less well behaved, and certainly less contented in their family life. Most people admired the Solo-Millers; Lincoln did not. What others admired as their strength, cohesiveness, and family felicity, Lincoln saw as snootiness, snobbery, repression, and plain luck. But other people felt the Solo-Millers were exempt from mortal status, and the fact that Wendy was scatty, that Henry, Sr., was aloof and somewhat cracked, that Paul was a stick, and Henry, Jr., an ape, only made them more appealing.

Lincoln felt that they did not properly appreciate their remarkable Polly. Polly was different. Catering to those quirky temperaments had made her mild and kind, sensible and tenderhearted.

Lincoln had had a spectacular show—the show at which Polly had met him—and Wendy was anxious to get him to one of her parties. One met so few painters, and he was after all a friend of Henry, Jr.'s. Besides, Wendy knew his nice aunt Louise. "That Leonard Barton," she would say, and Polly had often quoted this to Lincoln, "so attractive and so well behaved, for a painter."

Lincoln had been a prodigy. Now he was a lone wolf. His talent had manifested itself when he was very young, and he had been carefully encouraged. It had never occurred to him that he would make a living painting, so he had gone to college first and then to art school. In his late twenties, when he found himself spending weeks alone without talking to anyone, he began to panic. Surely he was meant to share his nest. He had grown up in a relaxed, casual household. Now his parents had retired to the country. His brother, Gus, and sister-in-law, Violet, were both architects. They had a daughter, Daphne, who was five, a dog, and a Persian cat.

His childhood had been a normal one, and his parents had given him freedom and encouragement. Furthermore, his parents were happily married, as were Gus and Violet. He could not account for his need for solitude. He knew this need to be excessive, but only when he was alone did he feel really comfortable and authentically himself. The fact that art requires solitude did not console him. The older he got, the less able he felt to deal in the real world—the world in which people socialized, went to parties, fell in love, and got married.

Lincoln was not a heartbreaker. He knew he wanted love, but he did not see how he could successfully get it, and he was uncomfortable with the conventional methods of finding it. Everyone was settling down around him. One day he had fallen in love with a girl named Audrey Warren. He and Audrey had gotten engaged and set up housekeeping together. It was a disaster for Lincoln. Domesticity rubbed against him like a hair shirt. How he could be so much in love and so miserable at the same time amazed him. It seemed overwhelmingly clear to him that he could not live with another person, and this made him feel unknown to himself. Audrey said his problem was psychological and had suggested to Lincoln that he go and talk to a psychiatrist. Dutifully he went, to a cultivated, sympathetic old Italian psychoanalyst who saw him twice a week. In the course of a year he learned a great deal about himself, and he came to see that his need to be alone was at the bottom of everything about him. He saw it as a problem: after all, he had the heart of a faithful husband.

The rest of him did not feel at all complicated. He felt that he was moving through a dense thicket of psychological vegetation and that if he cut it all down with a machete, he would still be left with his problem: that he needed love but could not bear to live constantly with another person. He and Audrey arranged to be together on weekends. For a while this worked very nicely, but what Audrey wanted was to be married to Lincoln. When it was clear this would never occur, she left him.

Lincoln had taken it stoically. He deserved to have Audrey leave, since he could not change enough to get her to stay. He felt that he had not been made for the chaos and tumult of early adulthood—of romance and mating and nest-building and childrearing. He had been born to be in his early seventies: peaceful, wise, and immersed in slow, painstaking work. In the meantime, he thought it would be immoral for him to have a social life. He did not want to fall in love or to be fallen in love with, since it led to such disappointment and pain. He was not interested in anything casual—he was not a bounder or a flirt—and eventually he got used to being lonely. He felt that since he was looking for love, he should stay by himself, lest he actually find it.

Polly was the answer to his prayers. Her marriage made everything possible. He had love and he had solitude, both guaranteed. He never had to wish that Polly would leave. She *had* to leave.

Lincoln's studio was on a little side street in a row of studios that had been built for artists in the 1920s. On the other side of the street were warehouses. It was impossible to walk down this street without coming upon a homeless cat. Some of the cats were feral and raced away. Some were lonely and followed you, throwing themselves against your legs and crying mournfully. These lonely cats brought Polly almost to tears. They reminded her of herself: so willing, so hungry for love.

Lincoln was waiting at the door for her. Seeing him, Polly realized, felt the same as coming home might to a sailor after a long voyage. She did not mean to feel this way but it was undeniable to her that she did. She saw him and her heart turned over. Once she had divided the world into the sort of women who had love affairs and the sort of women who did not. But now she, a woman who did not, did, and with considerable expertise. In her gravest moments she gritted her teeth and said to herself, "I deserve this."

"Hi, Linky," she said.

He took her into his arms and kissed her all over her cold cheeks.

"I am a woolly beast," Polly said.

"You are the most gorgeous, swell person that ever lived," Lincoln said. "Get your coat off. Where's my salmon?"

Polly took a sandwich wrapped in thick waxed paper from her handbag.

"That's not Solo-Miller salmon," Lincoln said. "That's from the delicatessen, isn't it?"

"Oh, Linky, I tried."

"I was only teasing, Doe."

"Next time," said Polly, "I'm going to make up a huge sandwich, wrap it in my napkin, and stick it into my bag—right in front of everyone. When they ask what I'm doing, I'll say: At these seminars I perform the miracle of the loaves and the fishes. This one sandwich is going to feed forty reading technicians."

"They'd never ask," said Lincoln.

"Probably, they wouldn't," said Polly. "That's the bliss of it. I never even have to lie. Nobody ever asks me what I do."

"Well, come over here, Dora," said Lincoln. "Put your arms around me and tell me everything you've thought or felt since Friday." He held her close. "I really do love you to pieces."

"I love you to pieces, too," said Polly. "Isn't it sad?"

Polly and Lincoln had met once the year before, at a group show that included a series of his landscapes in oil, and then again at Lincoln's one-man show the first week in September. Of course, they had met, long ago, as children.

Henry, Jr., and Andreya had taken Polly out for an evening when Henry Demarest was away on business. Their friend Lincoln Bennett was having a one-man show and they took Polly to it, since she had been so entranced by the group show they had taken her to. She had just come back from Maine.

At the gallery, Polly put her glasses on. She was slightly nearsighted but Henry, Sr., believed that unless you were almost blind, spectacles weakened the eye muscles. Polly had always worn her glasses on the sly and still felt sneaky about it.

The show consisted of portraits and still lifes, all oil on paper. They were all so beautiful that she was glad Henry and Andreya did not feel obliged to stick with her. She wanted to react privately to these pictures.

She realized, as she moved from picture to picture, that Lincoln Bennett had been in the back of her mind since she had met him in the spring. She had had an impulse to send him a letter—a fan letter—and she had composed it over and over in her mind but had never written it. She had thought of him as she had sent the children off to their grandparents in Maine for the summer, and as Henry's schedule invaded the time they had set aside to be alone together in June and July.

She had found herself reflecting on every scrap of information Henry, Jr., and Andreya had given her about Lincoln—chiefly that he was antisocial and that he lived alone in his studio. She imagined a studio. She imagined being constantly alone. She remembered the pictures from the show and wondered what sort of person would have painted them.

That August Henry had spent his Maine vacation on the telephone. It was impossible to be angry with him: his holiday was being spoiled, too. Polly was used to canceling appointments, juggling dates, and having to turn up at the last minute by herself. She was used to being by herself, after all, even when Henry was around. What, she had wondered, would it be like never to have to switch anything in behalf of anyone?

To be in a room full of Lincoln's paintings gave Polly a sense of intimacy with him, and she wanted to savor it. She suddenly realized that she had been thinking about Lincoln all summer long, more or less unconsciously. A little shiver of guilt went through her: she did not believe it right to think, consciously or unconsciously, about someone who had no connection to you.

But of course, she told herself, it was not Lincoln she had been thinking about, but clean, lean lives of solitude and work—Henry and Andreya had told her how very solitary Lincoln was and that Lincoln had been through some awful time or other (awful times were not in Henry, Jr.'s emotional range, so he could not imagine what would cause one) and had painted in white for a year. The past year they had hardly seen Lincoln at all. He had begun to paint in color again. The paintings in the group show, and this one-man show, were the result. They were not like anything Polly had ever seen and she wanted one fiercely.

Henry and Andreya caught up with her. "Look," said Henry. "There's Lincoln." Polly looked around and saw him at once: a tall, well-made man with an unsmiling boyish face, and a thick shock of straight hair that fell onto his forehead. He had a big, pouty mouth and, when he smiled, a crooked grin. He was wearing the sort of clothes an Irish fisherman might wear: a briary sweater, a pair of tweed trousers, and heavy laced shoes. He cut through the crowd toward Henry and Andreya, and when he saw Polly, he stopped and kissed her on the mouth.

"Oh, I'm sorry," he said, stepping back. "I thought you were someone else." He smiled a rattled smile. "Why," he said, "it's a little pack of Solo-Millers. Hello, Henry. Hello, Andreya." He turned to Polly. "You must be the Solo-Miller sister."

"Polly Demarest," said Polly.

"Dora," Lincoln said, "isn't it?"

"Everyone calls me Polly."

"Of course. Well, Andreya. What do you think?"

"I cannot understand these pictures, Lincoln," Andreya said. "They are about *things*. What do they mean?"

"Andreya likes for everything to have a lot of abstract meaning," Henry, Jr., said. "It's her European heritage. It's a shame we didn't bring the dog. He would really go for this stuff."

"Stop being such an oaf, Henry," said Polly. "These pictures are just beautiful. They don't need to be explained."

"I have to go and mingle with these art types," said Lincoln. "I'd rather stay here, but I'll be back."

Henry and Andreya wanted to circle the gallery once more. Polly went with them, and then Henry began to yawn and Andreya began to itch. Like small children, they expressed their boredom physically.

"Let's get out of here," Henry said.

"One second," Polly said. "Wait for me. I'll be right back."

She searched the room for Lincoln, and when she spotted him it seemed to her that he was looking in her direction. She went right up to him.

"I want to buy one of those oil-on-paper pictures," she said.

"You'll have to come to my studio," said Lincoln. "Tomorrow is good for me."

"Me, too," said Polly. "What time?"

"Any old time. Lunchtime. I'll write my address on this piece of paper. Here."

The next day Polly felt rather fevered. She was distracted all morning, then lost track of time and had to race out of the office and down to the subway, her heart pounding. She was going to have an adventure, she knew: lunch with a painter. She was going to buy a painting. Polly's life was full, but she did not get out much by herself. She and Henry had inherited pictures and had bought pictures together, but this was to be all hers. She would hang it in her office and no one would have to know that she had bought it.

She ran out of the subway and searched around for Lincoln's street. It was not a part of town she had ever been in before. She finally found the piece of paper to check his address, rang his bell, and waited. When he opened the door, Polly impulsively kissed him.

"Oh, I'm sorry," she said. "I thought you were someone else."

This gesture shocked both of them. They stood awkwardly at the door until Lincoln composed himself enough to smile and show Polly in. The front of the studio was his work space, with an apple-green floor. Lincoln was as precise as a Japanese master: his shelves were neat and his walls were bare except for his black-and-silver kite, and a large pencil drawing of a cat and a rabbit in the style of Dürer which Lincoln had done at the age of seventeen. His paintings were stacked against the wall, stretcher side out, so they could not be seen.

In the back, looking out on an overgrown yard, was his living space. Behind a painted screen was his bed, covered with a green-and-red coverlet. There was a table and four chairs, a green armchair and hassock. Way in back were his kitchen and bath. The table was set for lunch: bread, cheese, butter, a bunch of grapes, a bottle of red wine, and coffee. The sight of it touched Polly. Lincoln sat her down and asked her questions. During lunch, encouraged by Lincoln, Polly talked about her job, her family, and about the picture she wanted to buy.

And since this picture was still hanging in the show, it was necessary for Polly and Lincoln to meet to discuss whether it was exactly the picture she wanted. They met at his gallery. They met at the studio so that Polly could look through some of his watercolor drawings. She found it difficult to make up her mind.

Finally the show was taken down, and Polly went to see Lincoln for what she believed would be their last meeting. He had lunch waiting for her again, but she had no appetite. The bread was straw to her, and the wine tasted sharp. She sat looking out the window, drinking her coffee. She knew this was not correct social behavior but Lincoln wasn't saying anything either. Polly knew she was supposed to speak—to talk to Lincoln about his work, to ask him questions and bring him out—but all her training had fallen away from her. She felt totally miserable, and she did not know why. She decided to say something—anything. She decided to say the first thing that came into her mind.

"I'm sorry," she said. "I don't know what's come over me. I feel very emotional."

"I do, too," Lincoln said.

"I think it's because if I take my picture away today I won't see you again," Polly said. "I liked having lunch with you."

Lincoln was silent.

"I'm very old-fashioned," said Polly, her voice quavering. "I'm not very grown-up. I mean I'm not sophisticated. I'm just a wife and mother and a reading project evaluator. I don't know anything about the other world, anymore. I'm emotional because you kissed me at your show."

The great foolishness of what she was saying occurred to her and she stood up. Her eyes were full of tears. She was looking out the window as Lincoln looked at her.

"I can't stay here," Polly said. "I'm making a terrible fool of myself."

Lincoln grabbed her wrist. "Don't go," he said. "Sit down."

She didn't sit down. She stood listening to her heart beat. Lincoln stood up and took her into his arms.

"I'm so fond of you I don't know what to do," he said.

"Oh, Lincoln," said Polly, who was now in tears. "This is awful. I'm so fond of you *I* don't know what to do. I thought I was buying a picture from you. I told myself that over and over."

"I told myself over and over that you were just buying a picture from me," Lincoln said.

"It didn't work," said Polly.

"I told myself that girls like you don't go around kissing painters."

"How wrong you were," said Polly. They held each other close. Lincoln smelled of spice and wool. Polly smelled of talcum powder and slightly of lemons.

"I'm very confused," said Polly. "These things don't happen to me."

"Nothing has to happen," said Lincoln. "You can go home and we don't ever have to see each other again."

"Oh, no!" Polly said. "Oh, please, no." She cried into her hands until Lincoln took her hands away and then she cried onto his sweater.

"I barely know you," Polly said. "How can I feel so much about someone I barely know?"

"Apparently love works that way," Lincoln said.

"Apparently," said Polly.

Thus had they fallen into each other's arms. They were so innocent and open in their feelings that they declared themselves at once. That first afternoon, they sat up in Lincoln's bed and plotted. Lincoln said how he hated the telephone and told her to give him a ring-once signal, and then ring again. Polly explained to him that she worked Tuesday, Wednesday, and Thursday and told him at what hour she got to her office. She told him when the children left for school on Mondays and Fridays and when Henry went to work. They were both very organized, after all.

She had gone home in a blaze, fed the children in a fog, listened to them as if they were shouting at her across a meadow. She was amazed at herself. As she sorted the laundry the afternoon with Lincoln seemed as remote as a dream. She went to bed without taking a bath, and the plain truth was that she didn't want to wash the afternoon off her. Henry was away, and when he called, late that night, she was half asleep. It was his voice that reminded her of the enormity of what had happened. She had committed adultery, that's what.

The next morning she had paced around the bedroom trying not to call Lincoln. After the children left for school and she had the apartment to herself, she talked out loud—something she had never done before.

"Of course it's right that I should never see him again," she said. "This will only get me into terrible trouble. I mustn't call him and if he calls me I will have to tell him I can't ever see him." Tears she did not immediately notice slid down her cheeks. "I must do the right thing," she said. "I must not slide into self-indulgence. This is all *very, very* wrong."

Just then the telephone rang.

It was Lincoln. He was angry. He did not say hello. He said, "I believe Mr. Demarest is away, so I have taken the liberty of calling you. Good morning. This is Lincoln Bennett, the painter. Perhaps you remember me. You also remember that you said you would call me, but of course you had no clothes on at the time."

"Oh, Lincoln," said Polly. "I'm so confused and upset."

"So am I," said Lincoln. "But I hate a chicken. You should have called."

"I was about to."

"So you say. Would you like to be let off the hook? We can hang up and never see each other again."

"No," said Polly.

"Okay," said Lincoln. "In that case, can we see each other?"

"We could actually have dinner," Polly said.

"That would doubtless be a very enriching experience," said Lincoln. "Come and fetch me, okay?"

"Okay," said Polly.

"You don't have to," said Lincoln.

"Oh, Lincoln," Polly said. "I want to."

She had fetched him, and from that time they were as insep-arable as two people, one of whom is married and the other of whom likes to live as a hermit, can be. Each weekday morn-ing they spoke on the telephone. On the days they did not see each other they spoke in the afternoon as well. The first flush of love left Polly high and full of energy. It made life easier. That Henry was away so much and worked so hard when he was home was not so dire. If he was preoccupied, if he was snappish, if he was exhausted, Polly knew she would be restored. She did not love Henry any less, she felt. Some balance had been established that made life more . . . "bearable" was the word but she did not like to think it.

Four

Lincoln had finished his smoked salmon. Polly had finished her second cup of coffee. Now they lay under the heavy blanket in Lincoln's bed. They were holding hands.

"I hurl myself at you," Polly said.

"It's just the other way around," said Lincoln.

"I don't know how I got this way," said Polly. "I was never like this before."

Polly often said this, and Lincoln often wondered if she meant that she had never been so passionate, or that she had never swerved off her straight path. Polly did not say much about Henry. She was filled with a sense of propriety and mentioned him only when Lincoln asked. She always said that she loved Henry, and from her description of their courtship it was clear they had genuinely fallen in love. It was also clear that Polly felt that she was married to the right person. But Lincoln also knew she felt neglected and taken for granted—and as if she did not have much right to complain, since she had always been neglected and taken for granted but, as she was loved, honored, and revered, had never felt the need to complain in the past. She said of herself, "I'm just tireder now. I'm weaker."

"What way were you before?" Lincoln asked. "Please put your head on my shoulder and speak into my ear."

"I was like my cousin Janet," said Polly into his neck.

"Oh, yes," said Lincoln. "Saint Janet Solo-Miller. How often and eloquently you speak of her. Mother of four, professor of French, wife of the dashing and demanding Robert Felix, perfect wife, mother, and cook, and never anything but a perfect thought in her head. You wouldn't catch *her* sleeping with a painter at four in the afternoon, would you?"

"No," said Polly.

"My point exactly," said Lincoln. "Wonderful Cousin Janet. Why *isn't* she sleeping with a painter at four in the afternoon? Come along, Dora. Say why."

"Because she's such a fine, upstanding person," Polly said.

"Right you are," said Lincoln. "Let's hear it for Cousin Janet. I've been to your awful cousin Janet's house, you know. She's an old friend of Violet's. Every time she and that perfect husband of hers think it's time for a few live painters to round out their elevated social circle, they phone me up. They mostly like dead painters but the dead ones won't come for supper—that's the problem. Your cousin Janet is just too thrilled with herself, and what for? She's not half as nice as you."

Polly listened to this with a bleak smile, the only one of her expressions Lincoln didn't love. He felt he was set up by Polly to make seditious speeches—that she badly needed to hear them. They bucked her up, but the guilt in her smile hurt his feelings.

"Oh, to hell with your relatives," Lincoln said. "You were going to tell me everything you felt and did since Friday."

There wasn't much to tell, but Polly reeled off her list. She found herself talking to Lincoln about her job, and about the office.

"This can't be interesting," Polly said, as she had said dozens of times. "You can't really want to hear about the Board of Estimate's memo."

"I do," Lincoln said.

"I don't know why you do," Polly said. "You don't have school-age children and you can't possibly find this sort of bureaucratic nonsense fascinating."

"I find you fascinating, you stupid girl," said Lincoln. "Besides, is it so thrilling for you to hear how I had a fight with my gallery? Or how the green paint I ordered from Italy didn't come?"

"I'm not going to tell you another thing," said Polly. She was looking at the clock. "I want to kiss you some more and then it will be time for me to leave."

She hid her face in his neck. At this time of the afternoon —close to the time to go home—Polly wore a variety of expressions on her face: confusion, dread, guilt, and longing. Lincoln said these expressions were as visible as the snakes that grew out of Medusa's head. He pulled her away and made her look at him.

"Your cousin Janet is not fit to kiss the hem of your slip," Lincoln said. "She isn't pretty or nice or any fun, and she thinks she's perfectly wonderful."

"She treads the straight and narrow," said Polly.

"Any jerk can do that. Besides, how do you know? Maybe she's sleeping with two painters," Lincoln said. "I know that when you cry out into the darkness you cry: Oh, why can't my life be as perfect and effortless as the rest of my family's?"

This was so true that it caused Polly to smile.

"I love you the way you are," Lincoln said. "I think you're a good, brave soul. I think you are as straight as they come.

You are a loyal, true-blue person. You think such awful things about yourself."

"I can't help it," Polly said. "I used to read those women's magazines at the beauty parlor when I went to get my hair cut, about discovering new things about yourself, and expanding yourself. I used to think: Isn't it fortunate that my life is so orderly and nice? I didn't think there would be much to discover. I *hate* discovering new things about myself. They didn't say in the magazines that it hurt this much. No one in my family has had to do it. Why do I?"

"Be quiet, Dot," Lincoln said fiercely. "I really can't stand for you to compare yourself with those people."

"They're not having affairs!" Polly was now in tears.

"Maybe they are," Lincoln said, "maybe they're not. Who would want them?"

"You don't know what it's like for me to be in love with you," said Polly. "It's easier for you. You don't have to live a double life. You don't have to feel wrong all the time. Every day I think about giving you up."

Lincoln put her hand on his chest, right over his heart.

"Are you going to?" he asked.

"I can't. I just can't. It would break my spirit," Polly said. "It's just so full of confusion and pain. Maybe that's what love affairs are like. I know you love me, and I can also tell exactly at what point you really need for me not to be here. I lie in bed at home and wonder how you would feel here in this studio with Pete and Dee-Dee running around. I imagine us all around your table. When I'm down here at the end of the day, the same thing happens to me: I need to be home. I need to see the children. I go home and think about you, and you pace around here and think about me."

She looked at Lincoln, and there were tears in her eyes. Her face was soft and serious at the same time. Lincoln rarely saw anyone with her sort of refined, clear, serious beauty except the other members of her family, and none of them were quite so pretty as she. Every once in a while he saw someone who had some trace of those features. His adjective to describe this look was Polly's maiden name, as in "What a very Solo-Miller–looking person."

"We need each other," Lincoln said. "You saved my life, Dottie. I was a low, lonely, miserable soul until you came around. And as for you . . ."

"What was I?" Polly asked.

"You were so sweet and innocent and out of your mind," Lincoln said. "You should have seen yourself, Dot. You were quite a sight. I said to myself: This woman is either frantic, or cuckoo, or she is actually falling in love with me. Each time after you left I would drink whatever wine was left in your glass and say to myself: Am I ever going to get to kiss her?"

"Well, you did," said Polly. "And then some."

"I was so nervous," Lincoln said. "I used to get up early in the morning and go to the bakery, and I would stop at that Japanese flower stand and tell myself that I was only buying flowers to make the studio look nice, but they were for you."

"I wanted to bring you things," Polly said. "On the days we had lunch I used to take a bath in the morning, when I always take a bath at night. I used to think for days ahead what I was going to wear. I wanted to bring you flowers and I wanted to bake you some madeleines but I was afraid to. Oh, Lincoln! Is this what lovers do? Do they lie in bed talking about how they came to feel what they feel?"

"It's one of the best parts," Lincoln said.

"I wish my life were simpler," said Polly. "If only I could say to myself: It's heavenly to lie around like this, and it's perfectly fine, too. But it isn't, for me. I can't help thinking what my family would say if they knew."

By this time Lincoln knew whether "family" meant Henry or Polly's parents and brothers.

"You always hate it when I say this," Polly said, "but I feel unworthy. Don't be cross. My family puts a lot of stock by the straight and narrow. They believe in what's upright and true."

"If you don't mind my saying," Lincoln said, "they believe in it; you *are* it. It makes me mad that they don't know a thing about you. You let them crowd you."

"They don't crowd me so much that I don't get to you," Polly said. "Here I am in your bed, right up next to you. I'm a fallen woman in your behalf."

Lincoln sat up and pulled Polly up with him. He put his arms around her and held her very tight.

"I want to go away with you," he said. "There's a chance that a gallery in Paris may give me a one-man show. I'd have to be there. It would be this spring. Would you come with me?"

Polly wriggled from his embrace. The idea of going off to Paris with Lincoln had the effect on her that a roller coaster has on a stomach. Wanting rushed from her head to her toes in a gush, making her dizzy. Instantly she realized that she had never wanted anything so much in her life. Instantly she realized how impossible it was. She burst into tears. Her big, creamy shoulders heaved. All the Solo-Millers, even the lean Henry, Jr., were broad in the shoulders and long in the flanks. Polly had the body of a swimmer, but more lush. Her flesh was peachy and smooth. She had fine, strong hands. When she was upset her eyes darkened. Her thick hair was mussed and she looked wild with emotion.

"Come with me," said Lincoln.

"I can't. I can't. I can't," she wept. Then she collected herself a little. "I'm sorry, Lincoln. This really rips me up. I can't leave the country—it's too drastic."

"You didn't go to Vermont either," Lincoln said.

A month after their love affair had begun, Lincoln had asked Polly to go to Vermont with him, just overnight, to an inn. Henry was away, and it would have been easy enough for Polly to invent a reading conference, Lincoln said. Polly had balked. Her parents could have taken the children for the weekend, but what would she have told them? Suppose something had happened to Henry or the children and they had called the inn to find her? It had been too guilt-inducing, too complicated, and too overt for Polly to bear. And by not doing it she had condemned herself constantly to thinking about it: of herself and Lincoln walking through a stand of birches, of waking up together in the same bed, of going to sleep together.

"How wonderful it would be," said Polly, wiping her tears away with her arm. "I would love to go to Paris more than I can say, but when I got there it would be awful."

"Awful?" said Lincoln. He put his arms around her. His darling, tactful Polly almost never slipped. It was very clear to him how miserable she must be.

"You know what I mean," Polly said. "It would be heavenly—absolutely heavenly—but I can't do it. I know I can't."

"Well, it may happen, and it may not," said Lincoln. "You know how these things are. A woman from the Galerie Georges Deliel cornered me at the opening, but it may be just talk. Even if they have the show I might not have to be present. I'd miss you an awful lot if I did go, you know. Some day, Dolly, when we're both fifty-five and the grubs are in graduate school, we can astound everyone by running off together. We'll go to India on a sketching tour."

"What will I do while you sketch?"

"You'll sketch, too. I'll buy you a sketch book and some number-three pencils. You'll have to wear one of those English garden-party hats. We'll go into the countryside and sleep in hunting lodges under mosquito netting. Then we can investigate the local school system and find out how little Indian children are taught to read, and you can write an award-winning study. I'll illustrate it. We'll run away, that's what we'll do."

He kissed her on the cheek and she turned to him. Her eyes were blazing. "Oh, Lincoln," she said. "I love you so very much."

At five o'clock Polly called to say she was on her way home. Lincoln watched her as she got dressed. He loved seeing those thick, expensive garments transform her back into a respectable matron. He made her the farewell cup of coffee she loved and they arranged their weekly schedule.

"What do you have on this week?" he said.

"Partners' dinner tomorrow. Home Tuesday. Henry's in Boston on Wednesday. Thursday we have Paul, the Peckhams, and the Sterns for dinner. Friday we're going to the theater with Mum, Daddy, Aunt Lilly, Uncle Francis, and Henry and Andreya."

"I thought they hated art," Lincoln said. "Or don't they consider theater art?"

"Well, they do, actually," said Polly.

"That's how dumb they are."

"They like to go to the theater so they can misbehave," Polly said. "You know, the thing about them is that they can get away with murder. They sit in the theater and fidget, and they eat those awful Milk Duds and Henry rattles the box. And they talk and giggle and the people in back of them have to ask them to shut up, but they don't. I tell you, she and Henry look like those little plush brother and sister mice we used to get in our Christmas stockings and they're so adorable that no one ever gets annoyed."

"Except the people in back of them."

"Except for them," Polly said. "We always think that if the

people in the back saw them from the front they would be enchanted, too."

Lincoln gave her a bleak look. "Is that what you all think?" he said. "Milk Duds, for God's sake, why don't they grow up?"

"They're engineers," said Polly. "Maybe that explains it."

Lincoln shot her another baleful look. At this point on a Sunday afternoon, both were edgy.

These days the light faded early and fast. There was only one lamp on in the studio—one by Lincoln's bed that had a dark yellow paper shade. It threw long, bleak shadows everywhere. Lincoln's neatness, in that mournful, dusky light, looked singular and austere. This was a place you visited, the home of a hermit who had occasional guests. There were moments when that solitude looked delicious to Polly and when the thought of the Demarest household uptown sounded rich and happy to Lincoln. This was their worst time: when she was set to go home, and he was set to have her leave, and both were so ardent that they could not bear to part.

Polly sat down next to him at the table and nudged his arm with her forehead. He put his arm around her.

"What do you have on?" she said.

"Nothing Monday. An opening Tuesday. You Wednesday. Dinner with my old painting teacher Thursday, and Friday I may go to the architects' for the weekend." Gus and Violet were restoring a house in the Berkshires and Lincoln did not mind helping out. "I'd come back Sunday morning. Can you invent another seminar?"

"Probably," said Polly. "But sometimes I just want to put my elbows on the table and say: Here's the deal. I'm having a love affair and I must go to it. This love affair doesn't mean I don't love all of you, but there you are. This sandwich is for my sweetie-pie, not for a bunch of reading technicians. He's a very lovely fellow from a good family and so you have absolutely nothing to worry about."

"That would cause something of a commotion," Lincoln said.

"No, it wouldn't," said Polly. "They'd all smile and say: Polly! Our Polly! Having a love affair? How ridiculous!" The lamp caught her face just right. She looked as innocent and sweet as honey, and lonesome. It cut Lincoln up to see her. It seemed awful to him to be surrounded by so much family and be so lonely: surely it was better to be really all alone. He gathered her into his arms. She had a wonderful heft, his Polly, and a sort of spring to her flesh. She came back at you, instead of melting away, although she sometimes melted, too.

"All right," she said, standing up. "If I don't go now, I'll never go, and think how affrighted you'd be. Give me my coat and get me out of here."

They walked arm in arm down Lincoln's street, hailed a taxi, and kissed good-bye. Although they knew they could easily see each other on Monday, their Sunday farewell was always painful. Polly always turned to watch Lincoln walking away as the taxi drove off.

On the way home Polly imagined Lincoln savoring his solitude. He often told Polly that she had rescued him, that she was his sign of spring. She had seen his white paintings—layer upon layer of despairing white. These pictures would never be shown, but he kept them as a reminder of what the other side of his solitude was all about. During the year that Lincoln had spent almost entirely alone, his brother thought he was having a nervous breakdown. He saw almost no one, and almost never went out except to shop for groceries and art supplies. When he discovered he could not paint in color, he painted in white. He was amazed, he had told Polly, at its variety and texture. He had done landscapes, still lifes, and a self-portrait, all in white. These paintings were extraordinary, Polly thought, bleak, intense, and full of power. She felt they ought to be seen, but they were too potent a reminder to Lincoln of what he felt Polly had saved him from. Her warm hand had pulled him back into life. These small doses, these blissful visits, were nourishing.

Polly knew that when she left the studio Lincoln smoothed the bed, washed the dishes, lit more lamps, and sat down at his drawing table. After she was gone, he told her, he sketched her from memory, although he often sketched her while she was there, too. He had a large folder in which he kept his pictures of her. He worked in colored pencil and when she was not around he did cartoons for an oil portrait. When Polly saw these drawings she was stunned. In drawing after drawing she stood in a doorway wearing her gray skirt and sweater. The room before her was full of life: a bowl of poppies, a pot of lilies, a lamb, a fox, a house cat, a cage of doves. In another the room was full of babies in baskets. The tribute they paid to her made her feel shy and fraudulent.

Lincoln smoked while he worked—Polly loved to watch him. He smoked crooked little cheroots that made his clothes smell spicy. The thought of that smell sent a shiver through her. It was on his skin as well, especially on his neck. She often thought that she was in thrall to that combination of cigar smoke and the sweetness of Lincoln's flesh. Was it right only to want someone in the small doses Lincoln required? Every now and again he said he wanted to pry her loose, but if he did she would no longer be the Polly who made his present life possible for him. She and Lincoln were not, she knew, each other's destiny, but only their present destination.

. . .

The apartment was quiet when Polly got home. She hung her coat in the hall closet. Her first thought was that Henry and the children had died as God's punishment on her for committing adultery with Lincoln. Her second thought was that Henry, who was so pressed, tired, and work obsessed, had decided that Polly was not much use and had taken the children and moved out—as just punishment from God for having a love affair with Lincoln.

Henry was working at the desk in his study. The children were on the floor playing Silent Cows and Hedgehogs. Henry had invented this form of the game so that the children could play near him while he worked. Whoever made one sound had to forfeit a cow or a hedgehog, while a person who made no sound got a fifty-cent piece.

Pete and Dee-Dee were fierce. They uttered not one peep, not even when Polly appeared. They presented themselves to her, their lips pressed firmly together.

"How did it go, Pol?" said Henry from his desk.

"All right," said Polly. "May the children speak?"

"You may speak," said Henry.

"Mommy, Uncle Henry said bad words in the park," Pete said.

"You snitch," said Dee-Dee. "You said bad words, too."

"You may now not speak," Polly said. At this the children pressed their lips together again. "Darlings, take the cows and hedgehogs out of here and go look over your homework and then get washed for dinner."

The children trooped out.

"Henry," Polly said, "are you going to turn around and kiss me hello?"

"I am. Just a sec."

Polly wondered if other women were as familiar with the sight of their husbands' backs. When she thought of Henry these days she thought of him sitting at his desk late at night, hunched over a large pile of papers. She could see that he was making notes, and he did not turn around and kiss her. Instead, she put her arm around his shoulder and kissed his neck. He patted her absently.

"I'm so lonely," she said.

"I am, too," said Henry. "Come on. Let's go make the salad dressing."

Henry's Sunday chores were to make the salad dressing and open the half-bottle of red wine he and Polly shared on Sunday night. On most nights Polly had dinner with the children in the kitchen, and dinner later with Henry in the dining room. Henry did not like eating at the kitchen table, except on Sundays.

The food Polly liked best was nursery food. She fed her children shepherd's pie, mashed potatoes, deviled chicken, vegetable fritters, hush puppies, Queen of Puddings, and apple crisp. Henry admired a more complicated cuisine. He liked fresh ham stuffed with pistachios, carpetbagger steak, and veal, ham and egg pie, all of which Polly was happy to provide. Polly loved to cook, and she loved a dinner party, but most of all she loved dinner in the kitchen with her children, especially when the weather was cold or messy, or when Henry was away. Then her children could be as silly as they liked, and Polly did not have to worry about preparing a second meal.

The family sat at the kitchen table eating veal stew. The events of the afternoon were recounted. Pete's kite had gone up very high, but Uncle Henry's kite had been a dud, which made him say any number of bad things.

"Should I say what they were?" Pete asked with a terrible gleam in his eye.

"Just because your uncle Henry behaves like a chimpanzee does not mean that you have to behave like a chimpanzee," Polly said.

"Chimpanzees behave like beautiful animals," said Dee-Dee. "Uncle Henry does not behave like a beautiful animal. It isn't fair to the chimpanzee to say that Uncle Henry behaves like one."

"Aunt Andreya hit him on the head," said Dee-Dee. "Then she hit Kirby on the head."

"Kirby is like a chimpanzee," Pete said.

"That isn't fair to the chimpanzee," said Dee-Dee.

"It is so."

"It is not."

"Enough, you two," Polly said. On Sunday evenings her children were tired and fretful. When their voices began to climb the scale, she knew it was time to give them a bath and put them to bed. Polly felt tired and fretful, too. Her heart was divided and she was only half present. Henry cleared the table while Polly gave the children their baths. They were so tired they did not demand their usual story, but neither would go to sleep until they had been kissed by both Polly and Henry.

"You look a little peaked, Polly," Henry said.

"I'm terribly tired," said Polly.

"Go take a bath," Henry said. "Soak a while. Run it really hot. I'll be up late tonight: I've got a pile of work to go through."

In her bath Polly felt so tired that she thought she might collapse and drown. Her bones hurt; the insides of her bones hurt. Polly had been trained to explain this sort of thing away by thinking that she was overtired, and then taking a very hot bath and going to bed early.

She did not have the luxury of getting sick—mothers of young children never did—but she was an excellent nurse-maid when anyone else got sick. Wendy had trained her well.

Her children were allowed extra pillows, given hot milk and honey or hot lemonade, were allowed to have breakfast on a tray and their toast cut up into pieces the size of postage stamps. These were the treats Polly had been given as a child. As a teen-ager she had been an excellent nursemaid to Wendy, who liked to go into an occasional decline and have her meals brought to her in bed. Now, when Henry had his yearly head cold, she waited on him as well. No one asked her to do this, but it cheered her. Polly liked to make order out of chaos, to tidy up the mess, to give the sick crisp fresh sheets and a nourishing and savory meal.

But she was not overtired. The fact that she was having a love affair was a clear message: she had been troubled for a long time and had never admitted it and it had worn her down. She had labored cheerfully and without complaint. She came from a legal family and knew as much about Henry's work as someone who was not a lawyer could. She had felt it right to understand his work. For years she had listened and discussed the very things that took Henry away from her, and she had done it without a thought. She had never felt justifiably angry about anything, and now that repression had come back to bite her. She did not know much about other people's marriages. She had instead the example of her parents, whom she had never heard quarrel, bicker or snap, or say a cross word about each other. Polly loved Henry with all her heart, but that seemed not to be enough to prevent her from feeling hurt and angry. She had lost her stamina. She had given in. She could not imagine either of her parents angry or hurt; thus she felt she had fallen from grace.

Henry's sister, Eva, had been Polly's roommate at college; she had introduced Polly and Henry. The first time she met him Polly had said to herself: I want to marry that man, or someone like him. A few years later they found themselves at the same party. Henry was a young associate at his firm, and

Polly was teaching reading. Their courtship was open and uncomplicated: they knew without a doubt that they would marry, and they were thrilled to have found each other. Both felt that marriage was a step into the adult world. It made sense in every way. Their families were delighted. Her best friend would become her sister-in-law. All this gave Polly immense security in love.

She and Henry set about replicating the comfort and success of their parents' lives. Polly had never been so happy. She was madly in love with Henry, and if she felt that she never quite got enough of him, that was the consequence of being married to a rising young lawyer who sometimes had to work five nights a week, or was called away, or who was often so tired he did not care what he was being given for supper. A good wife's job was to create a haven in a heartless world, Polly knew, and to compensate men with understanding and love for the perils of their lives. Over the years the feeling that for all she gave she only came second to work and children grew within her until one morning she had woken up and pitched herself into Lincoln's arms. His attention, no matter how minimal, made her realize that her connection to Henry, no matter how profound, was not enough. She did not approve of the way she felt. After all, Henry's commitment to her was central, whereas Lincoln could only stand to have her around for several hours at a time. That she craved so much attention mortified her, but she could not fight it. She was too starved for it.

Once in bed, she was too tired to read, too tired to sleep. She left Henry's night-table lamp on, covered with a scarf. In the glowing darkness she let her eyes travel the room. It was massive and comfortable, a place in which a family might relax.

In that comfortable bed, under the blue-and-white Early American quilt that Henry's sister, Eva, had given them for a wedding present, Polly thought about Lincoln, about his kindness, his love for her, his ardor, his attractiveness. He was so lovable, so talented. He was becoming well known and would eventually be famous. Surely one day he would wake up and shake off his need for solitude as if it were an outgrown jacket. He would suddenly emerge; his love affair with Polly would have given him a taste for domestic and emotional life. Then some lovable, very talented, and beautiful girl would cross his line of vision and he would want to marry. He would marry that lovable, talented girl and Polly would never have access to him again.

Polly sat up in bed. The nice full life she had led had not prepared her for this sort of pain. When she breathed, her ribs hurt. She was suddenly glad that Henry was so absorbed in his work that he forgot to come and kiss her good night. She felt like someone shot full of arrows.

In a few hours Henry would come to bed, smelling of tooth-paste and wearing his English pajamas. He would be careful not to disturb her. He might or might not read a few pages of one of the English mysteries he read for relaxation. He was her husband and he loved her. And even if he was so buried in the difficulties of his work that she could not get to him, their marriage was safe. Perhaps that gave Lincoln a pang or two. She loved Henry—Lincoln knew that.

She got out of bed, went into the bathroom, pressed her face into a large bath towel, and cried so that no one could hear her.

PART TWO

Five

Paul Solo-Miller, who people in the know said would one day be appointed to the federal bench and then to the Supreme Court, had never married. He was a tall, stern, handsome man whose hair was clipped short enough so that the shape of his elegant skull could be admired. Within that skull resided his venerated brain. Paul was not easy to get along with. As a child and an adult, he had, with his silence, his indifference, his high-mindedness, made life difficult for the chatty, the passionate, and the lower-brow—Polly considered herself all these things. It seemed to her that Paul had never known childhood. As a little girl she had thought of him more as an uncle than as a brother, and had often gotten him a little confused in her mind with her father, whom he resembled. The tiny Polly was restrained from making noise when her father was thinking in his study, or when Paul was doing his homework. At the age of four Polly had thought that her nine-year-old brother, Paul, was a lawyer, too.

Wendy dithered over Paul. Polly tried to be sunny and open toward him. Henry, Jr., succeeded in not paying very much attention to him. No one, except for Henry, Sr., who had his son's admiration, quite knew what to do with him. He treated his mother with the tender but essentially distant courtesy you might give to a mildly insane but well-meaning relative. Polly he accepted as if she were a piece of pleasing wallpaper, and Henry, Jr., he ignored as if he were a mess on the rug. His place in the family was absolutely firm and no one expected anything of him. They were thrilled to see him when he showed up.

The apartment he lived in was devoid of everything except what he considered essential—in these matters he was very like his mother. He had a piano, a large dining-room table, some Persian rugs, a bed with an extra-firm mattress, and very good lamps. All the Solo-Millers were fanatic on the subject of proper reading lights.

Besides the law, Paul's passion was music, especially symphonic music. He loved the early-twentieth-century German composers and he spent a considerable amount of time and money on stereophonic equipment. His most lavish conversations with people not in his firm or family were held with a bunch of young dope heads at Sid's Stereo Hut who counseled him as he upgraded his sound system. Paul was also a strong supporter of the symphony, which he attended in the company of the person Wendy referred to as "this woman," a very attractive divorcée named Mary Rensberg. The fact that Paul did not marry Mary Rensberg or bring her into the family circle clearly indicated to Wendy that there was something wrong with her. She was divorced; Wendy did not approve of divorce and she assumed that Paul did not approve of it either.

Wendy had long ago despaired of Paul's ever marrying. Once she had assured herself that he was entirely heterosexual in purpose—she assured herself of this by simply believing it and by observing that he did not attend the theater or the opera more than socially necessary—she took it into her mind that Paul was not entirely of this world, and that for very brilliant people, Nietzsche's aphorism that a married philosopher is a joke held true.

Paul was in constant professional demand. He was lent out to foreign governments by his firm and asked to teach seminars at our nation's most esteemed law schools, and he lectured on panels to other lawyers. His energies were channeled into these ennobling works. His public and private manner were identical, but he was constantly invited to dinner parties. On his nights home he made notes for a book on the organic nature of the law in which he argued that the coherence of the human body had as its corollary a desire for order and an appreciation of structure. Thus man's perception of himself as individual territory was the basis of property law.

Polly, who often catered Paul's dinner parties when he had them, had for five years hoped that Paul would marry "this woman," Mary Rensberg, although she did not understand why Mary would marry Paul. Mary was small, wiry, and blonde. She smoked unfiltered cigarettes, wore men's shirts, real silk stockings, and diamond earrings. In her conversation she was breezy and slangy; she swore constantly. Every Sunday she went to church in the company of her teen-aged daughters, Dulcie and Daisy. She had been married to a banker named Charlie Rensberg who had gone through life fearing that someone would take him for an ordinary Jew. He was of an immensely rich German Jewish family, one that Wendy felt was very vulgar—Wendy knew the elder Rensbergs from afar. Polly thought that Mary's churchgoing was a revenge on Charlie and his awful, snobby family. Mary was a few years older than Polly, but the Demarests had attended the same dinner parties as the Rensbergs. Polly wholeheartedly liked Mary and had always hoped to know her. She had been privately glad that Mary and Charlie had divorced—Polly had never been able to stand Charlie Rensberg. When Paul had started to be seen with her, Polly's heart rose up in hope, but Paul did not encourage her in this. By some unspoken code he made it clear that Polly was not supposed to make friends with Mary, and he was fortunate in having a sister sensitive enough to pick this up.

Not only was Mary divorced, but she kept shop. She dealt in antiques—tables of all sorts and Victorian china. She sold these out of a corner store in Polly's neighborhood. Paul did not approve of shopkeeping among people he knew. Polly assumed that he must be in love with Mary, since she so thoroughly violated his sense of propriety. She said almost anything that came into her mind. When Polly had last run into her and asked about her daughters, Mary said, "They are perfect ducks, my sweet girls. They refer to your brother as Paul 'Night of the Living Dead' Solo-Miller."

It was the first week of the new year. Polly sat at her desk in her office wishing she had been able to get all last year's work taken care of, so she could start the new year fresh. The year-end report was sitting on her desk waiting for her evaluation; the memo she had drafted the week before was lying on top of her typewriter. In a large folder were printouts of the results of a series of experimental reading tests that would form the basis of the spring report. Each spring Polly's group presented to the Board of Education a review of all the new reading methods developed during the previous year, along with a re-evaluation of the old.

Lately Polly had begun to long for her office. At work she did not daydream about Lincoln; it occurred to her that when she said she had had a good or productive time, she meant that she had been involved in something that caused her not to think about Lincoln for as much as a whole hour. The more work she had, the better she felt.

She was sitting editing the year-end report when the telephone rang. It was Wendy.

"I have breathtaking news," she said. "Your brother Paul is getting married."

"Good Lord," said Polly. "That *is* breathtaking. I never thought Mary would marry him."

"That's the breathtaking part," Wendy said. "Your brother is marrying someone named Beate von Waldau."

"Who? Who is she?" Polly asked. "Do you know her?"

"The first I heard mention of her name was this morning. Your brother came for breakfast very early and broke the news. I haven't a clue who she is. Paul says she's a psychoanalyst of some sort. At any rate, she's a German." Wendy paused. "Your father is quite beside himself."

This meant that Wendy, who had nothing but contempt for modern Germans, was quite beside herself.

"Isn't it interesting," said Polly, "that both Paul and Henry have ended up with Europeans?"

"I never think of Czechoslovakia as a European country," said Wendy. "But never mind. They're coming for dinner tomorrow night, just the two of them, so this Beate can meet us all, and after that I expect she'll be introduced to the family at large."

The family at large included the Solo-Miller aunts and uncles, the Hendricks aunts and their husbands, all the first cousins, and Great-Aunt Harriet, who was very old and who claimed she had never in her life taken part in any social function that was not in some way connected with family. Henry and Wendy felt that only blood really counted. The married-in person was, even after fifty years, somewhat of a guest. For what family was the equal of the Solo-Millers or the Hendrickses? Henry, Sr., and Wendy had been the oldest in their families, and now that old Grandmother Solo-Miller was dead, they were the head of the family, with Henry's two brothers and their wives, and Wendy's sisters and their husbands, as second string. Henry Demarest said that only anthropologists could properly understand the Solo-Miller family, and Lincoln said the Solo-Millers functioned like a racist state and that their unwritten statutes were like the Nuremberg Laws on which Adolf Hitler had been so keen.

"About dinner," Wendy said. On both sides of the line, mother and daughter settled down for the conversation they enjoyed most: what to serve with what for dinner. Wendy's longtime housekeeper, Odessa Smith, helped Wendy with the cooking, but menu planning was one of Polly and Wendy's chief delights. "I thought roast leg of lamb or roast beef, potatoes Anna, and those lovely cold string beans of yours for a second vegetable."

"Don't you think a cold vegetable is too springlike?" asked Polly. "And what about Andreya?"

"Oh, dear. Andreya. Well, some eggs with cheese in a gratin dish. I think the green beans will be just fine. I feel rather springlike around now. This is the lowest part of the year, so all signs of spring are cheering. Lots of flowers, I think. I saw some lovely quince branches the other day. I think one cold vegetable dish will fit in very well. And apple pie."

"I think lamb," Polly said. "Spring lamb."

"Just roasted with rosemary, mustard, and garlic," Wendy said.

"Perfect," said Polly. "I could make peach mousse if you would rather have that than apple pie. Our grocery has hothouse peaches."

"Hothouse fruits never have enough flavor," said Wendy. "I'll ask Odessa to make her apple pie. It's a nice American touch. Goodness, there's the door. It's the window cleaner.

How can they bear to clean windows at this time of year? Call me later, darling."

The next day Polly was frantic with obligations. She had bought the string beans on her way home from work. In the morning, while she gave Henry and the children their breakfasts, she topped and tailed and steamed them, and made the dressing in which they would rest for an hour before serving. She got Henry's shirts together to be washed and ironed, left a long note for Concita, the Demarest housekeeper, sewed a button on Henry's suit jacket, checked to see whether her black silk dress needed pressing, put a ribbon in Dee-Dee's hair, found Pete's lost math homework, and arranged for a baby-sitter. She went through her briefcase, collected her notes on the spring report, and left for her office. Before beginning work she called her mother to see if there was anything she needed. There was. Would Polly please stop at the French bakery in midtown and buy ten baguettes, and then go to the cheese store and pick up two goat cheeses of the type Wendy called "Primitif," but only if they were fairly young.

"Pyramid," said Polly. "It's a snap to remember. That's its shape."

"Darling, I can't remember a thing," Wendy said. "This business with Paul has me absolutely rattled. I completely forgot that this Beate has a brother, so he's coming, too. He doesn't live here. He's visiting. Do you think you could call Henry and have him pick up some of that brandy your father likes so much? These people drink schnapps, I'm quite sure."

Polly wrote all this down on a little card.

When she hung up, she looked at the card and looked at her desk and realized with panic that she did not want to meet Paul's fiancée or his fiancée's brother. She did not care that Paul was getting married. Why had he picked a time when she was so pressed? She saw before her an endless procession of family gatherings—cocktails, lunches, prenuptial suppers, buffets, bridal dinners, wedding breakfasts, for all of which Polly would be called upon to make her *oeufs à la neige*, her chocolate cake, her mocha jelly roll, to say nothing of stuffed mushrooms, cucumber sandwiches, cream of sorrel soup, and spinach pie. Or she would be asked to find a caterer. Her desk was piled with work, Henry was getting ready to go away again, and the children both had scratchy throats. She was a monster of selfishness, she thought. She picked up her telephone, dialed, hung up, and dialed again.

"Hi, Dot," Lincoln said.

"It's only me," said Polly.

"You sound awful. How's the bridal couple?" He was enthralled by the subject of Paul's marriage and had talked of nothing else since yesterday.

"I'm just tired. I ought to be thrilled about Paul, but I'm not."

"Well, I am," Lincoln said. "I can't wait until you meet the little bride. Do you think she's won the Nobel Prize already, or is just about to?"

"She's a psychoanalyst of some sort," Polly said. "Did I tell you that yesterday? I can't remember anything these days."

"You did, and I think it's very nice that Paul has found an Aryan controller," Lincoln said. "Goody for him. I bet she dresses up in old Nazi uniforms."

"Oh, Linky."

"Come on, Dot. You know there's something weird about Paul. Why does this make you sound so low?"

"I'm just tired. I've got a thousand things to do. I have all these errands to run. I wanted to see you today, but I don't see how."

"I'll tell you what," Lincoln said. "I'll come see you. We'll meet for lunch, just like real chums. I'll help you run your errands and I'll carry the packages in my teeth. What about it?"

"Oh, Lincoln. You really shouldn't stop work to come have lunch with me. It'll disrupt your day."

"Not another word. I'll meet you at twelve-thirty. Where's that place you sometimes go to?"

"The Sublime Salad Works," said Polly. "It's right around the corner. We passed it once when you picked me up, remember?"

"I'll be there at twelve-thirty."

"You really needn't."

"I do need," Lincoln said. "After lunch I'm going to take you into an alleyway and kiss you and feel you up. And because I love you so much I have produced a German sentence for you to practice for tonight. Here it is. Write it down. *Ich bin ein baltischer Scharfrichter auf Ferein.* I've always found it a very useful phrase. It means: I am a Baltic executioner on vacation."

It took Polly five minutes to collect herself and get back to work. She was overcome, like a flooded car. She put her list aside and realized that in order to get the cheese and bread, and meet Lincoln, she would have to get the cheese and bread first, and that Henry was far too busy to go and buy the brandy, and so, either on the way home or after lunch, she would have to stop at the wine merchant's near her office and buy it. It would not be the kind Wendy wanted, and Wendy would notice. Polly wondered for a moment if she had time to take the subway downtown and go to the vintner near Henry's office, but that was out of the question. She would buy an expensive bottle of something else, and Wendy would have to put up with it. Two years ago, or even a year ago, Polly realized, she would have cheerfully taken the subway downtown to get a special brandy. But gestures of that sort were impossible if you were having a love affair. Of course the very fact that you were having a love affair meant that you no longer wanted to make gestures of that sort.

Polly's love for Lincoln was divided like a pie chart: part gratitude, part pain, part restoration, part consolation, and part pure lust as well as a lust for friendship. From week to week the proportions changed. There were times when she was as lovesick as any thirteen-year-old, but the nature of their relationship prevented any undiluted joy. Guilt, longing, confusion, and surprise mitigated everything. Polly discovered how volatile and emotional she actually was. She said to Lincoln, "If only I could have a specific lobotomy—if they could find the part of my brain where you are and take it out." In unguarded moments she felt that if she did not have Lincoln in her life she would shrivel. This filled her with sorrow. These days she felt her sorrow and confusion were like rainy weather, dripping on everything, making everything wet.

She felt she had been pitched from a safe, calm harbor into an unpredictable and turbulent sea; that she had woken up not from a dream but from a daydream. Falling in love opened the world up to her in a way it had not been opened before. Everything occurred to her: her place in her marriage, her place in her family, her place in herself. She had no precedent or guide for these feelings. Never in her life before had she felt lonely, bereft, agonized, or fearful. She had never felt that the road of her future was dark. Yet, with all her blessings, she had gone off to hunger after something else.

When she was feeling especially terrible Polly tried one of two things. First she would buck herself up by telling herself that her sufferings were tiny—that she was not sick or maimed or poor or alone and that she was simply a spoiled brat. This never seemed to work, and so she devoted herself to her job. She found that work really did take her out of herself.

She could burrow into it so intently that she did not hear someone call her name or tap on her door. When someone pounded on her door, Polly looked up. It was her office chum, Martha Nathan.

Martha was a *Wunderkind*. She was not as young as she looked but no one was as young as Martha looked. She wore the sort of clothes a child might wear to a child's party—smocks and shifts. The rest of her garments were made in India, Guatemala, or Afghanistan. Martha felt solidarity with emerging nations. "I am sort of an emerging nation myself," she said. Martha was the office computer genius and very much fussed over, but she found her present line of work pretty much a breeze. She was brilliant in the way that some people are left-handed or redheaded or beautiful—it was a fact of her existence. As a result she was somewhat restless. Before becoming a computer expert she had worked with a documentary team on a film about land reform in Chile, and because she had found the problems of Latin America so overwhelming, she had turned to computers for fun. Recently she had applied to medical school, since she felt being a doctor might be entertaining as well as useful.

"And after that," Polly had suggested, "there's always law school."

"I've thought of that," said Martha. "I love the process of learning a thing. It's doing a thing I find so boring."

In addition to being a genius, Martha claimed to be intensely neurotic. "I have had many years of expensive psychotherapy," she said. Certainly she was devoted to her moods. She was alternately furious, depressed, gloomy, silly, or simply full of good spirits. Polly was very fond of her and looked forward to the days when Martha, who worked on a free-lance basis, was in the office. Polly had never had an office friend before.

At the sight of Martha in the doorway Polly cheered up.

Martha's volatility made her the least exacting presence Polly had ever encountered. After all, she did not expect consistency from anyone else. As a result, Polly felt free to be any old way she pleased. This was as refreshing as several weeks at a spa, especially now that Polly generally felt so low or agitated or distraught, and most of the time struggled to conceal it.

"Hello, there," said Martha. "I've been pounding on your door."

"I was a little distracted," Polly said.

"You're a lot distracted, it looks like. What's up?"

"My brother Paul is getting married."

"Really! He's pretty old, isn't he? Who's he marrying?"

"Somebody nobody knows," Polly said. "This is a real bolt from the blue. My family likes to gather on every occasion, so we're gathering."

"My family can't stand it when they're all in the same room," said Martha. "I can't remember any family occasion on which we didn't have a fight. I'm not sure whether I think you're lucky or not."

"It's nice to have a united family," Polly said.

"It sounds like living hell to me," said Martha. "But now, for instance. Do you like your brother Paul? Everything you say about him makes him sound awful. You say he's silent and preachy and everyone is scared of him."

It had never really occurred to Polly to ask herself whether she *liked* her brother Paul or any other member of her family. They were *family*. They were not judged by the standards you might apply to other people.

"He's my brother," said Polly. "I love him."

"A beautiful sentiment," Martha said. "I quote my old dad, who says that everything is relative except relatives, who are constant."

"Another beautiful sentiment," said Polly. "Now I have to

run five hundred errands, and I've got to meet a friend, and I've got to go to the liquor store and the cheese shop and the bakery."

"Quite a little schedule," Martha said. "Big family dinner party?"

"They're all big."

"If you need any help," said Martha, "just ask. I could run an errand for you. I like to help out a person who likes their family and, as you can imagine, this leaves me with lots of time on my hands."

By the time Polly met Lincoln for lunch she was wilted. She had rushed out of the office, rushed back because she had forgotten to call Henry about the brandy, remembered that she was going to get the brandy herself, and rushed out again. The bakery was jammed and so was the cheese store. Still, she had five minutes to spare, so she bought two pounds of salted almonds, the only hors d'oeuvre of which Wendy approved. Lincoln was waiting for her in front of the Sublime Salad Works.

"Look at you," said Lincoln. "You didn't wait for me. You've done all your errands and now I have nothing to carry in my teeth."

"I ought to buy some cigars and an extra bottle of champagne. And I have to get a bottle of brandy after lunch," Polly said. "This was so nice of you, to come up here and have lunch with me."

"It'd better be worth it," said Lincoln. "Is this Sublime Salad Works as sublime as its name?"

"It's convenient," Polly said. "That is, if you can get the waitress to take your order. They're all art students and actresses."

The Sublime Salad Works was crowded, but Polly and Lincoln managed to squeeze into an uncomfortable table for two. When the waitress finally appeared, it turned out she had forgotten her pad, and when she came back she had forgotten where she had put her pencil and was forced to borrow a conte crayon from Lincoln, who had made a stop at the art-supply shop. Polly ordered the Swiss Health, which was described on the menu as "A life-affirming medley of low-calorie Swiss cheese, a piquant julienne of hearty beet, tender carrot, and powerful high-energy dressing." Lincoln ordered the Sublime Works, a salad that included crab meat. Eventually the waitress brought Polly a Chef's Salad and Lincoln the Egg Salad Supreme.

"It's hopeless," Polly said. "I never get what I order here and I always order the same thing. I ask for Swiss Health and as a result I have had everything on the menu."

It didn't much matter, because Polly was low on appetite. As they sat over their second cups of coffee, Lincoln held her hand under the table.

"Come along now, Dottie," he said. "Try to eat. You have to keep your strength up."

"I feel all broken down, Linky," Polly said.

"You're a fine figure of a woman," said Lincoln.

"The funny thing is," Polly said, "I've had such a charmed life, really. Now suddenly everything is out of kilter. I used to be so full of energy. Now I don't look forward to anything. I used to be so positive. It isn't right for a person like me to feel awful. I'm not supposed to. I tell myself over and over: My life is full of blessings. Including you."

"Everybody goes through this," Lincoln said. "It's part of growing up."

"Not in my family."

"Your family was put on earth to make everybody, including you, feel like hell."

"Linky, you don't know them."

"I know one thing," Lincoln said. "For all this gathering and family unity, you can't go to them and they make you feel bad."

"Family is just there to be family, Linky," Polly said. "They're my tribe. They don't have to know the secrets of my innermost heart."

"You're the only member of your tribe who has an innermost heart," Lincoln said. He looked up. "There's a child over there waiting for a table who's staring at you."

There in the doorway was Martha Nathan. The sight of her caused Polly to blush, but she motioned her over anyway.

"It's Martha," Polly said. "You've never met her."

"You better get that blush off you before she gets here," Lincoln said. "You look like the Woman Taken in Adultery."

"Hi, Martha," Polly said when Martha appeared. "Come sit down. There's a free chair over there."

"Oh, no," Martha said. "I've just come to read this article and bolt my lunch." It was perfectly clear that she had sized up the situation in one glance.

"Oh, sit," Polly said. "Martha, this is my friend Lincoln Bennett. Lincoln, this is Martha Nathan."

"I'm starving," said Martha, sitting down. "I guess no one will take my order. Is that girl a waitress or a customer? It's so hard to tell in these places. Oh, miss!"

An extremely sullen girl meandered over to the table.

"I'd like to order," Martha said. "What can I get fastest?"

"Our salads are all handcrafted," said the waitress.

"Bulgarian Eggplant Salad," Martha said, "and a cup of coffee right away, unless the coffee is handcrafted, too."

"I didn't get that," the waitress said.

"Yes, you did," said Martha. "Bulgarian Eggplant and a coffee. Just because you went to a progressive high school and studied modern dance at college doesn't mean you can't remember a simple order."

"How did you know that?" the waitress asked.

"A child could tell," said Martha.

"How *did* you know that?" Polly said.

"It's a snap. Modern dancers are a type. They all wear the same clothes. Everyone who went to progressive school holds a pencil funny. They don't teach them how to write till they're about twelve or thirteen. When they *feel* like learning." She looked at Lincoln. "I bet you're a painter."

"I am," said Lincoln. "You can tell from the paint on my sweater, my large bag from the art-supply store, and my sensitive, soul-stricken look."

They chatted with Martha until Lincoln could see how nervous Polly was.

"Okay, Dottie," he said. "Let's go run the rest of your errands and leave Martha to her handcrafted salad."

"She knows," Polly said when they got outside.

"Of course she does," Lincoln said. "But you can always say that I'm your little brother's pal. And besides, what would it matter if she did know?"

They were walking slowly toward the tobacconist's. Polly suddenly stopped. She looked exhausted and grim.

"Come on, Dot," Lincoln said softly. "You'll be all right."

"I don't know if I will," she said and pressed her face against Lincoln's shoulder. "Oh, Lincoln, I wish I knew."

That evening, as Polly left the office, it began to snow. There was not a taxi in sight and the bus, as it inched its way up the avenue, was packed. Polly had her briefcase, her handbag, and two large shopping bags containing the ten baguettes, the cheeses, salted almonds, a box of cigars, a large box of her family's favorite chocolate, two bottles of champagne, and a bottle of brandy. It was almost certain that one of the shopping bags would split. She had not worn boots or taken a scarf. As she got off the bus, one of the packages began to disintegrate and it was necessary to hold it in her arms. Snow blew into her eyes. She felt that juggling this many things was beyond her—she, who had juggled babies and prams and strollers and packages at the same time. She felt like throwing herself and everything else into the street.

Polly had had her adolescent swivets, her bouts of nerves, her small heartaches. She had read, good student of literature, novels in which great unhappiness and emotional tragedy unfolded. She knew these states of feeling existed. She had sat on the deck of an ocean liner going to France on her honeymoon and read *Anna Karenina*. Heroines in literature fell from grace little by little. Small mistakes were emblematic of terrible flaws. Suddenly the truth was revealed: these flaws were chasms, magnified and compounded. The heroine was then exiled from optimism, cheer, security, and the safety of the right thing. Did nice people ever feel this miserable? Lincoln said they did, but Polly did not really know many people outside her family; and no one in her family, she was sure, had ever felt the way she felt, or if they had, they had triumphed over it in secret. Her distress frightened her. It was not because she had fallen in love with Lincoln. It was what allowing herself to fall in love revealed: that everything was wrong.

Once at home, she flung her packages on the kitchen table. Both split, spilling out the contents. Pete and Dee-Dee came to the door and gave her a desultory kiss. They knew she was going out for the evening, and she was therefore of limited use to them.

Concita Croft, the housekeeper who came in on Polly's three workdays, had put the children's dinner in the oven.

"Hi, Polly," Concita said. "You look tired."

"I am tired," said Polly. "Did Nancy Jewell call?" Nancy Jewell was a sixteen-year-old girl who lived in the building and often baby-sat.

"She'll be here at seven," Concita said.

"I'm going to make a cup of tea," said Polly. "Do you want one, too?"

"Okay," Concita said. "Mr. D. called. He says he'll meet you at your parents', but he might be a little late. And the housepainter called. He said to call if you had the time."

"The housepainter?" said Polly. She looked at the number and went to the telephone. She dialed, hung up, and dialed again. Lincoln almost never called her at night, and never if he knew Henry was in town.

"It's only me, Dottie," Lincoln said when he picked up. "Your housepainter."

"Yes," said Polly.

"I just called to tell you how swell you are, and that everything will be all right. You know that, don't you?"

"I don't know," Polly said.

"I do," said Lincoln. "Have a wonderful time tonight and make mental notes of everything. I want dress, behavior, and any interesting, revealing, or bizarre remarks. I love you, Dot."

"Thank you," said Polly, and they both hung up.

Six

Beate von Waldau was one-half of a set of twins. She and her brother Karlheinz, who was called Klaro for short, looked exactly alike—tall, bright-eyed, hawk-faced, with the same sleek dark beautifully cut short hair. It was hair of the sort you want to pet, like beaver fur, but otherwise the first impression they made was forbidding and standoffish, in the way of modern furniture. They had elegant, bare lines. Their clothes were expensive and modern. To Polly they looked as chic as a pair of chairs by Mies van der Rohe. Klaro wore heavy gold cuff links and a gold watch identical to his sister's. Both had long, strong fingers. After careful scrutiny, Polly correctly guessed that they were forty-four.

The formality of this meeting militated against anyone's sitting down. The family stood clustered around the fireplace, fanning out from a center composed of Beate and Klaro, with Paul next to Beate. They drank chilled vermouth but no one touched the large silver bowl of salted almonds. Wendy had filled the house with forsythia and quince branches. There was nothing, she felt, so nice as the sight of spring branches near a wood fire. She was thrilled that it was snowing. Snow, a wood fire, and flowering quince in combination was her idea of sheer perfection.

Beate was saying, "I have lived in New York for eighteen years, but Klaro lives still in Berne, where we were raised." Polly watched her mother's face smooth out. A Swiss! What a tremendous relief. In these situations, Wendy was a master of disguise, and only her nearest could read her. Her best reader was Polly, the only one who paid close enough attention. The look on Wendy's face was complicated, but Polly knew what it said. Wendy was surveying her two sons and their European mates. "If only," her expression seemed to say, "Henry had not married Andreya, and Paul was not going to marry Beate, they would be free to marry . . ." A frown creased Wendy's forehead, for the logical conclusion to her sentence was that they would be free to marry each other.

Now Wendy was faced with two utter strangers. They looked perfectly well turned out, but how did you tell with Europeans? She felt as if Paul had been taken over by extraterrestrials. Who *were* these people? What, precisely, was their background? Several things had been made clear: their parents were in their eighties and lived in Berne—too old and, it was implied, too noble to travel. The implication was that if Wendy and Henry wanted to meet the von Waldaus they would have to fly to Switzerland to do so. Father von Waldau had been a professor of theology at Berne. Their mother had been the administratrix of a small, experimental hospital that rehabilitated amnesia victims. Had they been Americans, Wendy would have known exactly what all this meant, but the rules and forms of life in Europe were different and it was impossible to tell what sort of daughter-in-law she was getting. This made her cross; when cross, she became fretful and spent her fretful attention on small details, such as the two forsythia petals that had fallen from the Chinese vase onto the black marble mantel. Polly knew that from this point on, her mother would have very little left in the way of an attention span.

"I think we should toast Paul and Beate, and welcome Beate and Karlheinz to the family," Henry, Sr., said. He did not feel that Klaro was anybody's name.

Paul stepped into the center of the family circle, drawing the unsmiling Beate with him. "An announcement must be made," he said. "We are not engaged. We have been married for five months."

There was an appropriate hush of pure silence.

"We must tell the other thing as well, Paul," said Beate. She had a rather deep, lilting voice.

"Yes," said Paul. "We are expecting a child. By the time we go to Maine, Pete and Dee-Dee will have a little cousin to play with."

The family was struck dumb. How mean of Paul to spring this on them, Polly thought. She glanced at her mother, who looked as if she had been slapped, thrilled, and dazzled all at once. It would never occur to Wendy how weird a gesture on Paul's part this was, for she had waited all these years to hear this news. As soon as she got over her surprise, she would be wildly pleased. Paul's marriage and impending fatherhood made everything fit. With the exception of one minor irritant—two daughters-in-law she did not fully under-stand—Wendy's life was now all of a piece.

Polly could not help noticing how lofty Paul and Beate looked. She tried to repress the desire to kick them, but she was too tired. The only news she had to spring on her family was bad news. Her love affair with Lincoln was about as old as Paul and Beate's marriage. The contrast between these events made Polly feel like a pariah.

Henry, Sr., was not at all shocked. Rather, the horse he had bet on all his life had come in a winner. It made perfect sense that Paul should be married and now he *was* married. It seemed right to Henry, Sr., that Paul would break the news of his marriage and his future child in one sitting. It gave the family two good things to react to at once, and it put the whole thing into context. After all, Paul was too old for frills, young love, elaborate weddings.

As for Henry, Jr., and Andreya, they looked about to fidget. They had always regarded Paul as a married person, and the fact that he was now actually married made absolutely no difference to them at all. But soon, they knew, they would be the only childless Solo-Miller couple, and they both flinched as they anticipated the subtle pressure that would be brought to bear on them.

Henry Demarest always did the right thing. He had never understood Paul's unmarried state, and he was pleased to see that Paul had found a wife who matched him so well. He got the bottle of champagne that had been sitting in a silver bucket on the sideboard and popped the cork.

"This certainly calls for a toast!" he said.

At dinner Polly could hardly concentrate on the conversation, so anxious was she that everything go well, and so completely entranced by the thought of Paul in love. She could not imagine it, nor could she imagine Paul in bed, especially with Beate. Their mating, she imagined, might resemble the slow movement in one of those grave, serious modern ballets that take a Great Theme, such as The Freedom of the Individual, or Suppression of the Dissident Artist Behind the Iron Curtain, as their inspiration. Paul was neither a laugher, a grinner, nor even much of a smiler. He was an occasional head-nodder—this was as far as affirmation took him. Beate matched him in stately cheerlessness. They did not look joyless—Polly felt it was impossible to be totally joyless and wear such expensive clothes—but they looked stern and separate from the feckless lot of mankind that wiggles, tells jokes, and has fun. They were very much in the higher mind, Polly felt.

Klaro, on second glance, looked positively mischievous. The features that were imposing on the female twin looked foxlike on the male. He was seated next to Andreya. Wendy had planned this without a thought in her mind, but had worried all during cocktails: Germany *had* done awful things to Czechoslovakia in the war. Of course once she knew that Beate and Klaro were clean, efficient, neutral Swiss there was nothing to fret about. Klaro and Andreya were deep in their own conversation. Andreya listened closely while she attacked her lovely plate of vegetables, eggs, and cheese.

Klaro, it was revealed during dinner, was a composer, much respected in Europe but less well known in America. His visit to New York had accidentally coincided with his sister's marriage announcement. Actually he had come to perform in the American premiere of one of his compositions, which the family was duly invited to attend. His composition was an unstructured motet for piano and string trio and would be performed by the Manhattan String Trio with Klaro at the piano. This set off an exchange between Paul and Klaro about harmonics and the hexachord. But mostly the talk was about the baby, although Beate did not look five minutes pregnant. She was tall and flat and lean. Polly thought she had perhaps arranged to somehow carry the baby outside her body.

"We will have the child according to the most felicitous method," Beate said. Like Klaro's, her English was stiff but close to perfect. It was rather like listening to someone who had learned the language by reading *The Origin of Species*. "This baby will be born in accordance with the methods of one of my former teachers, the great doctor Rudolph Ping. There will be soft music and muted lighting. There will be calm and lull. We would have this child at home but this is not possible, so I have found a young Swiss doctor who will conform to the method of Dr. Ping in a hospital. This young doctor will birth us."

Polly looked at Paul. So he was having the baby, too.

"And you'll be with Beate in the delivery room," said Polly.

"Certainly," said Paul, as if attacked. "The birthed infant knows if the father has been there." The idea of the birth process and Beate did not jibe in Polly's mind. She looked so much more like someone who would be interested in having a baby in a test tube. But the idea of these two unsmiling, spotless people married and having a baby was preposterous anyway, so the rest, no matter how farfetched, followed.

"We've remodeled the apartment," said Paul. "While I was in Paris, Beate oversaw the construction and we camped out at Beate's. We now have a proper nursery, painted the color recommended by Dr. Ping: peach, but on the pink end of peach. Dr. Ping feels that a peach color reassures the recently birthed infant."

"I can't believe you're actually going to watch," said Henry, Jr. He and Andreya found the idea of birth disgusting. Sex was fun for children, but having babies was work for adults and of no interest to them at all. They did not connect the appearance of children with sex in any way.

The dinner plates had been taken away. The salad was consumed. Coffee was brought to the table along with an enormous apple pie. Polly had decorated the top, right before it went into the oven, with leaves and flowers cut out of the leftover dough. It was brought to Polly to serve while Wendy, at her end of the table, poured the coffee. Out of the corner of her eye Polly could see that Klaro and Andreya had reconnected. They were chatting away, in German. Henry, Jr., looked at them as if they were a pair of talking chipmunks—interesting for about five seconds. He was about to tuck into his dessert, ignoring the warning flash of his mother's eye. Henry, Jr.'s approach to any meal was that of a ravenous truck driver. Andreya had explained one afternoon at breakfast the difference between the German words *essen* and *fressen*.

"*Essen* is to eat as people eat. It is to dine," she said. "*Fressen* is to eat as an animal eats. It is to feed." Henry's great smile of recognition made it clear to all what side he was on. The quantity of food he could pack into his lean frame was amazing to almost everyone. He also liked to make a mess when he ate if he could, and favored things like shrimp boiled in the shell, pizza, French fries with catsup, and crabs. If he ate at a roadside stand he liked to have the hot sauce or mustard drip down his arm, and he liked for French fries to fall onto his shirt. Wendy had stopped putting out unshelled nuts when Henry came to dinner, because he left every surface, and the floor beneath him, littered with shards. He was good with chopsticks since they were a great aid in shoveling your food, a method Henry embraced heartily.

Suddenly Andreya laughed. It was a beautiful laugh—light, melodious, and girlish. From the looks this sound produced it was clear she would have to explain.

"Klaro knows the songs of my childhood," Andreya said. "He has put them into a composition. These are the songs my German nurse used to sing to me."

It became obvious that there would soon be singing at the table. Wendy looked around helplessly to see whether anyone might help prevent it.

"What songs?" asked Henry, Jr.

"Very silly ones," said Klaro.

"Well, sing one," said Henry, Jr.

"Yes, please!" said Polly.

Klaro's voice was a sweet tenor, Andreya's a contralto. They sang in the affecting, unassuming way of amateur singers. Polly felt the hair on the back of her neck lift. These days music brought her to tears.

> *"Was müssten dass für Bäume sein*
> *Wo die grossen*
> *Elephanten spatzieren gehen*
> *Ohne anzustossen."*

"This means," said Klaro, "What sort of a tree is it that the big elephants can promenade beneath without hitting their heads?"

Then they sang:

> *"Karbonade, marmelade*
> *Eisbeinschnitzel*
> *Blumen Kohlsalate.*
> *O! Mayonnaise! O! Weisskäse*
> *Rote Grütze, Bratkartoffel*
> *HUNGER HUNGER HUNGER HUNGER."*

"There is no translation for this," said Andreya. "It is merely some incoherent ravings about food."

The party moved into the living room, where Henry, Sr., stoked up the fire. There was more coffee, brandy, and hard, spicy little cheese biscuits—Wendy clung to the old-fashioned notion that all dinner parties should end with a savory.

At the far end of the room was the baby grand piano Henry, Polly, and Paul had taken lessons on. Paul could play, but he was only interested in reading music, and he used the piano in his apartment for picking out themes in symphonic scores. Polly could play well enough and would help Pete and Dee-Dee when they took lessons on the upright the Demarest and Solo-Miller parents had given Polly and Henry for an anniversary present. Henry, Jr., had hated the piano as a boy and had asked for a tuba. This instrument had been rented for him, but it was soon clear that his chief interest in it was its nuisance value and it had been taken away. Nowadays the music he liked best was the loudest and most atonal of rock and roll, or the sort of modern compositions that sound as if a piano is being hacked up with an ax while someone in the background is smashing glasses.

Klaro sat down at the piano and played quietly. He was fond of twentieth-century French music and he played Satie. Instantly savage breasts all over the room were charmed. Klaro played exclusively as background, but the expression on his face was that of an ingenious veterinarian who had quelled a room full of anxious schnauzers. Everyone sat a little more comfortably. Henry moved closer to Polly, and stretched his arm out on the back of the sofa. Polly's spirits had not been calmed. Music made her feel excessively emotional and she had been anxious all night that this party be a success, and worried that this family party took up Henry's time when he was so pressed at work. Klaro's playing had smoothed Henry out. He stretched out his legs in front of him. Polly could feel him relax. Her heart seemed to twist. How she loved him! And as she looked at him relaxed on the sofa, how distant and remote he seemed to her. How odd to have the source of her deepest and most profound feelings at such a remove. Had she changed? Or had Henry? Or was it simply that life changes things?

She sipped her coffee and turned her attention to Paul and Beate.

There was something about them that Polly could not quite define. Whatever it was, it was making Wendy nervous: exaggerated formality was one sure sign of stress in her, and she was speaking carefully to her family as if translating into English from a foreign language. Paul and Beate were not like one of those couples madly in love who have no attention left for anything else. Rather they were like mutant cells that had broken off from the larger organism.

Then it struck Polly: Paul and Beate were now their own tribe. Paul was soon to be a patriarch in his own right. All his secretiveness, his silence, his rigidity was nothing more than a preparation for forming his own club. Polly and Henry Demarest still belonged to the senior Solo-Millers, and Henry, Jr., and Andreya had set themselves up as mascots. And although Thanksgiving dinner had gradually been shifted over to the Demarest household, Henry, Sr., and Wendy were still the center, the monarchs of the family. But soon there would be a pull toward Paul's family, and into Paul and Beate's orbit. Wendy would know that the deference paid her was of the empty, formal variety and there would be nothing she could do or say about it. Paul and Beate would be treated like emissaries from a colonial nation that was now richer than the mother country. Wendy knew that Paul would take the family over, after she was dead.

Beate was talking about her parents. "Our father was a professor of theology and ethics, and the institution administered by our mother was run on the most modern lines. We are a family that believes in service toward society. Klaro is our only artist."

"There was Great-Uncle Clemens," said Klaro from the piano.

"A contemporary of Christian Morgenstern and, like him, a writer of serious nonsense poetry," Beate said. "Klaro has made a song cycle based on Uncle Clemens's and Christian Morgenstern's sillier verses."

"Has your great-uncle been translated into English?" Polly asked.

"I believe so," said Beate. "But you must go to the library to find it."

"The library system in this country is quite poor," Wendy began.

"It's actually extremely good," said Paul.

"I was thinking of the Bibliothèque Nationale," Wendy said. "Or the British Museum."

"Perhaps Klaro will sing from his song cycle," Andreya said. Wendy looked fretful at this possibility.

"No," said Klaro. "But Andreya and I will sing 'Heiden-röslein.' Since we know the same childhood music, she must know this as well." He turned to her. "You know it, do you not?"

"I cannot sing by myself in front of people," Andreya said.

"Oh, please," said Polly. "Please sing. Klaro will sing it with you."

Andreya got up and, looking like a chastened infant, went to the piano.

"This is not Schubert's 'Heidenröslein,'" Klaro said, "but the version one is taught to sing in childhood. It is a simple, sweet tune like a folk song. Do you know this poem? The boy goes to pick the heath rose and the rose warns him that if he picks her, she will hurt him with her thorns and he will never get over it. But he does anyway, and that is the end of that."

Andreya and Klaro harmonized the chorus: *"Röslein, Röslein, Röslein rot, Röslein auf der Heiden."* During this performance, Henry, Jr., ate the entire silver-bowlful of salted almonds. He then ate half a dish of the hard chocolate pastilles Wendy considered proper for after dinner. Henry, Jr., liked chocolates with filled centers—the kind he could squeeze to discover the contents—but Wendy did not approve of them.

Polly looked around the room. Here was her family, the people she was most connected to of any in the world. She was surrounded by the fragrance of wood smoke and the smoke from Henry, Sr.'s and Henry Demarest's cigars, but she felt very far away. At the sound of Andreya's voice she was suddenly filled with longing, longing for Lincoln. She imagined herself and him in his studio in the evening. The studio would be filled with yellow light from the oilpaper lampshades Lincoln liked. What am I doing here? she asked herself. Longing struck her like a shooting pain. She wanted to stick her head out the window and call his name, but she sat quietly on the loveseat next to Henry. As Klaro and Andreya sang, he held her hand. She sat in the crook of his arm. How well they fit! How handsome they looked! When Henry turned his tenderness toward Polly, her heart usually melted. But now she felt like a visitor from another planet, alone in the middle of her family.

It was time to go home. Everyone stood up. Wendy still looked fretful: This was not the family she had bargained for. One of her sons had married secretly, and the other, who had eloped, shared his clothes with his wife. Henry, Jr., and Andreya were both wearing suits—Andreya was wearing a silk edition of a suit, and Henry, Jr.'s one formal shirt (a shirt he had inherited from his father, which was how Wendy recognized it) with a silk scarf instead of a tie. Wendy's eye rested easily only on Polly. Polly made perfect sense to her.

If Polly had told her mother that the family Wendy had

gotten was more interesting than the family she had bargained for, Wendy would have told her that an interesting family did not strike her as an attractive idea. Families were not meant to be interesting. Wendy believed that life should be predictable. The unpredictable she considered rather vulgar.

Henry, Sr., was always the model of perfect rectitude. The small emotional arrangements made by mortals ran over him like water over an enormous rock: it made a little difference but only in the long, long run. His acceptance of his children was total. How could it not have been? They were his, and therefore they were above criticism.

It was not his style to say much. He either lectured, addressed himself to a question, or was silent. He cropped his hair short and favored clothes that were sober and manly. When he was not wearing a suit, he wore navy-blue Viyella shirts and twill trousers that were thirty years old. He was truly not much attached to things of the world. He had always had them: he had inherited them. There was almost nothing in his life that he had had to go out and get.

He wore on his face a look Polly knew well. It was The Look of the Higher Mind. In this case it meant that he was tired and had had quite enough dinner party, and his mind was now addressing some Important Issue. He had another look, a look that as a child Polly had dreaded to see. It was called Daddy's Horizontal Flicker of Disapproval—a look that darted across his eyes the way fish dart past you in the water. The wrong dress, a bad grade in Latin, a friend of whom he did not approve, a rebellious attitude or inappropriate hair style occasioned that look. It lasted but an instant, but had a devastating effect. Nowadays this look came over him out in public when he surveyed the eating, reading, or public behavior of others.

Henry, Jr., and Andreya were tired. When tired, they threatened to become cranky. Kirby was at home waiting to be taken for a walk. A little snow had stuck, and it was cold. There was every chance that their unreliable car wouldn't start. They felt it was unfair that Kirby was allowed to come to breakfast but not to dinner, and they had had enough of Paul and Beate.

"Hey, Andro," said Henry, Jr., at the door. "How come I never hear you sing?"

"I sing to Kirby in a language you cannot hear," Andreya said. She and Henry had their jackets on and were pawing at the door like colts dying to be let out of the stall.

Had all things been equal, Henry Demarest would have enjoyed himself entirely. He loved displays of personality, and the family he had married into always gave him an eyeful. If he had not had so much on his mind he would have enjoyed contemplating Paul and Beate. But all things were not equal. This dinner party had taken away a chunk of his time and now he would have to stay up for several hours after he got home. He was not in an optimistic frame of mind. Work was suspended before him, unremunerative, unending. Polly seemed tense and distressed. He felt pressured on every side.

Polly was exhausted and relieved: the evening had been a success. Now she wanted to get Henry home. She felt she could read his mind, and she knew he was thinking about how much work he had ahead of him. She had accepted this schedule of Henry's before, and she had catered to his preoccupation, too. Now she took it personally and was glad when she was too tired to care. She wanted to go home and go directly to sleep.

The family stood in the foyer saying good night with their coats on. The sight of Paul in his cashmere overcoat and Beate in her mink filled Polly with happiness. She had a rather simple heart after all and her wants were plain. She wanted Beate to like her, and Paul not to disapprove of her. When their baby was born she wanted to be able to go and play with it. As far as Paul was concerned, Polly always did the wrong thing. He did not like emotional gestures very much, and Polly had often been made to feel like an untrained puppy. Standing next to him now, she did not so much fling her arms around his shoulders as hug him.

"I'm so happy for you," she said, on the verge of tears, and Paul patted her as if she were a distraught child.

Seven

Now that the weather had turned icy and wet, it was natural for Polly and Lincoln to spend their afternoons together under the covers in Lincoln's underheated studio.

Polly gravitated toward a bed. She liked breakfast in bed, reading or work in bed, and she liked to talk lying down. The Demarest family often shared horizontal evenings, in which Polly and Henry read or worked, and the children did their homework or some quiet project other than watercoloring, all spread out on Polly and Henry's big bed. The sight of her family lying around her gave Polly a deep sense of pleasure. The sight of Lincoln lying next to her gave her pleasure as well, but in their situation Polly knew it was impossible to be simply happy. Still, no matter how many times she told herself that lying next to Lincoln was certainly sinful, she could not help giving herself over to the pleasure of his company.

It was three weeks after the dinner party and very cold.

Polly and Lincoln were fully dressed and huddled under a quilt. Polly had been talking about work.

"Last year," she said, "I dove right into the spring report. I had it pulled together, edited, and at the printer's in two months. This year I feel as if my head were full of gelatin. I can't seem to get started. Linky, can't you get a space heater in here?"

"I have you," Lincoln said.

"I mean for when you don't have me."

"Then I don't care," Lincoln said. "Don't scream, but I'm going to put my very cold hand under your sweater and right against your nice warm back. What you need, Dot, is a little vacation, in some tropical place."

"Yum," said Polly.

"You could lie in the sun like a lizard and I'd rub suntan lotion all over you. You could bring a briefcase with you and work on the spring report while turning a beautiful color."

"It's nice to think about," said Polly sleepily.

"Why can't you do it, Dottie? If not with me, then by yourself."

"I can't do it either way," Polly said.

"You can," said Lincoln. "You just think you can't."

"It's the same difference," said Polly. "Besides, if we went away together you'd feel cramped in eight hours and start looking for an escape hatch."

"I don't think I would," said Lincoln.

"Lincoln," said Polly. "I can feel you getting edgy about half an hour before I'm due to leave you. Being with you in a hotel would be like living with a trapped ferret."

"If we went away it would be different," Lincoln said. "Would you press yourself a little closer to me? Thanks awfully. My feet are freezing."

"Put them back under the quilt," said Polly. "Now I get

to put my very cold hands under *your* sweater. You feel so nice, Linky. You have such lovely velvety baby skin on your back."

"Scratch me right under my left shoulder blade," Lincoln said. "That's perfect. Now enough about you. Tell me about the enchanting Beate. Did you find out what sort of psychoanalyst she is?"

"Well, she *is* one," Polly said, "but not as we know them. Mum says she's a disciple of someone called Fitch-Grabner, or Horsefield-Finch. She believes in something called metaethics—it's all about character. It's about the great idea that motivates small behavior."

"She picked a perfect family to marry into," Lincoln said. "They're all bursting with meta-ethics."

At this Polly was silent. The recent torrent of family events overwhelmed her. Of course Paul and Beate deserved this attention. It was right that they should receive it. Their having a baby made them exempt from everything, although Polly remembered that being pregnant had not made her especially exempt. She had carried on as always. She had gone to fuss over her mother when Wendy was enjoying one of her little declines and needed to stay in bed for a few days. She gave her father dinner every night for the week that Wendy went off to her college reunion. Henry was away or working late, as usual. She went shopping with her mother and gave dinner parties. But Paul and Beate were somehow different.

When Polly withdrew she did not turn away from Lincoln but toward him, as if she needed to be warmed up. Sleet clattered against the window. She burrowed against Lincoln the way kittens press up against their owners. Lincoln worried about Polly—about the pressure she put herself under, about her secret unhappiness, about the standards her family had set, which she tried to live up to when no one else in her family bothered.

Polly sat up in bed.

"I know it's the lowest part of the year," she said. "But I feel so low. On Saturday, when we had the big party, I noticed how much my uncle Billy Solo-Miller drinks. He's my favorite uncle—the one from Philadelphia. He's the one who sent all his kids to Quaker schools and said, 'Some of our best Jews are Friends.' I found myself saying to myself: Lucky Uncle Billy to be able to be drunk so often." She turned to Lincoln, who was lying on his side watching her. "This is awfully boring, Linky. I'm sorry."

"Don't be silly, Dot," Lincoln said. "I've made you spend hours listening to me complain about a million things."

"You don't complain about *your* family," Polly said.

"My family is not my trouble," Lincoln said. "I have other troubles, as you have often pointed out, but family is not one of them. What I'd like to do is to go to one of your family dinner parties and give them all what-for." He pulled her down next to him. Their cold noses touched.

"You help me by just being here," Polly said. "Now I have to go back to the office."

"Sometimes I don't want to let you go," said Lincoln.

"Sometimes I don't want to go," said Polly.

She was glad to be back in her office with the door closed. It was not one of Martha's days on the job, and Polly was grateful that she didn't have to talk to anyone. This piece of time was her decompression chamber between Lincoln and home.

It was a quiet afternoon—no meetings, no telephone calls. The sky was dark gray. Polly thought about Martha with a jolt of guilt: only a very tired, sloppy, and needy person would have paraded a love affair past an office friend. She should never have let Lincoln come and have lunch with her. It was terrible to admit that you wanted to see someone that badly. Now Martha knew. That Martha might not care—that Martha might be sympathetic—did not occur to Polly. She had violated her own sense of propriety, and that was wrong.

The women in her office, the people in the elevator when she left to go home, on the street, and on the bus all looked like solid citizens making the most of their peaceful lives. As Polly waited at the bus stop she felt as isolated as one of the tragic heroines she had read about in college—set apart from the ordinary throng of men and women, who did not expect perfection, who were happy with what they had, whose inner lives and outer selves matched nicely. On Polly's desk at work she had three framed photographs: one of Henry, one of the children, and one of Henry and the children. These days she often looked at those photos and had cause to reflect that her inner and outer lives did not match at all.

She stood in the back of the crowded bus surrounded by men and women going home, reading their newspapers. As the bus crawled up Madison Avenue, Polly thought of a story Lincoln had told her, a story she frequently reflected on.

Between college and art school he had taken a summer job as a building inspector—miserable work that paid very well. He told Polly that he had once gone to inspect the sub-basement of an old tenement and heard an eerie noise from behind a door. He opened the door slowly and shone his flashlight. Confronting him was a wall of yellow eyes: the basement was infested with rats.

Polly felt that admitting your unhappiness to yourself was very much like opening a door and being confronted by a wall of yellow eyes. Her problem was not that she had fallen in love with Lincoln, or even what had made it possible for her to fall in love with him: her problem was herself. It was the yoke she put herself under, the standards she chose to adhere to, and the fact that underneath all the service, cheer, care, and nurturing was some other Polly she had not quite confronted.

Henry was not her problem either. *She* had chosen him. She had picked someone whose ways she knew: someone generous, kind, intelligent, and good, who loved and honored her for the excellent qualities he had come to expect and take for granted, and whose neglect, whose immersion in work, whose abstraction when engaged in work she was expected, as she had been trained, to accept, accommodate, and lighten when she could. Could it be that she had never been happy doing this? That this role had always been a burden? That she had never felt at ease in her family or cherished by her husband?

When the bus stopped at her street she was so tired she ached. She dragged herself from home to work, down to Lincoln, back to work. Her children had taken to patting her tenderly. The most ordinary details of life—lists, plans, menus, schedules—at which she was an absolute wizard—had begun to throw her. She had forgotten to leave Concita's check. She had forgotten to take Henry's two suits to the cleaners. She had forgotten a lunch date with her mother.

Once home she had the disturbing sense of having forgotten something else, and when she found Henry shaving in the bathroom she was sure she had, but she could not remember what.

"You're home awfully early," she said. "Do you have a dinner meeting?"

"Don't you remember?" Henry said. "Tonight is Klaro's concert."

"Klaro's concert," said Polly. "What concert is that?"

"It's not like you to forget," Henry said. "Haven't you and Wendy been on the telephone all morning? Klaro's premiere is tonight."

"It is?" said Polly. "Where is it?"

"Stringed Instrument Society," Henry said. "Afterward we're invited to Paul and Beate's to see what they did to Paul's apartment and to inspect the nursery."

Polly sat down on the edge of the bathtub. Henry was wearing only a pair of shorts—blue-and-white-striped ones. He had long, strong legs and a big, well-made torso. Watching him shave brought back her childhood, when she had sat on the edge of the bathtub and watched her father shave. How she had revered him! And how carefully she had been trained to revere her husband.

"I'm sorry I forgot," Polly said. "I'm just tired. Mum didn't call me all day, so it went right out of my head."

"Don't be sorry," Henry said. "There isn't any need for you to be."

Polly felt there was. She felt that she ought not to forget things and that any little slip made Henry angry.

"For God's sake, Polly," Henry said. "Don't look as if you're about to be shot. I'd give anything not to have to go. I've got a ton of paper to go through."

Polly buried her face in her hands. "I feel as if I deserve to be shot," she said.

"Come on, Polly, don't be melodramatic. Come over here and hug me. Then you ought to take a cat nap. You look wiped out."

"I can't take a nap," said Polly. "I have to sit with Pete and Dee-Dee."

"You do *not* have to sit with Pete and Dee-Dee." There was a note of frustration in Henry's voice which was as good a warning as Daddy's Horizontal Flicker of Disapproval. "Pete and Dee-Dee are sitting quite happily with Concita, and since we're going out, they don't have much interest in us."

"I'm sorry I behave so badly," said Polly, who was still sitting on the rim of the bathtub. If her husband wanted to be hugged, why didn't he come to her? Why did she have to go to him? Why, when she put her arms around him at night, did she feel she had to beg him to make love to her? Why did she feel that she was getting in the way of his precious rest? Her response to Henry was the most profound feeling she had— the feeling that she was entirely given over to him—but even that, she felt, was parceled out to her by the demands of his work. Lincoln, on the other hand, simply wanted her: nothing got in the way—an affirmation was so essential that the thought of doing without it made her weak. She looked at Henry and all she saw was someone she had to fight to get to.

"I'm sorry," she said.

Henry pulled her up by the elbows and held her close.

"Are you going to cry?" he said into her hair. "Don't cry, Polly."

She did not cry. She pressed her head against his big, consoling chest and did not feel consoled.

"My poor Polly," Henry said. "My poor darling Polly."

"I want you to love me," Polly said. Tears slid down her cheeks. Henry smelled sweet, like someone who had been lying out in the sun.

"I do love you," Henry said. "I love you with all my heart."

At this Polly wiped away her tears.

"Go take a nap," said Henry. "I'll wake you in half an hour."

Instead Polly went down the hall and sat with Pete, Dee-Dee, and Concita. That the sight of her children didn't cheer her struck her as rather grave. She imagined them sitting at the table with another woman—Henry's new wife, a better edition of Polly, or if not more providing of comfort and cheer, then better suited to him in temperament, someone less needy and less angry. It was not fair to sit with your children and not give yourself to them entirely. How she had hated it as a child when Henry and Wendy's attention had drifted away from her, and now she was doing the same thing to Pete and Dee-Dee. She got up.

"I'm going to have my shower now," she said. Like her father, both her children could raise their eyebrows. They gave her a pointed look.

"You're not any fun," said Pete.

"I'm your mother," Polly said. "I'm not supposed to be fun all the time."

"Flower Bernstein's mother is lots of fun," said Dee-Dee placidly, without taking her eyes off her dinner.

Polly wheeled around. "Who is Flower Bernstein?" she said.

"A friend," said Dee-Dee airily. "They always have fun at her house."

"Then go live at Flower Bernstein's," said Polly. "I'll help you pack."

"I made her up," said Dee-Dee. "She isn't a real person."

"Then I guess you'll have to stay here with your no-fun mother."

"Oh, Ma," said Pete and Dee-Dee and they turned back to their dinner.

Henry was dressing when she came into the bedroom.

"I thought you were going to take a nap," he said.

"I just went to sit with the children."

"Come on. Into the shower with you," Henry said. "It's getting late."

In the shower, Polly meditated. She and Henry dovetailed, as married people ought. They had everything the books say marriages need in order to thrive: a commitment to family, identical feelings about truth, honor, children. They had similar backgrounds. They agreed on the way life should be lived.

Perhaps, thought Polly, they had married because they had found each other to be so familiar, and had never given it another thought. She knew Henry loved her. His love for her was manly and grown-up. He approved of her so fully it went without saying, and that was at the bottom of her distress.

She thought about their courtship and the feeling of sweet correctness it had conferred on her. To be loved rightly, to love the right person ardently, seemed to her the most complete bliss; and it meant she could take her place in a long family line, producing, she hoped, excellent children, creating another family within her own family. What had all this excellence covered up? Even during their courtship Henry had been away, had had to work late, had not been able to meet her for a concert, had not had the luxury of time to loll, meander, or dreamily do nothing. A Sunday afternoon spent simply walking around was a treat, not a commonplace. An evening free of work was a rarity. She had always lived under the firm conviction that Henry's time was sacred. His attention was properly focused on the children or family or work. Polly, good sturdy citizen, who had been so carefully brought up by her mother to do without, thought she *could* do without, as long as it was clear she was loved and honored. Well, she was loved and honored, and she could *not* do without.

There were times when Polly was prey to the most elemental loneliness, even in the midst of all her good things. She had felt it for much longer than she knew, and it had helped to throw her straight into Lincoln's arms. Lincoln simply loved her. Her family *had* to love her—they were tied to her by blood. Henry had chosen her for all the right reasons: for her attractiveness and charm, for her good sense and high ethical standards, her love for children, her kindness, her sense of fun. To have been chosen thus, and then to be neglected, had hurt her badly. As a young bride she had not dared to suggest to Henry that if he loved her he might make more time for her, but she had felt it. Henry Demarest, like the rest of her family, relied on her pliant nature and understanding heart. It was not Polly's role to be praised but to praise, not to be singled out but to single out. Excellence in her *was* a commonplace, nothing to get excited about.

But something had happened—Polly did not know what. She felt as if she had woken up one morning after a profound and lucid dream whose content she could no longer remember but which had changed everything. A gate had opened up and through this gate walked Lincoln, who singled her out and praised her for her excellence, and wanted to know everything she thought and felt.

Could everything she had always believed be wrong? That her life with Henry was essentially flawless, that she had no grounds for complaint, that she could accept his absences since she so cherished his presence, that his frequent abstraction was more than compensated for by his focus? She knew that people were often unkind, selfish, petty, ungenerous, small-minded, gutless, and untruthful. How could she be angry with a person who was none of these things, simply because she had suddenly discovered that she was starving for attention? Wasn't that a very second-rate thing to long for compared with the excellent things she had? Did she have any right to be angry? She was riddled with every feeling she had been taught to believe petty and unworthy: shame, remorse, confusion. But it was safe to feel these things in the shower, where the water drowned out the sound of a person who was crying hard.

The family took up an entire row at the Stringed Instrument Society. They looked unified and splendid out in public, like visiting royalty. Only Wendy, who always sat beautifully straight, turned to see who else was there: a purely music-loving and mostly badly dressed crowd.

The two works on the program were Klaro's *Unstructured Meditation for Piano and String Trio* and the Brahms Piano Quartet in C Minor. Klaro was pianist for both, but his composition was to be played first. Polly thought this brave of him. In the program notes he was quoted as saying: "Most audiences have traditional ears, so I wish to approach them before the great traditionalists get to them. In this piece I strive to have a melodic line emerge from structured form-lessness, rather as a statue emerges from stone." Of his music in general, the esteemed music critic Julian Dretzin had said: "Von Waldau likes to ambush his listeners with beauty."

Polly was a little frightened of this concert. In her present state, music went off like a depth charge, and Brahms was the composer she loved best. She did not need to be afraid of Klaro. His music was of a highly cerebral sort, gorgeous and remote. Polly knew you were meant to listen to music purely as music and not have it remind you of other things, but the melody—austere and rather mournful—made her think about herself, about her present sadness, her fear that her life would never be innocent again, and about Lincoln, who was an artist, too. As for the others in the Solo-Miller party, with the exception of Henry, Jr., who looked slightly moronic, and Henry Demarest, who was a plain, old-fashioned music-appreciator, the look of the higher mind was all over them. Beate seemed absolutely elevated. Music to them was philosophy, mathematics. They liked to be challenged by brain food of a very sublime order. And best of all was criticizing the performance at dinner. Wendy adored a bad performance, especially of anything written for the flute, an instrument she loathed. A bad flute player was all her joy: "So breathy and *spitty*," she liked to say. From the expressions of mathematical rapture on the faces of her family, Polly knew they realized Klaro for the real thing. How nice to have a first-rate composer to show off! Underneath that rapture, of course, was pure relief.

There was no break between pieces, which Polly took as a sign of Klaro's self-confidence. It robbed everyone of a chance to shake his hand and congratulate him, while giving the audience the briefest moment in which to read the program as instruments were retuned.

According to the notes, the Brahms Piano Quartet had been written during one of the unhappiest periods of Brahms's life. Composition had been an agonizing struggle for him, he was unknown in his home town, whose recognition he badly craved, and he had fallen hopelessly in love with Clara Schumann, who was older than he, and whose husband, Robert, was his dearest friend.

These days Polly had a working interest in what unhappiness might produce. She was reminded of Lincoln's white pictures, those intense products of what he called his "reign of terror." Color had hurt his eyes. His bones had ached and he had had both insomnia and bad dreams. His brother, Gus, had encouraged him to see another psychiatrist, but still he had suffered for months and months. Those white pictures were more evocative of suffering than any representational picture Polly had ever seen. Eventually he had met Polly and fallen in love. He said, "Unhappiness isn't the worst thing in the world. It doesn't last forever and it usually teaches you something about yourself."

When the Brahms Piano Quartet was published, Brahms had suggested illustrating the title page with a picture of a man pointing a pistol at his head, since that was the spirit in which the piece had been written. Polly put the program down, and listened. She was waiting for the third movement, which the program informed her was something of a love song, a testament to Brahms's devotion to and love for Clara Schumann.

This movement began with a theme so grave, so ravishing, and so touching that Polly was afraid she might cry out. Penned in on either side by family but secure in the darkness, Polly lowered her head so that no one could see the tears that slid down her cheeks.

It was childish to be listening to the most beautiful music in the world and have the reactions of an overwrought teenager, but no one noticed, and by the time the lights came on, Polly was herself again.

Eight

The weather became more severe: it sleeted, it snowed again, and then everything froze over. The torrent of family parties ebbed. Everyone had taken a look at Beate, acknowledged Paul's new standing in the family, and gotten used to the idea of Paul and Beate as a married couple. They had now been absorbed and would never again, except briefly when the baby was born, be subjected to such intense scrutiny. They would establish their own rituals. This would draw the family into their orbit, but would not conflict at all with those occasions specific to Wendy or Polly. Andreya had no rituals; she and Henry were the family guests.

Beate's festivals were Twelfth Night, New Year's Day, and Holy Thursday—the von Waldau family holidays. On Twelfth Night she would make a Twelfth Night cake, on New Year's Day she would have pancakes, and on Holy Thursday —Gründonnerstag—she would follow the von Waldau tradition of putting branches over the door and serving spinach soup and fried walnuts. Years of Twelfth Night, New Year's Day, and Gründonnerstag had unraveled before Polly's eyes as Beate, at a family dinner, explained the festivals by which she would enrich the Solo-Millers. This, of course, sat well with Henry and Wendy, who were medieval in their outlook and liked to build a network of fortified castles close to one another.

Lincoln said that Polly was set into her family the way a sapphire was set into a bracelet. He brooded mightily on Polly. Those family obligations forced him to see somewhat less of her, and when he saw her she was very low.

When the family went back to normal Polly did not. She had stood next to Henry through all those family parties, in her heavy silk dress. She wore the diamond earrings Henry had given her as an engagement present, her plain wedding ring, and her grandmother's watch. She knew what she looked like: a happy and successful matron. Her younger cousins looked up to her and Henry. This gave her an overwhelming sense of being a fraud. Only she knew the truth: that she felt as if she had a stone in her heart. That she often found it difficult to breathe. That she felt thousands of miles away from her own husband. That she had a lover. That Henry's abstraction upset her wildly. That his distance made her almost crazy for his affection. If she threw her arms around his neck, he patted her absently and then unhooked her hands and put them at her sides. She looked at Henry and she knew she loved him, but she could not get near him. Had it always felt like that to her? Had she been so intent upon having life proceed in a certain way that she had never noticed what it felt like to be lonely, rejected, and unsure? Even their most elemental connection left her lonely: she was sleeping with two men.

Her own discomfort was so neatly hidden that she wondered what Henry might be hiding from her—the charges, accusations, and hostilities he might be harboring. Perhaps he was in love with someone else. She could hear herself saying in a frightened, modest voice, "Oh, Henry, I'm so worried about us. I feel so far away from you." And she imagined him telling her gravely that he loved and respected her, but that he was not happy; that he had turned to his work, that he had never been in love with her, but in the *idea* of them.

Polly was sophisticated enough to know about projection. Was this what *she* felt? She and Henry might dovetail, they might fit as married people ought, but did they actually have a taste for each other? Had she stopped noticing Henry? Did he surprise her? A husband, like a wife or a daughter, is part of a household and can be taken for granted as easily as a chair or lamp. Polly wanted things to be right, but now she did not know in what way she meant this. Would everything be right if Henry paid more attention to her? Or was it more complicated? If it was, she did not yet know in what way, and there were many times when Polly felt that her life might explode before her eyes and shatter into pieces before she found out.

Henry was as low as she was, and neither could turn to the other for comfort. The prettiness of her household, the sturdiness of her children, the very handsomeness of her husband shamed her—she did not deserve these things if she did not relish them. She felt that she and Henry were prisoners. A lovely meal, a weekend at the seashore, a long talk were not going to make things better. She did not know how these things were made better. She only knew that she felt condemned to undergo her sense of panic, confusion, and eventual loss the only way she knew how: by putting the best possible face on things, keeping going, smiling, making conversation, and trying to keep everything firmly in its normal place.

She was quieter than Lincoln had seen her and he was afraid to ask what was on her mind. If it was Henry it was none of his business; if it *was* his business he was afraid to hear it. Perhaps what was on Polly's mind was giving Lincoln up, and this alarmed him horribly. Life was not going to put another Polly in his path, someone good and kind and dear whom he might see enough of to make life sweet, but not enough of to threaten him.

As for Polly, she looked at Lincoln with longing, and knew that he would never rescue her, but that she needed someone to love her without complication or encumbrance, and he loved her in exactly that way.

One icy afternoon, Lincoln told Polly that the Galerie Georges Deliel in Paris had definitely offered him a one-man show in April. They were sitting at the table having coffee.

"Oh, Linky! How wonderful," said Polly.

"I've got to be there for about a month," said Lincoln. "Maybe longer. I want you to come with me, for a week."

"I can't, Lincoln," said Polly. "You know that."

"You can so, Dot. Tell Henry you need a week to yourself. Tell him you're overtired and overworked, just like him. Tell him the society of reading project analyzers is meeting in Paris. Get Concita or Concita's cousin to take the grubs, or send them to your mother's. You *can* do it."

"I can't, Lincoln," Polly said. "You don't know how it is." She got up and began to pace around the kitchen, coffee cup in hand.

"I do know how it is," said Lincoln. "You have a million more moving parts than I do. All right, if you won't go to Paris with me, give me one night with you. Just one. If I've got to be away from you for such a long time, let me wake up one morning with you next to me." He grabbed her by the hand.

Polly's features closed up, a sight Lincoln knew her well

enough to observe with tenderness. Henry, Jr., knew how to look like a closed door, too. Lincoln and he had been kite-flying friends for years before Lincoln had known Polly. He knew a variety of Solo-Miller looks, which most Solo-Millers wore a great deal of the time but which lasted only a moment in Polly. This one was replaced by a complicated expression that included longing, desire, perplexity, struggle. Polly's essence overcame her family every time, Lincoln thought. Her eyes changed color when emotion overtook her. It was not possible to see her looking like this and not take her into his arms.

"Oh, Lincoln," she sighed. "You really are as free as a bird. I wish I were, but I'm not. It isn't loving you that makes me sad, but what I have to do to get to you."

There was nothing Lincoln could say to this. His life was light and clean as a palette knife and he had no one to answer to, no one to look after, and nowhere he was expected to be.

"Maybe we can have a sleep-over date. That's what we used to call them in fifth grade," Polly said. "Right before you go, if Henry is away. I'll make dinner for you. We can go to the zoo in the afternoon and stroll around and then come home, have dinner, take a bath, and sleep in the same bed, like normal people."

When she left to go home, she was as sad as Lincoln had ever seen her.

Henry was due home late that evening, but when Polly got home, there was a message that he would be back tomorrow. On the sideboard in the kitchen was the tray Polly had set in the morning—a tray that would have contained a pot of tea, a plate of sandwiches, a peeled orange, and some shortbread for Henry's late snack. She always made up these trays for Henry, as she had made them up for her father when he came home late from a trip. Now she dismantled it, feeling the combination of anger, disappointment, and relief she was all too familiar with.

In the kitchen Pete and Dee-Dee were ready for dinner. One night a week, Concita cooked *arroz con pollo*. It had begun to sleet and it lifted Polly's heart to note that she was glad to be in the kitchen with her children, who ate happily, mashing everything together. Pete liked to entertain Dee-Dee by describing the natural life of whatever it was they were having for dinner. For this reason the idea of vegetable dinners did not appeal to Pete. He tried very hard to get Dee-Dee to cry, but Dee-Dee was a born hardhead, and the idea that a real bird with feathers had died for her dinner plate had no sentiment attached to it at all. Chickens were very nice to look at in the country but in no way resembled her *arroz con pollo*.

"They flap and scratch, and make little noises like this, Dee-Dee," said Pete. He then uttered a series of very lifelike chicken clucks.

"Where did you learn to do that?" Polly asked.

"From those chickens Mrs. Dunaway has in Maine. She let me sit on the fence and watch them."

"I did, too," said Dee-Dee.

"Yes, but you were too little to learn how to make their noises," Pete said. "See that leg you were going to eat? Maybe one of Mrs. Dunaway's chickens used to have that leg and now you're eating it."

"You're eating some part of a chicken, too," said Dee-Dee.

"I don't have a leg," said Pete. "I have these other parts that aren't as sad as a leg." He lapsed again into chicken sounds.

"These aren't Mrs. Dunaway's chickens, anyway," Dee-Dee said. "The chickens we get don't come from Maine, unless we're in Maine. They come from New Jersey, and from the DEL*MAR*VA Peninsula."

Polly was appropriately awed. One of her children could imitate domestic poultry, and the other knew where it came from.

"Dee-Dee," Polly said, "did you learn that at school?"

"Yes, Mommy," said Dee-Dee with becoming modesty. "It's Delaware, Maryland, and Virginia."

Most nights Polly could have listened endlessly to her children, whom she admired a great deal. They constantly surprised her. They were just as inventive and imaginative as the books say children are meant to be, and they had very sweet temperaments. Pete had never expected that his depictions of animal life at the dinner table would faze Dee-Dee. A few years before, the thought of one of Mrs. Dunaway's chickens would have caused *him* to burst into tears. The fact was that he liked to scare himself and make himself cry. At the most frightening horror movies, when Pete, who always insisted on going to these movies, burrowed his head into his mother's coat, Dee-Dee sat placidly eating popcorn by the handful.

But Polly was tired, and she ached. It hurt her that her attention was wandering, that a lump rose in her throat, that she wanted her darling children to go right to sleep so that she could be alone to think.

But Pete and Dee-Dee demanded a story. Polly sat with them after dinner while they did their homework, and during the half hour of their baths. The story was the most important nightly ritual, unless Polly and Henry were going out, and then Pete and Dee-Dee read to each other.

Once they were in their pajamas and robes, with their bunny slippers on their feet, they snuggled up next to Polly on their parents' bed. Polly read them a Grimms' fairy tale. They were crazy about Grimms' fairy tales—the more gruesome the better. She read them "Fundevogel."

"There was once a Forester who went into the woods to hunt, and he heard a cry like that of a little child," Polly read. The woodsman finds a little boy way up in a tree, where a bird had carried him. He takes the child home with him to be the companion of his little daughter, Lina. He calls the child Fundevogel because he had been found by a bird.

"Fundevogel and Lina were so fond of each other that they could not bear to be out of each other's sight," Polly read. Her eyes filled with tears and a lump rose up in her throat. She took a deep breath.

"Go on, Mommy," said Dee-Dee.

Polly began to read again. One day Lina sees the wicked cook boiling a big pot of water. She asks the cook what the water is for and the cook says that she is going to catch Fundevogel, throw him into the pot, and boil him up. The next morning Lina wakes Fundevogel and tells him what the cook has in mind. The children run away, and when the cook discovers that they are missing, she flies into a rage and dispatches a party of hunters to bring them back.

In the woods, the children hear someone approaching.

"Lina said to Fundevogel, 'Never forsake me, and I will never forsake you,'" Polly read. Her voice wavered, so she stopped and took another long breath.

"Go *on*, Mommy," said Dee-Dee.

Polly read: "And Fundevogel answered, 'I will never forsake you as long as I live.'"

Lina turns into a rosebush, and Fundevogel into a rosebud. The hunters pass them by and the cook tells them that they should have torn the rosebush to pieces and sends them out again. This time Lina turns into a church, and Fundevogel into a chandelier. Again the hunters pass by. The cook tells them they should have torn down the church and smashed the chandelier, and then she goes out with them herself. Lina turns into a pond, and Fundevogel turns into a duck. When the cook bends down to take a drink, the duck pulls her into the water by her hair and drowns her.

Polly read: "Then the children went home together as happy as possible, and if they are not dead yet, then they are still alive."

She closed the book abruptly, collected her children, put them both to bed, and kissed them. Then she fled down the hallway to the bathroom, where she buried her head in a bath towel and cried until she hurt.

She sat at the kitchen table, drank a glass of water, and turned to the telephone. She dialed Lincoln, hung up, and dialed again.

"Hello, Doreen. I thought you would call," Lincoln said.

"It's only me," said Polly.

"I know it's only you, you sad little thing. Are you all right? You looked pretty far down the road when you left here."

Polly began to cry. "I'm sorry, Linky. I'm not much fun. All I do is weep."

"I don't care if you weep. What are you sorry for?"

"Just for feeling so awful. I love you, and it isn't making anyone happy."

"It makes me happy," said Lincoln. "Besides, it's not your job to go around spreading happiness like a fertilizer machine. The lawyer isn't coming home tonight, I assume. Do you want me to come and visit you, now that the grubs are asleep?"

There was nothing Polly would have loved more than a visit from Lincoln, but everything in New York conspires to keep life on the up and up. Polly would never have left her children alone for even five minutes, and what would the doorman think, letting a man up to the Demarests' at this time of night? What would the elevator man think? Surely they knew that Mr. Demarest was away. Supposing Lincoln spent the night? What would the morning elevator man say?

Lincoln had been to the apartment once, when Henry was out of town and the children were staying with their grandparents overnight. Polly had worked late, picked Lincoln up, and brought him home with her. Her heart had been in her throat the whole time. Lincoln had gone prowling: after all, she knew his studio, so why should he not know hers? She had made him an omelette, but was so nervous that Lincoln had wolfed his dinner and then taken Polly out to the movies.

"You could get into a cab and come down here," Lincoln said.

"I don't have anyone to stay with the children," Polly said.

"They're too old for crib death," said Lincoln. "Can't you leave them alone for an hour?"

"It wouldn't be an hour and you know it," said Polly. "I don't like to ask our sitter downstairs at the last minute. She's too precious. These teen-age baby-sitters have to be treated like rare porcelain. It's all so complicated." And besides, when Henry was away he called late at night, and where could Polly say she had been? She was not the type to take off to the movies at the last minute. It was hopeless.

Everything was hopeless. At night she lay in bed next to a man she loved, and craved the love of another man. Her husband did not come back from business trips when he said he would—she had never gotten used to it, although she thought she had. The sight of the tray she had set for him, with his big cup, and teapot, and the glass he liked to drink his brandy and soda from, and the plate for his sandwiches, and the linen napkin, made her realize that for years she had simply turned away and told herself that these were the things of life, plain and simple, and they did not matter one bit.

But she could not deny it: the fact that Lincoln actually loved her kept her going. If Henry was working late, if he was away, if he was distracted, so much the better. It gave her more time with Lincoln; it gave her justification to be with Lincoln; and it would never be noticed that she had been with Lincoln.

Lincoln was angelic, but only in context. He hated noise, the company of most people, ordinary life. He did not go to the movies or to the theater, although he once in a while went to a dinner party. He said, rather proudly, that he had missed almost every major event of the past decade. He was scarcely interested in other painters. His society consisted of his brother, a few old friends from college, and a painter friend or two from art school. Once in a while, he bestirred himself from his studio and went kite-flying with Henry and Andreya. And he saw Polly. He could have done without almost anyone except her. Late at night it pained Polly that she contributed to his hermitage. She believed that all people unless impeded wanted family, needed family, that family was what life was for. In her secret heart she felt that there must be something wrong in Lincoln's anti-family feelings, and that his stance was useful to her made her feel immoral. She sometimes hoped that one day she might be her old self again, a happy wife and mother, and Lincoln, woken up to the joys of love, would seek a mate and build a nest. This rosy vision filled her with longing and dread, and she did not believe it for a second.

At first it made no difference to Polly that their love affair had no future. She had simply been in love. The early stages of romantic love are like the world before the Fall: sweet, innocent, full of pure, unadorned feeling. The sweetness of that feeling flavored everything. But now alone in her household, her children asleep and Lincoln in his studio, she saw the futility of their situation. She could not go to a tropical island with him, or to Paris. They would never spend a night together. His desires in the world were few. Polly's were many. She loved him; would never have him; and didn't want him.

"I wish you could come up," Polly said.

"Well, I would," said Lincoln, "if you weren't so afraid of what the elevator man might say."

"Don't be mad at me because I'm afraid of the elevator man," said Polly. "I *am* afraid of the elevator man. It's my nature."

"I'm not mad, Doe. I'm sad because I'd like to come up and be with you and I can't."

"Think of me, Linky," said Polly.

"I always think of you," Lincoln said.

The next day she sat at her desk in her office trying to work but she was exhausted, distracted, and tense. She had not slept well, and when she had finally fallen off to sleep, she had had two terrible dreams. The first was that her whole family had gone off to Maine without her—they had simply forgotten all about her. Then she dreamed that Pete and Dee-Dee were lost and she had run to Lincoln's studio to find them. When she got there, the door was open and the room was empty. It looked as if no one had lived there for a very long time. The windows were thick with dust and the walls were covered with cobwebs. Wind blew through a broken window in the back across the bare, dirty floor. These dreams had upset her so terribly that she had gone to check her children. She found them as she always found them. Pete was curled up at the foot of his bed with all his bedclothes on the floor. Dee-Dee slept like a medieval knight on a coffin, with her hands folded on her chest, neat as a pin. She was so still that it was not unusual for Polly to bend down to make sure that she was breathing.

Polly had not been able to get back to sleep and now she could not start to work. She felt as if she were the only person in the world in trouble, and that her trouble was herself.

When she looked up from the papers she could not make herself concentrate on, Martha Nathan was standing in the doorway.

"You look pretty tired," Martha said.

"Didn't sleep," said Polly.

"That's consoling," said Martha. "I always thought you slept the sleep of the right and just."

"I think only the right and just get to do that," said Polly.

"If you're not right and just," said Martha, sitting down, "then there is no hope in this world. I *never* sleep. I am a bat. I think I've gotten about four hours of sleep in the last six months. As soon as I lie down, my life flashes by me and causes me to sit up faint with dread."

"Your life isn't dreadful, is it?"

"Well, not my life per se," Martha said. "It's my head. It isn't life. It's what's inside that counts."

"What's inside?" asked Polly.

"I am the world's most neurotic woman," said Martha grandly. "See how cheerful I am about it? My years of expensive psychotherapy have made me positively sunny on this depressing subject. Yes, at least half a dozen well-known shrinks have peered inside my alleged mind."

"And what do they discover?"

"Oh, this and that," said Martha. "For instance, why do I like to learn a thing and then hate to do it? Why is it that I have hung around with the same person for seven years and have never once thought of getting married?"

"Not once?" Polly said.

"Well, what I mean is that when I think of it I sort of recoil as from a snake," Martha said. "It isn't really nice to feel that way with such a nice saintly boyfriend as Spud, but of course even though he is nice and saintly, I sort of can't stand him."

Spud Sawyer was Martha's longtime beau. He was a mathematical genius, and Polly had met him when he came to pick Martha up at the office. He had silvery-blond hair and looked almost as young as Martha did.

"You're my model of the way things ought to be," Martha said. "I mean, you have it aced. You know how you feel about all the things that cause me anxiety. Husbands. Children. Family."

It occurred to Polly to set Martha straight, but she could not. The notion was too distressing.

"Oh, Martha," she said instead. "You have everything in front of you. You haven't made any mistakes yet. You haven't done anything irrevocable. You don't have to marry Spud, you know."

Martha yawned. "Gee, this makes me sleepy," she said. "I compare myself with you. I really do. I wish I *wanted* a life like yours. Don't take that the wrong way. I think the way you live is right. You love your family. I love mine but I can't stand to be in the same room with them. You got married. You have Pete and Dee-Dee. What do I have? I have my neurosis and a nice boyfriend I can't bring myself to marry. Sometimes I say to myself: Martha—that's what I call myself when I'm talking to myself—Martha, I say, why don't you marry Spud? Spud always says to me: Martha, why don't you *try* to shut up? Why don't I? Why don't I try to shut up and get married? Besides, how will I ever experience adultery if I don't get married? After all, I say to myself, I don't live in a country under Islamic law. I could get married and then if it got too intense I could have a little affair to make me feel better and I wouldn't even run the risk of being stoned to death, although in the case of someone as neurotic as me, maybe being stoned to death might be a reasonable solution."

Polly was silent.

"I ought to try to shut up," Martha said. "I just blab along. Did I say something awful?"

"No," said Polly, who was staring at her hands. "It hurts me that I'm a model for you. I'm not a model of anything. If I lived in an Islamic country I would be stoned to death because I am having a love affair."

"Oh," said Martha. "The painter at lunch. Lincoln."

At the sound of his name, tears came into Polly's eyes.

"Was it so obvious?" she said. "I was afraid it was."

"I guessed. And if I hadn't, it certainly would make sense now that I think of it," said Martha. "You looked awfully related to each other, and he called you Dottie. I figured he might be an old friend."

"I love him," Polly said. "I believe it's ruining my life."

"What do your pals think of this?" asked Martha.

"You're the only person who knows."

"I am? That's not right. Why doesn't anyone know?"

"I don't have anyone to tell," Polly said. "I can't tell my family." She looked down at her desk because she was about to cry.

"But I'm safe," Martha said. "Because we don't know anyone in common."

"I suppose that's right," Polly said. "You are safe."

Martha considered this.

"I'm glad you told me," she said. "It cheers me up. It's nice to know that other people who you think have perfect lives have trouble, too. It must be awful not to have anyone to tell."

"I never thought of it until recently," Polly said. "In my family, we have family. I used to tell my mother things, but I never had anything like this to tell."

"My family is always on the outs," Martha said. "We're forced to have pals. Come on. Let's go out to lunch."

At lunch Polly learned what sweet relief there was in talking about The Beloved Other. Martha was a wonderful listener. Polly talked about Henry, about Lincoln, about everything.

"Something happened to me," she said. "I grew out of something—I don't know what, really. This isn't my language. I don't *know* anything anymore. I'm not sure of anything. I used to be so sure of being sure. I walk down the street and see people who are really in trouble, who are sick or disabled, or poor or crazy, and here I am. I have a wonderful family. I don't have to worry very much about money. I have a job I like, my children really are marvelous, and I am married to a man I admire and love."

"Maybe you just want the terms changed a little," Martha offered.

"That's exactly it," Polly said. She sat very straight in her chair with her hands gripping the table, as if she were making a point at the debating society. "I want the terms changed. I'm tired of my same old self. But it seems so selfish, so greedy, and so ungrateful when I have so much."

"It isn't what you have," Martha said. "It's how you feel about it. Just because you have a nice life doesn't mean you can't get in trouble."

"It isn't *real* trouble," Polly said.

"It isn't sickness or grief," Martha said. "It isn't death or war. It's the sort of misery you have to have the luxury for, but that doesn't make it less miserable or serious."

"I'd like to believe that," said Polly. "Mostly I just feel shamed."

"Listen," said Martha as she leaned over the table for the

sugar. "Once you have food and shelter, you start agonizing over how you want your life to be. Next to that, food and shelter is a snap." She stirred her coffee.

"This is the first serious trouble I've ever been in," Polly said.

"Yes?" said Martha. "Welcome to the club."

As they walked toward the office, Polly reflected that Martha was light as a feather. Her life was not mired and entangled. When she said as much, Martha turned on her.

"That's what married people with children always think," she said. "It's like phobics. The person scared of elevators thinks the person who's afraid of centipedes is ridiculous. You think your trouble is more serious than mine because you're married and have children. When you wake up at four o'clock in the morning you think your anxiety must be the worst kind and that if you were single life would be a snap. I wake up and think about how I'm too conflicted to get married and that you have it all. Tonight when I wake up at four in the morning I will say to myself: At least Polly has a husband and children. So there."

Polly put her arm through Martha's. "I'm glad I know you," she said. "I wish I had known you a long time ago."

"I'm not so nice," Martha said.

"You're clear," said Polly. "Anyone can be nice."

But at four o'clock in the morning, when Polly woke up, the thought of Martha's trouble did not console her. The notion that everyone gets into trouble at some point or other did not console her. She felt that she had been caught in a snare. Falling in love had not set her free—it had pushed her into an unfamiliar landscape in which everything was askew. Falling in love was like being inoculated with a virus that gave you a disease you could not shake. It dogged you and got in your way, and never for a moment could you forget that you were sick. You woke up with it in the morning, lived with it during the day, and took it to bed with you at night. There was no cure, no relief. Nothing made it better—nothing even made it less.

Nine

Happy marriages! How blatantly they flourished around Polly's distress. As the last of the winter spun on, Polly was surrounded by happy love affairs, the engagements produced by these love affairs, wedding plans, and weddings. Eventually she would see honeymoon photos and be invited to the first apartments of a squad of happy young couples. Two of her cousins became engaged. Her Philadelphia cousin got married. Another had fallen in love with someone perfectly suitable. And, of course, there were Paul and Beate.

At every family party Polly was aware of how well matched these couples looked. She and Henry looked well matched, too. Did this mean that trouble would come to all these matched sets? She regarded Paul and Beate. It was impossible to imagine them discussing their relationship or having an argument, or to think what trouble they might have. They moved with a grave, institutional dignity that precluded such things as spats, tiffs, and disagreements. Their relationship was like a monument or a war memorial and did not need to be discussed. Even Andreya and Henry, Jr., who resembled a pair of golden-retriever puppies more than anything else, seemed quite above the ordinary trouble of married people.

Polly, of course, did not actually know what ordinary trouble might be. Her family, as far as she could tell, were immune to these things.

"Darling, I just don't understand these books about marriage," Wendy had said to Polly more than once. "There's almost nothing else in the bookshops! How to live with your mate. How to live without your mate. How not to live through your mate. How to mate. How not to mate. And the people who buy them! I suppose it's no accident, poor things. That's what modern life has come to. No one knows what anything is supposed to be *for*. People simply don't have much sense, after all."

It was clear to Polly that human relationships, in the modern psychological sense, struck Wendy as rather silly. There had been one divorce in the family—poor Ellen Hendricks. She had married a very unsuitable man, divorced him a year later. Then she married a very suitable man, to everyone's relief, and produced a family; her divorce was entirely forgotten about.

Struggle was not admired by the Solo-Millers. Unlike Martha Nathan, they did not believe in change and growth and enlightenment. They believed that nice people were born so perfectly formed that change and growth were quite unnecessary. All really nice people *were* enlightened. How grateful they were that they were spared those dreary, ordinary struggles that got in the way of life and work—the sort of struggle that fell to the upwardly mobile, the social climber, the striver, the unworthy.

In her present state of mind, her family did not console Polly. She knew she had fallen from grace. She knew that in her family setting she was a liar—a person with a horrible secret. She wished that she could emulate her family's posture fully and truly: so firm, so unwavering, so strong in purpose. On this subject Lincoln had but one sentence. "How clever of them," he said to her, "not to have taught you the word 'smug.'"

What had been expected of Polly when she got married was simply that she be perfect and that her life run smoothly—a simple task for which most Solo-Millers seemed equipped. She was looked up to by her cousins, who came to her for advice on all domestic subjects or when their friends' children—this of course never happened to them—had reading problems. Henry Demarest was the most available, the nicest man in the family. He was not intimidating and formidable like Henry, Sr., or unintelligible like Henry, Jr., or a stone wall like Paul, and the younger cousins could confide in him their law-school problems, their feelings about their firms or the judges they clerked for.

In modern life, people either knew more than they ought or less than they should. The family knew a great deal about Polly and Henry, and, of course, they knew absolutely nothing at all.

There had been no break in Henry's bad year. He had had to cope with a long trial, an incompetent judge, a great deal of travel, and an expert witness who had died before giving testimony. It looked unlikely that this case could be won, which meant a lengthy and enervating appeal. He already had a case on appeal—another unrewarding job. He felt caught in a massive flood of paper. The result of this was that his appetite for the law left him. The joy and pride he was used to taking in his work had disappeared. Henry's trouble was easy to see. It had a real cause. Under such conditions, a woman cannot expect a man to console her in her formless, inexpressible distress, and she cannot accuse him of being distant and hurting her feelings.

It was Polly's job to cheer Henry on, to make his life sweet, but nowadays he radiated a nervous concentration she was frightened to interrupt, or was it that she had never interrupted him before? Was the fierce look he often wore familiar to her?

He was going away for a week and Polly sat on the chaise and watched him pack. His shirts were stacked on the bed. His suits were laid out over a chair.

"Take some wool socks," Polly said.

"They have holes in them," Henry said.

"They don't," said Polly. "I darned them all. Are you going to take something to kick around in?"

"There's not going to be very much kicking around for me," Henry said. "This trip is fairly grueling."

Polly's heart sank. How awful for Henry to have to have a grueling trip. He was going from Geneva to London and stopping in Boston on the way home. It frightened her to see how tired he looked. What if it was too much for him and he got sick? Tears came into her eyes.

"I wish you didn't have to go," she said, quavering.

"Polly, this is the worst time," Henry said.

"I didn't say, please don't go," Polly said. Even to herself her voice sounded frantic. She was instantly ashamed. She made everything worse, and Henry was violently touchy these days.

"I'm sorry I snapped at you," Henry said. "Come help me figure out what ties to take."

"With what suits?"

"Those," said Henry, nodding toward the chair.

Polly contemplated the suits. She looked at Henry. He was absorbed in his packing. Of course he had a great deal to figure out—what to take, how to schedule his appointments, how to arrange time to think. Men's clothes were so heavy. Henry would have to carry his briefcase and a suitpress as well as a suitcase. She imagined him at the Geneva airport, strained and tired, carrying his suitpress and wishing he were home asleep.

It was almost midnight. Tomorrow night Polly would sleep in their bed alone. She would have the week to herself. If she wanted, she could see Lincoln every night—but of course she would not allow herself that luxury. Henry and Andreya had asked her to dinner at their loft. She felt she owed it to them as the only member of the family who ever went to see them. She had planned dinner with Paul and Beate a week ago, and that she knew was an unbreakable obligation. And she had to spend time with the children, who deserved her attention. And Martha wanted her to come for supper. How was she going to fit all this in, when her one desire was to be with Lincoln? Henry's leaving made this possible. She watched him pack. How she longed for him to stay home with her, to be close to her, to save her. How she longed for him to be away. The air between them was full of strain. Often the sight of him remote and preoccupied produced in her a piercing loneliness she had never felt before.

Henry was packed. His suitcase lay open on the luggage holder. His suitpress was zipped, and his briefcase was lying on the chair with a neat stack of papers on top of it.

Polly wanted to say, "Henry, will you come to bed, or must you stay up?" but she could not bear to. It made her too angry and hurt. Finally, she could stand it no longer. "Henry," she said, "it's your last night home. Please come to bed with me." Why did she have to beg her husband to want her?

"I'm beat," said Henry. "Turn the covers back. I'm half asleep on my feet."

He came out of the bathroom in his English pajamas, smelling of toothpaste. Polly sat staring at the two bedposts. Henry slid in next to her.

"Turn the light off," said Henry.

"I don't want to," Polly said. Henry also smelled of shaving cream. She looked closely at him. He had shaved. She rubbed her cheek next to his.

"Oh, Henry," she sobbed. "I'm so lonely for you."

"I'm lonely for me, too, Polly." He kissed the top of her head.

"Kiss me for real," Polly said. "Oh, please, kiss me for real." He kissed her for real and she felt as she had always felt. "Henry," she whispered, "you don't ever want me anymore."

"I sometimes feel I hardly have myself," Henry said softly. "I do want you, Polly." She looked at him longingly, and in an instant they were in each other's arms.

Polly sat on her side of the bed and watched Henry sleep. How tender and handsome he looked. How odd it seemed to her to feel so far away, so angry, so troubled, when Henry could make her feel so overwhelmed, so profoundly moved, so deeply satisfied. How odd that this did not make her feel any different. He stirred next to her and Polly covered his shoulder with the quilt. He shrugged it off and held out his arm. She crept beside him and he enfolded her. They fit perfectly, but, then, they always had.

He left the next morning, after breakfast, with the same haggard, preoccupied look on his face. Nothing made any difference, Polly thought—not love, not comfort, not the idea of a safe haven. Henry kissed her good-bye and patted her absently. He was already on the plane before he even set foot out the door. She waited with him until the elevator came, and when the doors closed she was too tired to bother pretending that she was not relieved. As soon as the children had left for school, she dialed Lincoln. This is what I have come to, Polly said to herself. My husband goes out the door and I am instantly on the telephone to my lover.

"Hi, Dot," said Lincoln. "All alone at last, huh?"

"Hi, Linky," Polly said. "I've only got a second before I fly out of here to the office. I've got to go in today."

"Well," said Lincoln, "have you managed to book yourself solid with Solo-Millers so that you can't come down and pass the evenings with your devoted friend?"

"I have to have dinner at Henry and Andreya's," Polly said. "That's always an early night. They get sleepy and I usually leave around nine-thirty. I could come to you after that, if I get the baby-sitter until midnight."

"Keep going."

"Paul and Beate want to have dinner. I'd like to cancel, but I don't see how I can. But I want them to come here. I can work at home and you could come and spend the afternoon with me. I'll just have to change the office around a little."

"And then?"

"Martha wants me to come to dinner, but I'm going to tell her I can only have a drink. If you picked me up . . ."

"My, my," Lincoln said. "Quite a schedule."

"Oh, Lincoln," said Polly. "Don't be cruel to me. I feel as if everyone has the right to know where I am all the time. I have to see my brothers, and I have to have time for the children."

"All right, Dottie, don't get upset. Call me when you get to work and we'll figure it out."

Polly sat down at the kitchen table. She made a list for Concita, called Nancy Jewell's mother to confirm that Nancy would baby-sit. From her office she called Paul to see if he and Beate would come to dinner, instead of her going to them.

"We'd much rather you came to us, Polly," said Paul.

"It's a little hard for me this week," Polly said.

"It's much harder for Beate to come to you. She has patients all day."

"I'll be working at home and I'll cook. It will be easier for Beate since she'll get waited on."

"I'll have to speak to her about this," said Paul, "and let you know."

When he did let her know, he did so grudgingly. Polly said, "Why don't we just cancel this and make a date for after Henry gets home and we can all go out to dinner?"

"We scheduled this dinner with you, Polly. Beate and I make very few plans these days, and we like to stick by the plans we do make."

A cold, wet sheet of fury tore through Polly.

"I have a wonderful idea," she said. "You and Beate have dinner and pretend I'm there. Then your plans won't go off schedule."

"I'm afraid I don't understand you, Polly," said Paul.

"I work as hard as you and Beate, and I have the children," Polly said. "This is a bad week for me, so if you can't come here, let's put it off until Henry gets back."

That afternoon Wendy called.

"Your brother Paul is very upset," she said. "What on earth is wrong?"

"Nothing is wrong," said Polly. "I'm having dinner with Henry and Andreya tonight and with Martha Nathan on Wednesday and I don't want to be out so much. It's too much for them to come here. If Beate can't manage it, we'll do it some other time."

"I don't see why you can't cancel this Martha Nathan," Wendy said. "Isn't she your little office friend?"

"Yes," said Polly. "She is my friend and I'm not canceling her. I am going down to Henry and Andreya's tonight and I can easily see Paul and Beate next week."

"Darling, they do have rather a strict life," Wendy said.

"That's entirely their problem," Polly said. "I have work and the children. Let them bend to me a little."

"Well, what about the other nights?" Wendy said.

"I have a meeting Thursday and I would like a night with myself and the children, that's what."

"It seems rather a lot of time out," Wendy said. "Why can't Henry and Andreya come to you? It can't be very nice to go to them."

"I love to go to them," Polly said. "And I'm the only one who does."

"I think you're being rather selfish," Wendy said. "It isn't right for your job to leave you so little energy and time. It isn't worth it."

At this, Polly was silent. She had all the energy in the world to see Lincoln, but not the inclination to see Paul and Beate. Didn't she deserve to see Lincoln if she needed to, even if she had to lie to do so? After all, she had baked a huge plate of brownies to take to Henry and Andreya's—it was part of the deal that she always brought the dessert—and she would have fed Paul and Beate a delicious meal. Even if she was only going to have a drink with Martha, even if her real intention was to be with Lincoln, what was so terrible about doing that? She tried to do right by everyone, and she often felt that she was spread as thin as butter on a Danish sandwich.

"I don't want to talk about this," she said to Wendy. "I have work staring me in the face and that's more important at the moment than Paul and Beate's social schedule."

"Very well," said Wendy, and she hung up with one of her well-known huffs.

Henry and Andreya's loft was bare, white, and immaculate. It had almost no furniture. They slept on a Japanese cotton mattress atop what looked like a giant chest, but was actually a custom-built bureau in which they kept most of their clothes. They had two drawing tables, a large redwood picnic table at which they had their meals, and a sofa made of squishy pillows. On the wall hung their kites. The sight of these always gave Polly a pang and made her think of Lincoln's black-and-silver kite, which hung on his wall. Scattered around were large squashed-looking cushions filled with pellets that made an appealing crunch when sat on.

They had no interest in *things,* and since they had eloped they did not have the usual complement of wedding presents. The silver they had inherited from Henry's Hendricks grandmother they used as if it were plate and threw it into a drawer after dinner. They had sold Grandfather Solo-Miller's Empire furniture to buy the picnic table, which they had bought, at Paul's suggestion, from Mary Rensberg. It was polished redwood, made by a monk at a California mission, and had fruitwood pegs. The plates they used were enameled tin in primary colors. For dinner they gave Polly what they usually gave her—vegetable mess. Andreya was indifferent to food except for chocolate. Her only kitchen skill consisted in making chocolate sauce, and the only thing of interest in the larder was the large store of chocolate bars. These, Polly suspected, were Andreya's principal form of nourishment.

They sat down to dinner with Kirby under the table. The cold weather had made him quiescent and in this mellow state he became very loving toward Andreya, whom he followed all over the loft.

"I am teaching him to sing," she said. "We started singing lessons with the sound he makes when he hears police and fire sirens. Now I am training him with dog biscuits. I will demonstrate this after dinner."

The brownies Polly had brought for dessert were Henry, Jr.'s favorite, known as "slumped brownies" since they were slightly undercooked and had a chewy, custardy center. Henry could not take his eyes off them. He was not comfortable in the presence of two women, even if one was his wife and the other his sister. He believed that women were either about to do things to him, or get him to do things—for example, to behave correctly or modify his table manners. He also felt that women wanted to be left alone to talk about nail polish and babies. But a vestige of his early training remained, and he opened up the dinner-table conversation.

"Boy," he said, between shovels of vegetable mess, "you certainly pissed off old Paul and Beate. Ma actually called me. She wants me to find out if you're all right. You look all right to me. Are you all right? What the hell did you do, Pol?"

"I told them to come to me for dinner instead of me going to them."

"Oh, yeah? Geez, you'd think you put a nuclear device in their elevator. Well, they're pretty hived off."

"Hived off?" said Polly. "What does that mean?"

"It is as a swarm of bees leaving their nest," Andreya explained. "It is horrid how fast you eat, Henry."

"It gets me more food," Henry said. "Pass that dish over here, Andro. Geez, Polly, I can't believe you got everyone so riled. Paul and Beate are very hurt, Ma says."

"Oh, be quiet, Henry," Polly said. "I'm tired of Paul and Beate."

"Don't say that, Pol," Henry said. "It makes me nervous."

"Andreya, please make Henry sit up and eat like a person," Polly said. "Henry, sit up and say why it makes you nervous." She looked at her brother, whose posture resembled a slumped brownie. He had spilled rice on his sweater.

"Henry," Andreya said. "Sit up. Be dainty. Do not shovel your food. Say to Polly why you are nervous."

Henry sat up. "If *she* doesn't like Paul," he said to Andreya, "then what am I supposed to feel? Can I be excused, girls? Please?"

"Do meals around here always take three minutes?" Polly asked.

"Henry eats like a vacuum cleaner," Andreya said. "Sit down, Henry. We have not yet had Polly's brownies."

"Can't I take one with me? I'm sure you girls have a million things to talk about."

"No," said Andreya. "Stay here to have coffee. We will talk about Paul and Beate's baby and then I will read Polly's Tarot cards."

It always surprised Polly that someone as scientific as Andreya was interested in fortunetelling, but the Tarot deck was a hangover from her Czechoslovakian childhood, when her nurse had taught her how to use the cards. Every time Polly came to dinner, Andreya read her hand.

"Tell Polly what you think about the baby," Andreya said.

"I can't," Henry said. "The whole idea is too disgusting."

"Henry says the baby will be born in a little suit," Andreya said. "Whether it is a boy or a girl. It will have little shoes and black stockings and it will have a gold fountain pen."

"Maybe it'll be a big, jolly baby like Pete," Polly said. "Although when I had lunch the other day with Beate she seemed to feel that since Pete hadn't had the proper birth environment, he probably wouldn't be happy when he grew up."

"What about Dee-Dee?" Andreya said.

"Dee-Dee was born in the hospital elevator," Polly said. "God only knows what will become of her."

Henry, who had gulped his coffee and eaten three brownies, was very fidgety.

"Do we have to talk about this?" he pleaded. "Why does it have to take nine months? Why do we have to talk about this all the time? Andro, show Polly how Kirby sings and then I'm leaving the table."

Andreya sat Kirby on one of the cushions. She held a dog biscuit in front of his nose.

"I command you, Kirby," she said. "Sing!"

Kirby looked at Andreya with an expression of intense love and then threw back his head and gave forth a series of low, musical hound howls. Then he wagged his tail and licked Andreya's hand.

"You are a wonderful dog," Andreya said, patting him. "I love you always. Here is your biscuit. Now go with Henry." She turned to Polly. "Is that not a beautiful sight?"

Andreya was wearing black trousers and a striped football jersey. Henry wore almost the identical thing. If only, Polly thought, dogs wore football jerseys, they could parade around as triplets. The sight of Andreya and Kirby was, however, undeniably affecting.

"Kiss Andro good-bye," said Henry. Kirby threw his paws on Andreya's neck and licked her nose.

When Polly later reported these events to Lincoln, he said, "If they get any more adorable, someone will want to strangle them."

Henry went to his drawing table and took Kirby with him. The dishes were cleared and Andreya began to shuffle the Tarot deck.

"This is how I was taught," said Andreya. She said this every time, as a preamble. "Some people read the entire deck and some do the Celtic Cross, but I am reading what I was taught, which is called the Roman line. It is six cards across to show first your present condition, then your self alone, then the two issues on your mind, then how others see you, and finally the essence of all these things. Now you must shuffle for a long time."

As Polly shuffled, Andreya went on.

"The person being read must handle the deck—that is how the deck knows whose essence is infusing it."

"What a lotta junk," called Henry from his corner.

"Be quiet, Henry," Andreya said. "You must shuffle more. Now cut. Cut again and again. When you feel the deck is as you wish it, stop."

Polly cut three more times and stopped. She was suddenly terrified that the cards would give her away.

"Now," said Andreya. "Put down six cards one next to each other."

Polly threw the cards and Andreya turned them face up. Polly's heart was pounding. The first was a red Valentine heart pierced with three swords. The second showed a woman patting a lion. The name of this card was STRENGTH. The third card showed two lovers, and the fourth depicted a family standing under a rainbow. The fifth showed a woman in a garden with a bird perched on her shoulder, and the last was a person sitting up in bed, hands over eyes, as if waking from a terrible dream. A quilt covered his legs, and the wall beside him was hung with nine swords. There it was, for all the world to see.

"What does it mean?" Polly said. She suddenly wanted Andreya to know. Wouldn't that give her a surprise!

"It is very strange," Andreya said. "It does not seem to be

at all about you. Have you a friend with a broken heart? Do you have a friend who is having some trouble in love?"

She looked at Polly. Her brow was creased and her eyes were dark. She was sincerely puzzled. Polly's heart raced. I could tell everything right now, she thought. It's very plain to see. But when she saw how puzzled Andreya was, she felt half rage, half pain. I will never be taken seriously, she said to herself, so what the hell?

"Yes," she said. "There is a woman at my office who is having a love affair. She is very anxious and confused."

"She has come to you for help," Andreya said. "Now it makes sense. The heart with swords is of chaos and sorrow in love, but the woman with the lion is a wise friend—you. The card of the lovers reflects your friend and you—the two sides of love. Next is you and Henry standing under the rainbow. This is what the friend sees and envies. The woman in the garden is you, I think. The person in bed with the swords is your friend. This is a reading of contrasts and oppositions, because your friend is in your mind. You think of her. She longs to be wise and tranquil as you are wise and tranquil. I think this reading explains itself, or would you like to hear more?"

"It explains itself," said Polly.

"Now we must give you coffee," said Andreya. "As a child my heart was slow, and I was made to drink coffee three times a day. Even now, if I do not have my cup in the evening, I became so full of lethargicness that I cannot sleep right. Kirby! Coffee!"

Andreya made very strong, muddy coffee. For the sake of Polly, Henry, and Kirby, who was always given a taste, she boiled up milk. She herself drank from what looked like a child's cup without milk or sugar. Henry hunkered over his mug, blew on it violently, and drank it in a couple of gulps.

"Polly," asked Andreya, "why is your brother eating like a savage? Your family are not savages."

"He's our noble savage," said Polly, who could not help doting on her oafish brother.

"Food doesn't interest me," Henry said. "I use it for fuel."

"Really," said Polly. "Well, in that case I won't have to bake slumped brownies anymore."

"I mean regular food," Henry said. "Vegetables. Stuff like that. I don't mean the good stuff."

"He thinks of food day and night," Andreya said. "Come here, Kirby." She turned to Polly. "I put the coffee in his dish and he becomes offended. I must put it in my saucer or he does not drink it happily."

Polly sneaked a look at her watch. She was getting edgy. Half of her wanted to go to Lincoln's. Half of her was tired and cold and wanted to go home. Supposing Wendy called Henry and Andreya after she was gone, and then called Polly, who was not home? How would Polly explain those two hours? Oh, love affairs! Polly felt she was becoming something of a seasoned trooper. Everyone in her office took a long lunch. There were a number of people who took an extra hour for their psychoanalytic appointments. As long as the work got done, no one was very sticky about time, and Polly, who had never missed a deadline, was a past master at schedule juggling. It certainly wore a person out, she thought.

"I'm going home," she said. "Henry, Andreya, put on Kirby's leash and you can all walk me to a taxi."

At Lincoln's she was edgy. "Stop watching the clock, Dottie," Lincoln said. "I must say, you're no fun at night. You get all antsy."

"Oh, Lincoln," Polly said. "I am consumed with guilt."

"Well, inch over a little closer," Lincoln said, "and you can be consumed with me." They were under the covers, pressed together. Lincoln's hands on her were cold.

"It's always one or the other of us," Polly said sadly. "Either you're watching the clock, or I am."

"It's all right," said Lincoln. "It's what we have. Pretty soon you'll be snug at home with the grubs. Close your eyes and think of that."

Polly closed her eyes and what she thought of was the particular smell of Lincoln's flesh. Smoke from his cheroots perfumed his clothes, and left a spiciness on his neck. He smelled of cigars and lavender aftershave. One day, in a fit of abstraction, Polly had found herself automatically following the scent of cigar smoke down the street to find its source—a tiny old man smoking the same kind of cheroot Lincoln smoked.

When she left Lincoln she felt she had to be torn away, but once she was in a taxi on the way home, despair settled over her. If life held in store for her more sorrow, more anger, more chaos in love; if she would tear herself from one place to another; if true enjoyment—of her family, of her children, of her husband and household—left her; if her life would always be divided and split, she did not see why she would want to go on living. In the dark back seat she felt that her heart was pierced, that she was like the person in the Tarot deck who woke up in a room hung with swords.

The instant she got home, the telephone rang. It was Wendy.

"I've got to settle up with the baby-sitter, Mum," Polly said. "Hang on just a second." She treated Nancy Jewell with reverence: good baby-sitters were very rare. She kissed her good night. "Bye, Polly," Nancy said. "We're set for Wednesday, right?"

"Yes, and if I need you once more this week are you free?"

Nancy nodded yes, and left by the back stairs to go home to her apartment.

"You let that child call you Polly?" Wendy asked when Polly got back on the telephone.

"Mother, she's sixteen years old. Of course she calls me Polly."

"You let Consuelo call you Polly, too."

"Mother, did you call me at eleven o'clock at night to tell me not to let Concita and Nancy Jewell call me by my first name?"

"Of course not, darling," Wendy said. "I called because Beate will probably call you tomorrow and ask you to have lunch."

"I can't have lunch with her tomorrow."

"Darling, please do. She really longs to see you and she and Paul are so disappointed not to be able to have dinner with you."

"They can easily have dinner here. All they have to do is come here."

"That isn't how they work, darling. You have to bend a little. You're less rigid and more open than they are. You have to extend."

"Why do I? I always bend to Paul, and he never bends to me. Besides, I don't want to have another conversation about proper birth environments."

"Your temperament is stronger and sweeter," said Wendy. "Poor Beate is just nervous, that's all." Polly knew Wendy's tone well—it was a warning. "I've told her you'd be glad to have lunch with her."

Polly's blood froze. "You don't have the right to do that, Mother," she said. "Supposing I had a meeting."

"Well, in that case, darling, call her up and cancel her!" said Wendy.

. . .

Polly had lunch with Beate in Beate's chaste office. The walls were white with apple-green trim. All the furnishings were apple green. On the wall was a painting in the style of Paul Klee. Polly sat in an apple-green upholstered chair, and Beate sat in an apple-green leather chair. They ate salad, bread, and mushrooms.

"We have here a little fridge," Beate said. "Dr. Jacobson, in the other office, and I share it. There is also a little stove, so I can make us some herbal tea."

Polly had never eaten such plain food. Nothing tasted of anything at all. Where had she found it? Polly wondered. This was her diet for pregnancy, Beate explained; she believed that exciting and therefore overstimulating food crossed the placental barrier. She wore a green wool maternity smock, gold disks at her ears, heavy green stockings, and beautiful suede shoes. Perhaps she felt the bright colors crossed the placental barrier, too.

"Most natural of births would be a home or field birth," Beate was saying. Polly found it entertaining to think of Paul, who never took off his jacket even for dinner, assisting Beate as she delivered in a field. "We are having as homelike an atmosphere as possible, but there will always be harm to the infant and future adult from the intranquillity of hospital birth."

"I had both Pete and Dee-Dee by natural childbirth," Polly said. "Dee-Dee, I think I told you, was born in the hospital elevator."

"I cannot consider birth in an elevator as natural," Beate said.

"I mean without drugs of any sort," said Polly.

"The American standards for these things are so low," Beate said. "I and Klaro were born at home. My mother was forty-five when she bore us. Her mother was forty-four when she was born. I hear the tea kettle. Just a minute and I will bring the tea."

Eventually Polly was given something that tasted vaguely of moss.

"Now I will tell you something," Beate said. "Tonight we will tell Henry and Wendy. There are two fetal heartbeats. Paul and I will have twins."

"How wonderful!" Polly said. "Two little future Supreme Court justices!"

"We have had such trouble with the contractor to build the right sort of double nursery. The twinned infants should be separate, but not apart, we feel. We do not want them to think that they *are* each other."

Polly wondered how a twin might feel that.

"Oh, it is quite amazing what twins feel. I know this from being a twin myself," Beate said. "Klaro and I, although fraternal, have such connection. When he broke his arm in Paris I was in Berne and did not know, but my arm was in pain. When he called to say that his arm was broken, I understood all."

There was little Polly could say to this, not being a twin. So she asked what Paul and Beate had come up with by way of names.

"In our families names are simple," Beate said. "If two boys, Heinrich for my father and John Felix for your grandfather."

"Another Henry," Polly said. "That ought to confuse everyone once and for all."

"I see nothing confusing," Beate said. "In our family girls are called either Beate or Matilda from one generation to the next. My great-grandmother was Matilda, my grandmother Beate, my mother Matilda, and I, Beate. If two girls in our family, they are called Beate and Matilda. No one is confused.

As to our twins, if one twin is a girl she will be Matilda. If both are girls, Matilda and Elizabeth, for your great-grandmother. If a boy and a girl, Heinrich and Matilda."

She passed Polly a plate. To go with the tea, Beate provided a dish of hard wheat biscuits that tasted very much like compacted sawdust.

"I've been wondering for a long time about your work, Beate," Polly said. "Now that I'm in your office, it seems a good time to ask. I'd love it if you could explain to me a little how you differ from traditional psychiatry."

"I am so sorry," Beate said, "but really I cannot speak of my work. It does not lend itself to conversation. In order to understand it, you would have to go through the process of it."

"I see," Polly said. "But what about Paul? Isn't it hard on you not to be able to talk to Paul about your work?"

At the mention of Paul's name, something like a smile settled on Beate's features. It was not a true smile but, rather, an expression of uplift and recollection, as if inspired by a memory of some noble event.

"The world of the Law is not my world," Beate said. "We each understand the *Gestalt*, if you will, of the other's work. Is more necessary? I think not. We have our home and our impending birth. That is a great deal to talk about."

Polly imagined Beate and Paul at dinner, dining in state. She imagined them walking down the hallway to the bedroom, removing their clothes in some magisterial, methodical way. In bed, not asleep, but lying in state.

Beate had stood up. It was time for Polly to leave: her fifty minutes were up. In Beate's presence Polly felt fussy and over-agitated, the sort of woman who gives birth in hospital elevators after having allowed chocolate, coffee, red wine, and other exciting foods to cross the placental barrier.

Polly felt it might be appropriate to kiss Beate's ring and

ask for a blessing, but instead Beate kissed both her cheeks.

"Thank you for coming to lunch," she said. "Now I must call Paul before my patient arrives."

"Do you call him often?" Polly asked.

"I do, rather," said Beate. She seemed almost to blush. "I do call him often. During the day, I find I miss him."

She looked flushed and bridelike, even in her maternity smock. How private private lives were, Polly thought. How hidden were the real lives people lived!

It was not like Polly to fill up a week with plans. Usually when Henry was away she liked to stay at home with Pete and Dee-Dee, except for an evening with Lincoln. She usually limited herself to one since in her heart she knew she would have liked to spend every evening with him, and she could not quite bring herself to announce or act on this desire. It showed her up, she felt, for what she really was: a mother who would rather spend time with her lover than her children; an adulterous wife; a sinful, unfit person in a state of moral lassitude.

Lincoln accused Polly of viewing their love affair as if it were a dangerous drug whose dosage had to be carefully controlled, and he was right. But where, Polly wondered, did this love affair go if it got out of hand? Her real life was with Henry, and Lincoln's real life ought to have been in serious combat with his craving for solitude. Their love affair was especially unfair to him: if she turned back to her real life, what would be left for Lincoln? If she were the upright, sensible, and helpful person she had been brought up to be, Polly would have insisted that Lincoln find a replacement for her, but it broke her heart to think about this. Instead she frequently hectored him on the subject, knowing very well that if a replacement turned up she would be desolate.

She did not think she ought to spend a great deal of time with Lincoln, but on this trip of Henry's, she did not want to be alone. She had made plans out of desperation, and also to prove that Lincoln was not uppermost in her mind.

"You do exactly what you accuse your mother of doing," Lincoln said to her. "When you want to believe a thing, you simply think it."

"I don't," said Polly, who feared this tendency greatly.

"Sure you do," Lincoln said. "You make all these plans. They make you feel normal. You *know* you're going to see me after Henry and Andreya, and after Martha, and if Paul and Beate had come to dinner we could have smooched at your house all day long. So you end up seeing a lot of me after all but don't have to admit it. You tell yourself one thing, you do the other, and it makes you feel as if it all worked out fine."

"I don't like to say to myself how much I like to see you," said Polly. "It's undeniable, and I wish it weren't."

Polly rushed home from work, sat with Pete and Dee-Dee while they had their dinner, waited until they were being read a story by Nancy Jewell, and dashed over to Martha's. She had been promising Martha that she would come and visit.

"I'll never get you here," Martha had said. "It's too dingy. And after all the times you've dragged me to your house and fed me! It isn't fair. I'm just a convenience because I'm always around and you can always bring me home at the last minute."

This was true, and Polly did enjoy bringing Martha home. It was easy to sit her down with the children and feed her whatever they were having. Pete and Dee-Dee loved her, and she kept Polly company effortlessly. It was not necessary to plan a dinner party to get Martha to come for dinner. But it wasn't fair, and Polly knew it.

"I can't believe I got you here," Martha said as she opened the door. "I pushed all the mess under the bed and I even washed out the wineglasses."

Martha's apartment looked like an enchanted paradise to Polly. It was a rabbit warren of a flat, cluttered, filled with books, journals, knickknacks, and cast-off furniture. One end of the couch rested on a Latin dictionary, and the braided rug on the floor had a hole in it the size of a salad plate. Polly had lived in groups all her life. Martha's apartment and Lincoln's studio were both arranged for the comfort of only one idiosyncratic spirit—something Polly had never known.

"It's wonderful here," she said. "It's so comfortable."

"It's so little and mingy," said Martha.

"Oh, no," said Polly. "It's heavenly. It looks like a perfect place to curl up and read."

"I can also curl up and listen to the girl next door having a fight with her boyfriend. Now, come sit down and tell me what time you have to leave."

"I'm being picked up," said Polly.

"Oh?" said Martha. "By an unnamed person?"

"Lincoln is picking me up," Polly said. She was so unused to anyone knowing about their relationship that she winced when she said his name.

"Is he going to come up?" asked Martha.

"He's going to ring the bell and I said I would meet him downstairs," said Polly.

"That's pretty fastidious."

"Do you think it's a hollow gesture?"

"Sure," said Martha. She held a wineglass up to the light, squinted at it, and poured Polly a glass. "I mean, I know about him and you, so what's the big deal?"

"It's the gesture," Polly said. "Being with him in front of a third person."

"It's too free," said Martha. "If you keep it a secret, it

makes it feel more sinful. If he came up here to pick you up, you think it would appear that you accept it as a normal part of your life."

"You're right, of course."

"Of course," said Martha, pouring herself a glass of wine. "You have just gotten the good of my years of expensive psychotherapy. Now lean back and tell me how you got married."

"In a white linen dress with a square neck," Polly said.

"I mean, how did you decide?"

"It made perfect sense," said Polly. "I was programmed for it, like one of your computers. I *wanted* it. I was in love, and I wanted to get married and have a family."

"And then what happened?" Martha asked. She and Polly were curled up on opposite ends of the couch.

"I got what I wanted," said Polly. "We had a beautiful, small wedding, and a wonderful honeymoon in France, and then we came back and started living our life, and then Pete and Dee-Dee came along, and everything was just as I always thought it would be."

"And then what happened? How did Lincoln happen?"

"Sometimes I can't remember at all," Polly said. "Sometimes I think it all happened to someone else. It hit me all at once. I met Lincoln at a gallery show and he must have made a big impression on me because I thought about him all summer long. He says that we were bitten when we first met but the disease had to incubate. Then I met him again in the fall. I didn't know what was happening. Henry was away a lot. We had had such a bad summer—I mean, I thought Henry had had a bad summer—that awful case, always being interrupted. I was busy thinking I was making everything hum, but actually I must have been waiting for something and Lincoln was it."

"Aren't you glad it happened?"

"It's either the worst or the best thing I've ever undergone," Polly said. "It certainly makes a great many things clear, but I often think that most things are better left unclear. Now, give me just a little taste more of wine. I don't want to talk about myself anymore. Tell me about you and Spud." Martha sat up straight on the couch.

"We have three styles," she said. "We bicker, we have serious discussions about big issues, and we talk a disgusting form of puerile baby chatter. Mostly we bicker. Don't you and Henry?"

Polly and Henry never bickered, and Polly and Lincoln had nothing to bicker about.

"No," said Polly. "And we don't ever have puerile baby chatter. What do you two bicker about?"

"Oh," said Martha, leaning back against her couch pillows. "He comes over after work. I say, Spud, did you have dinner? He doesn't answer. I say, louder, Spud, did you have dinner yet? He looks at me and says, I was thinking about whether or not I had dinner. I don't think as fast as you. I say, That's ridiculous. How can you not know if you have had dinner? He says *I* can not know. I say, It's just that you hate to answer a direct question. He says, Oh, Martha, try to shut up and give a person room to relax, and so on."

"Fascinating," said Polly, "but what does it accomplish?"

"It's just a method of getting information across. Some people don't have to bicker to do that, but we do. It's our little way."

"You ought to get married," Polly said.

"Spud mentions that from time to time. Maybe I could get married the way people used to have babies—out cold. You could chloroform me, and when I woke up I'd be married."

"It isn't that awful," Polly said.

Martha gave her a bleak look.

"My trouble isn't marriage," Polly said. "It's me."

The doorbell rang and it was Lincoln.

"I'm sorry, Martha."

"It's all right," said Martha. "But you're not off the hook. You have to come for dinner. Go and have a good time." She kissed Polly at the door and Polly went down the stairs feeling that a wise and understanding older person had sent her on her way.

Lincoln and Polly had dinner in a small Hungarian restaurant.

"Just like normal people," Lincoln said. "A real date. Do I get to walk you home?"

"Okay," said Polly.

"And can I come up for a nightcap?"

Polly looked at him for a long time. "All right," she said. "There isn't any reason for you not to."

"The grubs will be asleep," Lincoln said. "I'm not going to stay very long. I'll try not to kiss you in your own home."

"Let's go," said Polly. "Before I lose heart."

Once at home, Polly hung their coats up in the closet. She took a deep breath and walked into the study. There was Nancy Jewell curled up on the sofa doing her homework.

"Hi, Polly," she said.

"Lincoln," said Polly, "this is Nancy Jewell, the best baby-sitter in New York. Nancy, this is our friend Lincoln Bennett."

"Hi," said Nancy. She began to gather up her homework. "Your mother called. The kids are fast asleep. I read them an extra story and I just checked on them a second ago."

After Nancy was paid, chatted up, and kissed good-bye,

Polly came back to Lincoln. He was prowling and snooping like a cat in a new house.

"I loved the 'our' friend," Lincoln said. "Never mind. I know you have to say things like that. Now, tiptoe me past the grubs and take me to your desk."

They crept down the hallway to the bedroom. Lincoln knew the way, and Polly stopped to check Pete and Dee-Dee. In the bedroom she found Lincoln at her desk reading her mail. On her desk and on the wall above her desk were framed photographs—of Polly and Henry, of Henry and the children, of Henry wearing a battered hat and a pair of blue jeans, of the children with blueberry pie all over their faces.

"Give me all the photograph albums," Lincoln said. "I'm sure you have dozens. I've been waiting to see them, so hand them over."

There was not one photo that did not pierce his heart, but he was hungry for more. He tore through them with no expression on his face. He could not stop staring at pictures of Henry, or of Henry and Polly together. He looked through their album of wedding photos twice. Then he stacked them all on the floor.

"It's an awfully pretty life you've got here, Dottie," he said grimly. Polly stared at him.

"If I were a true gentleman, I would get into that elevator and never see you again."

Polly put her hands over her mouth.

"There will never be any pretty pictures of us, Dot."

At this Polly sat down. "You don't want any pretty pictures," she said. "This *is* my life. I *am* embedded here. How do you think I feel in your studio? Everything is perfectly arranged for one person. Everywhere I turn I see things that aren't mine, and will never be mine. Your house announces that I'm just a guest. I look at *you* and you aren't mine.

You're just somebody I love. I know it looks like a fortress in here. But it isn't so strong a fortress that I didn't fall in love with you."

She was sitting on the chaise, and Lincoln came to sit with her.

"I know you love me, Dot. I've only been here once before. I was dying to mooch around where you live. I wanted to see where you sit when you talk to me on the telephone. Now take me to your kitchen and make me a cup of tea."

They both stood up and flung themselves into each other's arms.

"It hurts a lot to be here," said Lincoln.

"It sometimes hurts me to be here," Polly said. "And sometimes it hurts me to be in your house."

"I know it does," said Lincoln. He kissed her eyebrow. "See? I lied to you about not kissing you in your very own home."

They stood entwined until Polly broke free. "This is torture," she said.

"I'm a gentleman," Lincoln said. "I wouldn't dream of misbehaving with you in your own home. However, I expect you at mine tomorrow. Now give me my tea."

They sat at the kitchen table, holding hands. Lincoln had cased the pantry and the kitchen, the refrigerator, and all the shelves and cupboards.

"Can I smoke a cigar?" he asked. "Or will Concita or the grubs remark about the smoke?"

"Smoke away," Polly said.

They sat in silence, holding hands.

"This is much worse than sleeping together," Polly finally said. "Anybody can go to bed with anybody, but not everyone sits around the kitchen holding hands."

"While that may be true," Lincoln said, "I want you for my lunch tomorrow."

"You'll get me," said Polly.

After Lincoln had gone, Polly looked in on Pete and Dee-Dee again and wandered back into the kitchen. She told herself that she was there to wash the cups and saucers, but she knew she wanted to be near his cigar smoke. She did not wash the cups and saucers. She sat where he had sat and the smoke was like his ghost.

A love affair is a secret from a spouse, but what is in the heart of one's lover is a secret, too. Polly knew how well she fit into Lincoln's life. She watched him wince if she stayed too long—he could not help it. She knew he functioned very well on the limited doses of her he got, and she knew that their relationship was limited, futureless, and very sweet. And she knew that even though the thought of Polly unattached, of Polly without children—of an eligible Polly—was not at all sweet to Lincoln, and that Lincoln did not want her very close by, the fact of her marriage caused him pain anyway.

The bonds with her husband and children were the strongest she had. Her marriage, for all its stresses, was a vault. In his weak moments these thoughts made Lincoln feel like a little orphan boy—a little match boy out in the cold, looking at the bright yellow windows of a big, rich house.

Polly sat quietly. She was afraid that if she moved around the smoke would dissipate. But after she had washed and dried the cups, she went to hang them in the pantry. It seemed to her the smoke had settled there. Her pantry shelves were neatly stacked with dishes, pots, staples, and supplies. She stood in the doorway and the scent of his cigar made her feel much less lonely—she could not deny that to herself.

Ten

One afternoon the idea that they might separate came over Lincoln and Polly. They were in Lincoln's bed, entwined so tightly that had they been a sculpture in marble, it would have been impossible to tell whose limb was whose. The sweetness and rest Polly felt in Lincoln's long arms made her quite miserable: she could never be entirely happy in his presence, she knew. It would have been difficult to get any closer together, but Polly pressed herself against Lincoln anyway.

"What's the matter, Dot?" Lincoln asked.

"In a little while you'll be in Paris," Polly said into his chest.

"That gives you time to rig up some excuse to come with me, you know."

"Okay, Linky," said Polly. "I'll come for the whole time."

"Don't tease me, Dottie."

Polly sat up. "I'm not teasing. I'll come for the whole time."

Lincoln sat up, too. "You are teasing."

"You hope and pray I am," said Polly. "A whole month or two of me! Even in Paris. You'd see me walking down the street toward our little hotel with a loaf of bread and a little string bag and terrible alarm bells would go off in your head. Every morning you'd wake up and instead of just your own peaceful self, there would be an alien creature lying next to you."

"Isn't it funny?" Lincoln said. "I always think I'd love it."

"Linky, listen to me. Do you know what you were like the week Henry was away? I know I was watching the clock—you know Henry calls me late at night—but you were *really* watching the clock. You came to my house and snooped around to tell yourself how much better things would be if you weren't in my life."

"Oh, come on, Dot. Five minutes of rain on a Paris roof, you and I strolling around the Luxembourg Gardens, us at a shabby little restaurant, us feeding the goldfish."

"That's all lovely, for three days. Look at you! When I teased you and said I'd come for the whole time, panic took you right over."

Lincoln grabbed her by the elbows and pressed her against him.

"Then come for three days. Come for two. Come for the whole time," he said.

"Lincoln," said Polly. She shrugged herself out of his arms. Her face looked pinched and mournful.

"What is it that's wrong, Dot?"

"I'm ruining my life," Polly said. "I'm ruining yours, too. It's all wrong for us to be having a love affair."

"It isn't wrong," Lincoln said. "It isn't a love affair. It's a romantic friendship of the highest order and not outside the moral law."

"I don't care about the moral law," Polly said. "I care about the logic of the thing. I prevent you from finding someone to love. I don't approve of your being a hermit and I aid and abet you in it. You ought to think about why you don't want to live with the person you love. You *know* you can't live with me. I don't think it's solitude you like so much as that something else scares you. You don't have to think about that so long as I'm around."

"And what do I prevent you from doing?" Lincoln asked. He was sitting up, too. Their voices had softened, like the voices of a pair of frightened children in a forest.

"You made me see that I wasn't happy," said Polly. "You made me see things about myself and my life. You gave me courage. But you and I don't have any future. You know that."

Lincoln grabbed her wrist. "We could have," he said fiercely.

"No, Linky," said Polly. "We can't. Think of it. You and I run off, but it's not just the two of us. It's Pete and Dee-Dee, and me changing their schools and giving them their dinner, and arranging when they see Henry, and sitting up at night with them when they're sick or have bad dreams, and making their Halloween costumes and taking them to museums, and amusing them on a rainy weekend. And there's my family, too. It isn't just me. It's only just me down here with you. And then when it gets late, off I go to my household, and I leave you to the solitude you want."

"I love you so much," said Lincoln.

"I love you so much, too," Polly said. "I want to have you in my life—I can't bear to think of life without you. But don't you see? If we can't bear to think of life without each other and we both know that we aren't destined to be together, then at bottom it's something we can't bear about our lives as they are. I do love you, and I know you love me, but that's not the only reason we're together."

"All right," said Lincoln. "All right." He leaped out of bed, put on his shirt, and handed Polly her underwear. "All right. What do you want to do? Shall we not see each other?"

"I think that will have to happen," said Polly.

"Can we wait until I go away?" Lincoln said. "Can we make that our natural break? We'll have more than a month to think things out. That's quite a long time, really."

"We ought to stop now," said Polly.

"Is that what you want?" said Lincoln. "Is it? To go home every night to Pete and Dee-Dee and have Henry be away, or late at work, or at home at work? Do you want to be alone and surrounded by that bunch of prigs you call your loving family who can't help you and don't care about you unless you're their perfect Polly? Do you want all that without me to sweeten the deal?"

"You do sweeten the deal," said Polly. She put her slip on, but she was so upset she put it on backwards.

"Come here, you poor kid," said Lincoln. "I'm sorry. I'm sorry. We'll figure something out. Maybe we can take this love affair by the neck and strangle it until it behaves itself and turns into a friendship. I do think of running off with you, Dot, and you're right. I only think of running off with you all by yourself. Come over here and let me fix your slip."

Polly let herself be helped and managed to get the rest of her clothes on without mishap. She sat down at the table. Lincoln went to make her a cup of coffee.

"You know," she said, "I used to be a really cheerful person. I wasn't optimistic: I didn't have to be. Real optimists take a stand on the side of hope but I didn't even have to do that. As Martha says, I had the big things aced. I don't think I was spoiled. I think I was afraid to think. Maybe I was just smug. I stumbled into you, but I always wonder if I was looking for you."

"I never saw anyone looking for love as much as you," said Lincoln.

"I want everyone to love me," said Polly. "Now that the genie has been let out of the bottle, there will never be enough. I let down my guard for a second, and look what happened."

"What happened?"

"I went from being an upright matron to a woman having a love affair. I went from being a faithful wife to an unfaithful wife. What else am I capable of? What will some other false move make happen to me?"

"Hush," said Lincoln. "You're a brainwashed creature. What's so wonderful about being upright? I've told you over and over again, any jerk can tread the straight and narrow. Is it so terrible to have things get out of hand? Is it so awful to have to see things? Or to feel them? Or to have them really strike you instead of you being either completely used to them or having them right where they're supposed to be?"

"Yes," said Polly. "It's so terrible."

"Well, your over-analyzed little chum Martha would be the first to tell you that what you get after you've been through this is your authentic self."

At this Polly burst into tears. "I don't even know what that means. If it means that I have to fall in love, cheat on my husband, find myself loathing my family, the people dearest to me—I don't mean that, Lincoln, but they make me so angry these days—I don't want to feel these things, I don't want my authentic self. I just want my old self."

"You don't have any old self anymore," Lincoln said. "You're a fallen woman. Now come over here and make it worth your while by kissing me."

She threw her arms around his neck and rubbed her cheek against his face the way cats rub an object to mark it as their own.

"Dot," said Lincoln, "don't deprive me of you. Let's make Paris the official break. Okay?"

"I'm a fallen woman," said Polly. "I can't hardly help myself."

"Come drink this cup of coffee and say you'll be my girl friend."

"I am your girl friend, Lincoln," said Polly. "I love you."

For the next month Polly crowded her days. She took the children shopping for spring and summer clothes, took Martha out to lunch, had the rugs and curtains cleaned, sent a chair to be slipcovered, rearranged the bookshelves, made curtains for the children's rooms, and baked five cakes for the annual book and cake sale at Pete and Dee-Dee's school. She saw Lincoln as often as ever. At night she was glad to bring work home with her—something she had rarely done before. Polly was responsible for coordinating, supervising, and editing the spring report to the Board of Education. Usually she worked rigorously at her office so that she would never have to bring her briefcase home at night, but these days, after dinner, she sat at her desk and Henry sat in his study and they both worked.

Henry had come back from his trip worn out. He looked so exhausted that Polly's anger melted. She gave him dinner in bed on a tray. She fluffed up the pillows. She brought his coffee to him in bed every morning. She felt that the two of them were delicately balanced and she did not want to tip anything over. They were both so frazzled that a cross word might bring everything down.

Surely a less absorbed husband might have paid closer attention to his wife, and the strain of constant lying might have worn her down. But Henry was too tired and preoccupied to ask much. Over dinner they discussed the children, Henry's case, the spring report. This, Polly said to herself grimly, is what is called "making dinner conversation." When she saw

Henry at work in his study, she realized how ardently she always strove to please him, to exempt herself from his criticism, to enable his work to go smoothly. No one had ever asked her to be efficient, enterprising, to set such a good table or run such an attractive household. It always surprised Polly that other women, who were not so good at making things sweet, whose households were not so sparkling and comfortable, whose children were not so well turned out, behaved as if they, too, deserved love. Paula Peckham's house was usually in some state of mess. Before a dinner party she agonized on the telephone to Polly, who usually helped her with the dinner: Paula was a hopeless cook. She could not quite keep track of her children. Little Joe Peckham had not said a word till the age of four, and his brother Billy, who was now ten, was a hitter. For all this, Paula seemed a happy enough woman, and her husband, Frederick, appeared to adore her. When dinner at a Peckham dinner party was actually edible, everyone was thrilled.

No one had ever asked Polly to be excellent, or to do excellent things. Rather, she had been encouraged in that direction by Wendy and now everyone was used to her. They were all used to getting a splendid dinner. The children knew—unlike Gwen Stern's children, for example—that their mother would never go out and leave them with a baby-sitter when they were sick—even when they had mere colds. Polly believed that one wrong move and people ceased to love you. Other people—her parents, her brothers, Gwen Stern, Paula Peckham—had some magic charm that allowed them to live any way they wanted. These effortless beings existed on some higher plane. Next to them, Polly was a drudge, the one who could be counted on to do the donkey work without complaint.

These days, if Henry called from out of town and asked Polly to pick up the shoes he had taken to the shoemaker, or to take a folder off his desk, slip it in an envelope, and call his secretary to send a messenger up for it, she was glad to do it, furious that he had asked, alarmed that she was angry, and relieved that she was there to do it. Without me these things could not go forward, she said to herself. Then she said: What do I care if these things do go forward? What does it profit me? This confusion of voices, this recent tendency to have four reactions to any one thing, caused Polly sorrow and despair. She often felt that her true nature had been revealed. Once she stopped striving so hard to be good, the armor fell away and she was simply the cranky, dissatisfied, and not very nice person all the rigid specifications that had been drilled into her had prevented her from being. And worst of all, the one step she took away from being amenable made her resent those she was closest to.

But at night, when Henry slipped into bed beside her, she often woke up from a half sleep and, before the complexities of her present life could crowd it out, all she felt was her love for him. She yearned for her husband. They lay side by side, or pressed together; their physical connection was very strong. But what did it matter? What did a smoothly run house, good meals, sweet children, and an admirable husband matter if you felt your heart being torn to pieces? When these thoughts woke Polly up in the middle of the night and gave her the first insomnia she had ever had, she told herself that she was a bad, spoiled, selfish woman who wanted everything. Where had she gone wrong? The things she wanted, the things she had, the things she worked for didn't fit her somehow. She felt a stranger to her own life, an outsider to the things she had created, and an outcast from her own heart.

The awful day came. It was Polly and Lincoln's last afternoon together. This was to be a real separation. The rules were clear: no writing, no cables, no phone calls. Their separate missions were to reflect and meditate on what they were doing together, to see clearly that they had no future, and to figure out what they ought to do. Even if Lincoln had not had a one-man show to go to, Polly said, they would still have had to part.

Polly fretted while Lincoln packed.

"You ought to take more clothes, Linky," she said. "You hardly have enough for a week."

"Stop fussing, Dot. I hate clothes."

"At least take the other blue sweater."

"I hate sweaters. I hate blue."

"Lincoln, you can't have just one pair of shoes. Take your boots."

"I hate those boots."

They were both distraught. Polly had cried so much that she felt bleached. Youthful weeping and adult crying are two entirely different things. Tears in youth are cleansing, like naps or bracing showers. A good weep makes the youthful sufferer feel that something has been accomplished. Tears in adulthood leave the victim drained and exhausted. They dry up the eyes. They leave behind a pain under the ribs and forehead. Polly had cried that morning in the shower, behind the closed door of her office, in the taxi, and all over Lincoln's shirt. Lincoln had tears in his eyes, too.

"You're crying," said Polly.

"No, I'm not," said Lincoln. "I didn't sleep last night. I'm overtired. That was a physiological tear, not a tear of emotion."

"You dog," said Polly. "Admit how bad you feel."

"Will that make you happy to know?" Lincoln said. "I'm sad enough to die."

While Lincoln packed, Polly paced. She paced and poked at things: this was most unlike her. She was the least snoopy person Lincoln had ever known. She picked off the table an announcement of an opening at the Museum of Contemporary Art.

"This looks familiar," she said. "Why do I know the name Fred Train?"

"Because your parents own a Fred Train, and so does your brother Paul."

"You know, I think I've lost my mind. Of course I know who Fred Train is. My parents have that little oil of six blue bottles, and Paul has a lithograph of three babies, three knives, and three hearts. Do you know him?"

"Fred Train," said Lincoln, "is a small, bald, expensively dressed painter in great demand amongst rich people, but only the nicest sort of rich people. Your mother would doubtless think him a social climber, but then your mother thinks that anyone who wants to know her is a social climber. Two bits your parents will be at that opening, and so will all their friends."

"When is it?" Polly said.

"Tonight."

"Tonight," said Polly. "What's on tonight? We're supposed to have dinner with Mother and Daddy—of course, after the opening. I can't remember anything at all. We're supposed to be going, too. I don't think I can stand it. You won't be there, Lincoln, will you?"

"Maybe yes, maybe no," said Lincoln. "Probably I will go. It will do me good to get my last look at you in the midst of your perfect family. Look through the catalogue. He's a good enough painter but I can never understand why he calls his paintings the stupid things he calls them."

Polly read out loud: *"Still Life in the Middle of Snowfall, Then Sleetfall Then Transmogrified into Fogbound Figures." "A Basket of Turkey Eggs and a Red Dish, All Struck Blue as Night Alters the Statement of the Light."*

Lincoln said, "I've always thought it would make a good

parlor game. You take a great painting, make up one of those titles, and get your friends to figure out what it is. For example, *"Untouched Girl in Blue Robe, a Grape Baby and a Man with a Stick Poised in the Middle of Travel."*

"Rest on the Flight into Egypt," said Polly. It was one of Lincoln's favorite pictures.

Lincoln had finished packing. His small leather suitcase stood at the bottom of the bed. The light in his studio was bleak and silvery. When he looked at Polly, his face was open. Everything he felt was on it.

"Come here, my Dora," he said. "I don't care how bad you feel. I don't care if this is our last time together. Come over here and get in bed with me. I want you near me."

Both of them were neat by habit and temperament. They folded their clothes and hung them on the back of the armchair. Lincoln's hands were cold. Polly's flesh was hot. They went at each other like people who have been deprived of love for centuries. Tears slid down Polly's face. Lincoln's eyes were dark and full of longing. They lay entwined without speaking, without the merest fraction of distance between them.

No sooner had Polly walked into her kitchen than the telephone rang.

"Darling," said Wendy. "Do you want to come here to pick me up, or shall I meet you at the opening?"

"I simply can't go, Mum," Polly said. "I'm too exhausted and Henry will be exhausted, too."

"He just called," Wendy said. "Both of us have been trying to get you all afternoon. Where were you, anyway?"

"I had a thousand things to do."

"Henry will meet us there. He's coming with your father.

We must support our local painter, and I do like that nice Judith Train—that is her name, isn't it?"

"Edwina," said Polly.

"She has such interesting clothes, don't you think? We'll have a lovely time. Who's coming to stay with the children?"

"Pete is at Willie Jackson's and Dee-Dee was invited to stay at Jane Rosenman's."

"I know her grandmother," Wendy said. "Wonderful woman. But I don't like this idea of farming out the children, Polly. I didn't farm you children out."

"Oh, for goodness' sake, Mother. I used to stay at Annie Talbot's all the time and Henry practically lived at Danny Sanderson's."

"That certainly isn't true," said Wendy.

"It is true," said Polly.

"But if the children are out, I can't think why you don't want to come to the opening. You sound a little peaked. Are you coming down with something?"

"I'm perfectly fine," said Polly. "I just don't really want to go. I'm awfully tired. It's been hell at work."

"But darling, we're all going," Wendy said. "You must, too. If your job makes you so very tired, perhaps you ought to think about giving it up."

"All right, all right," said Polly. "I'll pick you up at seven."

"Take a nap, darling, and get into a better mood. I'll see you at seven. Look beautiful."

Henry came home at six. He wore on his face an expression that caused Polly's heart to shrivel. It was one of worry, defensiveness, and exhaustion. It said: Don't ask me anything. Don't ask me how my day was. Leave me alone but don't go too far away.

"Would you like a drink?" Polly said.

"No," said Henry.

"I thought you were picking up Daddy," Polly said.

"I decided to come home first. I called him. We'll meet there."

"Do you really want to go?"

"I said I did," Henry said.

"Do you want a bath?"

"No, I'll just shave. Are the kids sleeping out?"

"Pete's at Willie's and Dee-Dee's at Jane's. Mother gave me a strong lecture on the subject of farming children out."

"Yes? I think I will have a drink, Polly. Just a little one. What a terrible day."

He hung up his coat and stalked down the hall to the bathroom. When Polly brought him his drink he was sitting on the chaise. He had taken off his shirt and wrapped a towel around his neck. Polly put the drink down on the table. Under it was a glass coaster and under the coaster a linen napkin.

"Thanks, Pol," he said without looking up.

"Henry," said Polly. "Are you in love with someone else?"

"For God's sake, Polly. No."

"You didn't kiss me hello," Polly said. Her voice was ragged. Henry stood up and kissed her on the cheek.

"Oh, Henry," she cried. "I don't make you happy anymore. I don't think you love me anymore."

"I love you fine, Polly," he said, patting her on the shoulder. "I don't think I make *you* very happy. And times at work are very hard." She threw her arms around him and he held her for a minute. Then he took her arms from around his neck.

"I'm going to shave now," he said. "You get dressed."

. . .

The Train show was hung in the stark white halls of the Museum of Contemporary Art. The admiring throng gave off the scent of cigar smoke, expensive perfume, leather, and barber shops. Polly's family cut through the mob, as solid and effective as a flying wedge. As usual, the whole family was in tow, including Henry, Jr., and Andreya in matching charcoal-gray suits. Henry wore a tie and Andreya wore a silk blouse with a bow. Beate wore a green silk maternity dress and gold earrings the size of half dollars and looked more like someone holding a shield than she looked pregnant. Polly wore black silk, as did Wendy. They stood together and received, as if at a family wedding. The Solo-Millers did not go to congratulate Fred Train—he came to salute them.

Fred Train was as tidy and precise as a china miniature, but his gaze was so fixed it seemed as if it might burn through paper. His bald dome reflected the muted light. Henry Demarest whispered to Polly, "Do you think he waxes or shellacks it?"

Wendy, of course, called his wife, Edwina, "Judith." she was as pretty as a fox and had little fox teeth. Polly could not stop staring at her. Both she and her husband wore clothes so plain, so beautiful, and so expensive that they seemed a parody of soberness. Who had made those gorgeous clothes for them? she wondered. They looked like rakish bankers or respectable hoodlums.

The air in the museum halls was cool, but Polly felt that she was burning up. Every member of her family was talking to someone else. Henry Demarest was talking to Henry, Sr., and Wendy was talking to Fred and Edwina Train. Henry and Andreya always talked to each other, and Paul and Beate were surrounded by a group of tall, well-dressed people Polly recognized as Paul's law partners and fellow symphony lovers. This left her free to wander through the halls looking at the pictures. Out of the corner of her eye, she saw Lincoln. She knew when he had come into the room, she felt a little jolt, the start you feel when the doorbell rings. Tension washed over her. Her hands felt hot. The glass of champagne in her hand seemed to tremble slightly. They both walked into the main room at the same time, and Polly could see that Lincoln was wearing a terrible, evil smile. He went straight up to Wendy.

"Hello," he said, his smile widening. "I'm Leonard Barton."

"No you are not," said Wendy. "You're Lincoln Bennett. I got that right, didn't I?" She looked very pleased with herself.

Lincoln shook hands with Henry, Jr., and kissed Andreya on the cheek.

"Hello, Polly," he said. The sound of the nickname he never used sounded like a caress to Polly. He shook hands with Wendy, with Henry, Sr., and was introduced to Henry Demarest by Wendy. Then he wiggled into the Solo-Miller wedge, right next to Polly. Everyone had turned back to someone else, and Polly and Lincoln were left together. Surely, Polly thought, it is obvious to everyone that Lincoln and I are having a love affair. It is perfectly visible and everyone will know. But no one paid the slightest attention. Here we are, Polly thought, on the eve of a terrible separation, surrounded by the Solo-Miller family on all sides.

"I had to see you this one last time," said Lincoln. "But it's awful to see you and see how perfectly you fit."

Polly was silent.

"I shouldn't write to you, should I?" he said.

"No," said Polly, swallowing hard.

"And should I call when I get back?"

Polly was silent. Her eyes were burning.

"All right, Dot," said Lincoln. "I'll send you a note when I get back. Everything you said today was right, but that doesn't make anything easier, does it?"

"No," said Polly.

"I'm going to take a spin around this show and get out," Lincoln said. "Look at all these types, will you? I'm going to go pay homage to *Two Idaho Potatoes in Marital Conflict.* My plane leaves in the morning, but you know that. I love you, Dot, and if you love me, take my hand and squeeze it as hard as you can. Don't blush—nobody's looking at us."

Polly pressed his hand with all her might.

"Jesus," he said, "I didn't mean for you to break it."

"That's how strong my love is," said Polly.

"Good-bye, Dottie."

"Good-bye, Lincoln," said Polly, and she watched him walk away.

An hour and a half later, the family withdrew their presence from the opening and went to La Vaucluse, a restaurant they all felt proprietary about. Henry and Wendy had been patrons of it for thirty years. It was the setting for the only family celebrations they held outside the home: birthday dinners, welcome-homes, graduations. These celebrations were by their nature not communal—they were not family rituals or holidays—and their proper celebration was in public.

They all sat down and immediately began to gossip.

"You and that Lincoln Barton seemed quite chummy," Wendy said to Polly. Polly was silent.

"He's our kite-flying friend, Ma," said Henry, Jr. "You remember. He went to my school but he's older than I am. He's a painter."

"Is he a friend of the Trains'?" Wendy said. "Probably he isn't. They only seem to know bankers and lawyers."

"Painters don't have to stick to other painters," Polly said.

"I'm sure that's true, darling, but you'd think a painter would want to know another painter."

"It's hard to tell them from the bankers these days," said Henry Demarest. "They all wear the same clothes."

"I think Fred Train looks sort of *louche*," said Polly.

"Darling, he does not," said Wendy. "He looks perfectly sinister with that shiny head and those little bitty teeth. But I'm sure they're very nice people. Their daughters go to your old school, Polly. They talked quite a lot about that. I just feel that a painter ought to talk about art. Now, your aunt Hat wants to talk about paintings night and day, and when I run into an actual painter, all he wants to do is talk about the people we know in common. I don't understand it. It's his *job* to talk about art, especially to people who own his pictures. Andreya, dear, please prop Henry up. I can't stand to see any of my children slumping."

"I'm not slumping, Ma," Henry, Jr., said. "I'm wilting. Where's Paul and Beate?"

"Home," said Wendy. "Beate said something about smoky rooms and rich food poisoning the prenatal infant. Isn't that sweet?"

"When Polly and I were pregnant," Henry Demarest said, "we used to go to smoky places with booze and rich food and everything. Do you suppose there's something wrong with Pete and Dee-Dee?"

"Paul and Beate are just a little over-concerned," Wendy said.

"I think Paul and Beate are ridiculous," said Polly.

"Polly!" exclaimed Wendy. "You mustn't be so critical. They're just nervous older parents-to-be."

"She gave me a disgusting lunch," Polly said, "and never once asked me anything about what it was like when I had Pete and Dee-Dee. After all, I have had two children and she hasn't had any yet."

"Darling, that's just the way she is," Wendy said in her warning tone.

"She's a pill," said Polly, using one of her father's favorite expressions.

"Darling, you're just tired," Wendy said. "Now, what are we going to eat?"

It was not necessary to consult menus. Everyone always had the same thing. A plate of steamed vegetables with green mayonnaise was brought for Andreya: Polly and Wendy had the salmon; Henry, Jr., the tournedos; and Henry Demarest the special. Henry, Sr., always claimed to want the veal chop and was always talked out of it by the waiter, who had been waiting on him for many years and knew him as well as his doctor. He knew that Henry, Sr., wanted the medallions. He also talked Henry, Sr., out of the wine he asked for and into the wine he really wanted. After that, the family was satisfied. All the appropriate rituals had been performed.

The conversation then returned to Paul and Beate. The idea of twins in the family was discussed. Henry, Jr., said that having all these nieces and nephews was going to make a pauper of him when Christmas rolled around.

"They'll just have the one me. I'll have four of them," he said.

"You can send them all lovely kites and model airplanes," Wendy said.

Polly could hardly swallow. She was suddenly exhausted, and powerfully sad. She wanted to be by herself, alone, in Lincoln's studio, so that she might cry her eyes out and then throw herself on his pillow, which might still smell of him. The family looked to her at these gatherings for cheer, and she had no cheer. Instead she had a stone in her heart. Andreya did not speak. Henry, Jr., grunted or made other loutish noises. Henry, Sr., maintained his imperial silence. It was often up to Polly to keep a conversation going. Henry Demarest was skilled at this, too, but the burden fell to Polly by custom since Henry was so often away.

Where was Lincoln now? Had he found one of his few friends at the opening and gone out to dinner? Had he been spotted by someone he knew and dragged off to a restaurant? Lincoln did not like going out in public. He told Polly that the few times he went out he generally had several glasses of wine too many and then behaved badly. He became cross or surly. He claimed he said beastly things to people. Polly had never seen this side of Lincoln. She tried to imagine it, but she could not. It was undeniable that they saw the best parts of each other. At the moment Polly was too tired to think about the realities of Lincoln's life. So what if he hated children? If his fix on solitude was neurotic? If they could never be together? To be deprived of him for such a long time was so terrible to contemplate, she did not know how she would be able to stand it.

She stood up. "I'm going home," she said. She knew this was a truly abnormal thing for her to do, but she could not stop herself.

"Darling," said Wendy, alarmed, "are you sick?"

"No, I'm just tired," said Polly. "Really, Mum. There's nothing wrong. I think I will come down with something if I don't go at once. I can't keep my eyes open."

"I'll take you home," said Henry.

"Please don't," said Polly. She was beginning to feel unhinged. She had never wanted to be alone so desperately. "You haven't even started your dinner. Andreya can take my salmon home and feed it to Kirby."

"Polly, this is most upsetting," Wendy said. "Henry, take her home, please."

"I don't want Henry to take me home," said Polly, who was near to tears. "I'll get into a taxi and go straight home. I had a terrible day, that's all. My head hurts. I just want to get in bed."

No one was used to Polly's having had a terrible day.

"Darling, are you sure you don't want Henry and your father or me to come with you?" Wendy said.

"There's nothing wrong," said Polly. "I want you all to have a nice dinner. I'm so tired I can't see straight. I'll be quite happy by myself."

It was clear from the looks at the table that everyone thought something *was* wrong. They looked as if Polly had just announced that she had murdered her children and set fire to her house.

"Darling, really," said Wendy, fretfully.

Henry walked Polly to get her coat. It was obvious that she had upset everyone, but she couldn't help it. She felt too bereft to sit at the table another minute. They walked outside to get a taxi. Polly shivered. The look on Henry's face was terrible but he put his arm around her.

"Are you sure you don't want me to come with you?" Henry said.

"I'm fine," said Polly. "I'm perfectly fine. I'm just tired, that's all. Stay and amuse them."

As the cab drew up, Henry held Polly's arm. He held her very tight. She looked into his eyes, which were perplexed, frightened, and concerned.

"Oh, Polly," he said sadly.

"I'll be all right," said Polly. Henry kissed her on the top of her head and she got into the taxi, which drove away.

PART THREE

Eleven

Each year in the early spring, Wendy and Henry made plans to go up to Priory Lagoon to open their summer house, and this year they arranged to take Pete and Dee-Dee with them for the weekend. They liked to get things in order way in advance of the summer and they liked to spend an occasional cold, spring weekend in Maine.

Polly had spent her childhood summers in the Priory house, as had her father, and his father before him. It was a big, odd-shaped clapboard cottage with woods on two sides, and open to the water in front. Because no one wanted to cut down any trees in order to build, Polly and Henry rented a small cottage a little way down the lagoon from an old lady who had promised to sell it to them before she died. Polly loved that her children could have a childhood like her own, and she hoped that Pete and Dee-Dee would bring their children to Priory, too. As for Henry Demarest, Maine reminded him of *his* childhood summers in Wisconsin, full of pines and cold water.

Henry was off on another trip and would be gone through the weekend, so for the first time in years, Polly would be all alone. At first the prospect attracted her. She thought of walks she would take, solitary meals she would have, and the pile of books next to her bed she would read; of not having to make breakfast; of sleeping late. But as the week wore on and she started to pack Pete and Dee-Dee's suitcases, she began to brood. The idea of coming home to an empty apartment on Friday with a long, lonely weekend spread before her gave her a feeling of panic. There would be no one who needed or wanted her—no one to help or serve, no noise or interruptions.

When she expressed this fear to Martha, Martha promptly invited her to come for dinner on Saturday night. "You can come Friday, too," said Martha. "I know exactly how you feel."

At night Polly brooded about her weekend. The children were leaving Friday morning, and so Polly would go to the office. That left Friday night to get through. If she was going to Martha's for dinner on Saturday, she would bake something elaborate for dessert. That would occupy Saturday morning with shopping, and the afternoon with baking. What she really longed for was a friend—a woman friend her own age to have lunch with. The idea of calling Mary Rensberg floated before her. If she called Mary, would Mary find it odd? And if they did have lunch, what would they talk about? The next noon at her office she took a deep breath and dialed.

"Rensberg Antiques."

"Is Mrs. Rensberg there?" said Polly.

"No. Sorry. She's gone to Brazil. Who's calling?"

"This is Polly Demarest."

"Oh! Polly! Gracious. This is Mary. I was just ducking customers. I haven't heard your voice in the longest time. How are you? I've got some lovely tables just in, if that's what you've called about."

"I called to see if you would have lunch with me on Saturday."

"Saturday. Saturday. Let me see. It looks fine. Why don't you come to the shop and I'll give you a picnic in the back? I'm dying to hear everything about Paul and Beate. It's so nice to hear from you."

Polly hung up, limp with relief. How very simple it was! Normal people made this sort of telephone call all the time, but Polly did not feel herself to be normal in this regard. It was the easiest thing in the world, and no one thought it a bit strange. Why hadn't she done this years ago? Why hadn't she just gone ahead and made friends with Mary? Would Paul really have minded, or was that something Polly had liked to imagine?

Friday night Polly came home to an empty apartment. In a happier moment, she would have savored her time alone. She would have made a big salad with anchovies—Henry hated anchovies—and red onions, and would have read while she ate. She would have drunk the salad dressing right off the plate, and she would probably have eaten the watercress with her fingers. Then she would have made a big pot of coffee and spent the hours reading, puttering, sipping her coffee, and enjoying herself. But she could not deny it: she was afraid of how terrible she felt.

She tried to push it away, but it would not go away. She went to her desk drawer, where in a back compartment she kept things pertaining to Lincoln. She had a little bound book that contained ten sketches of her. She had a pair of gold earrings he had given her, the silly postcards he had sent to her office, and the silver pin he had won at art school. Polly had given him a gold Saint Christopher medal, which he had never taken off; a picture of herself as a child, in an enamel frame, which he had asked for; and a pottery vase she had made at school as a girl, which he kept his brushes in.

How much they knew about each other! There was not a friend, not an incident of personal history, not a joke or a reference unknown to them. They knew each other's lives back and forth. A love affair, a marriage, a family—these things were built, like houses or like paintings. They were constructed. Polly had opened that drawer simply to touch something Lincoln had touched, but she missed him too piercingly to be consoled. She did not want the things: she wanted him.

The roles of Henry's wife, the children's mother, of daughter, sister, of Lincoln's beloved, dropped away as if they were heavy ceremonial robes. She stepped out of them light, lonely, and functionless.

There was not a person she could go to for help, and that was her own fault. Her pride, her image of herself as a person who ought not to need to seek help, prevented her.

She did not know whom to miss first. This caused her grief; did she really miss anyone, or was it that she could not bear to be alone with herself? She was an unfit mother. Every act she did in her children's behalf—when she tucked them into bed, sewed their buttons, made them cup custard, soothed them when they were sick, and laughed at the wonderful things they said—was fraudulent because in her heart she was corrupted.

As for Henry, now that he was away, she realized that in some way he was always away. This made her angry in her adult heart. In her child's heart she said: If he loved me, he would not be away.

If you let the tiniest crack appear on the surface of things, some one-celled something might slip through and begin, imperceptibly, to grow. One morning you woke up and the house was covered with it. Polly felt she had woken up from a comfortable sleep and found everything—Henry, her family, her place within it, her sense of herself—all askew.

She walked to the kitchen, sat down at the table, and covered her face with her hands. Missing Lincoln caused her a physical sensation, like pain that takes the breath away.

"I must not let this get out of hand," Polly said out loud. "I must get after myself. I should *do* something." But there was nothing to do. Her orderly house was in perfect order.

She made herself some scrambled eggs and a cup of tea. There was no point reading anything serious—she could hardly concentrate. She skimmed three magazines and the morning paper with amazing speed, reflecting unhappily that time is the enemy of an anxious person. There were two things she dreaded: a call from her mother, and a call from Henry. To head the one off at the pass, she called to Maine.

"Hello, darling," Wendy said. "It's cold up here. We went to Ronnie's Clam Box for dinner and the children went straight to sleep an hour ago."

"Ronnie's open early this year," Polly said.

"His wife appears to have left him," Wendy said. "He looks awful. He has that nice sister of his—Denise, who's married to Vern at the gas station—helping in the kitchen."

"Denise is the wife, Mum," Polly said. "She's Vern's sister. Dianne is Ronnie's sister."

"Darling, how can you expect me to keep these things straight? You know, your father and I think you ought to have come up with us. You don't have anything else to do."

"I'm fine where I am," Polly said. "I'm having a little vacation. I have plenty to do."

"But, darling," said Wendy, "you could have been with us. What will you do all by yourself?"

"I'm having lunch with Mary Rensberg tomorrow and Martha invited me for dinner."

"Which one is Martha?" Wendy asked.

"Martha Nathan, Mum. From the office. I've told you about her."

There was a slight silence which made clear to Polly that Wendy did not see having lunch and dinner with friends as anything important to do.

"Now, this Mary Rensberg," Wendy said. "Where on earth did she come from?"

Suddenly Polly was embarrassed, and reluctant to admit that she had made this date herself.

"We ran into each other on the street," she lied.

"Hmmm," said Wendy. "Won't that be a little awkward? After all, your brother jilted her."

"Mother, he did not. Mary would never have married him."

"Darling, she certainly would have," Wendy said. "Look what she's come to. Charlie can't have done very decently by her. She keeps that little shop, after all."

"That little shop is extremely successful," Polly said. "Henry and Andreya got a gorgeous table from her."

"I'm sure they did. With the money they got selling Grand-father's really *good* things."

"I think Mary does very well," Polly said. "Believe me, she never would have married Paul."

"I'm sure you're wrong," Wendy said. "I think she was dying to marry into the family to show up those ghastly Rensbergs."

"She wasn't," Polly said. "Never mind. Is it muddy up there?"

"Clear and gorgeous and cold, but not muddy. Your father is going to get the boat in shape tomorrow and take the children for a little spin around the lagoon. And you? Tomorrow night that little friend of yours is coming for dinner?"

"No," said Polly. "I'm going to her."

"Well, darling," Wendy said. "I'm sure you'll have a lovely

weekend, but you really ought to have come up with us."

An hour later the telephone rang. Polly looked at the clock. It was too early to be Henry, who always called late. Her heart rose up: perhaps it was Lincoln. But it was a wrong number. If I can only last until ten o'clock, Polly said to herself. To go to bed this early is a sign of something awful, but it is perfectly normal for a tired person to go to bed at ten o'clock. She put her head down on the kitchen table and began to cry. All she wanted was for Lincoln to call her, but she had told him not to. And if he did, it simply meant that they longed for each other and that was wrong. There was just no end to it.

Once in bed, she was too anxious to sleep. Her limbs were burning. Her mind was burning, too. Maybe, she thought, Henry is the right person for me, the person I love, but even so I'll never be happy with him again. If I can't it is either my fault or his fault. I'm not good at fixing things. Besides, I don't know what to fix. Did I ever really love Henry, or was he simply so right for me to marry that I didn't have to really think about it? Perhaps he felt the same way about me. Maybe I am not his real type, but just the sensible person to have as a wife. Supposing, she said to herself, the real truth is that I have been trying to get loose from my family and Lincoln is only my secret way of doing it. Maybe I don't want either of them for any pure reason. Maybe the truth is that I am so spoiled and so smug and so lucky that I have never had to batter my way toward what I want. Maybe I never wanted any of this. Maybe everything I think is what has been drilled into me.

Adrift in her upset, Polly fell into a light, unrefreshing sleep which was interrupted by the ringing of the telephone. It was Henry, who was not fond of the telephone and hated chatting on it. This was just as well. Polly was too fuzzy to talk. She asked Henry how he was and he said he was tired. The case was going fairly well. He would be home sometime on Sunday, and it was not necessary for Polly to fuss. They would go out for dinner.

Instead of falling back to sleep, she replayed Henry's telephone call. What was the use of calling someone if only to tell that someone how tired you were? What was the point of being married to someone if you never asked how *they* were? The kind of marriage Polly knew was based on family, on the creation of family, on keeping family together, on family events, circumstances, occasions, celebrations. It had to do with loyalty, unity, and strength. It had to do with family goods and services. She felt like a mechanical toy, performing like mad. Did anyone love her just for herself? If she never cooked another meal, ran another errand, remembered another strange craving or favorite food, listened patiently for another second, would anyone have any use for her? Would Henry love her?

The weekend stretched before her ominously. The idea of lunch with Mary Rensberg was now threatening. How could she see a virtual stranger when she felt so shaky? What if she lost control and broke down in front of Mary? How would she explain herself? All she looked forward to was her dinner with Martha Nathan. That was the way life worked. If you were frightened or lonely you planned a dinner party. Then you had to figure out a menu, go shopping, set the table, wait for the guests, talk to the guests, feed the guests, and clear up. Or you went to someone's house for dinner and thought of what elaborate thing you could bring. Time passed without a serious thought. Did people create families in order to keep themselves from wondering what the purpose of life was? With children it was a snap. Children *were* a purpose, and generally there was so much to do in their behalf that you might never stop to think at all.

The first thing she did on Saturday morning was to call Martha, waking her out of what Martha described as her first sound sleep in several years.

"Are we still on?" Polly said.

"Are you kidding?" said Martha. "I called my sister in California last night for menu advice."

"And what did she tell you?"

"She said: Martha, go and get everything already cooked from one of those expensive places. Or give her baby lamb chops. I'm doing the combination—baby lamb chops and something from one of those places."

"I'm bringing dessert," Polly said.

"I hoped you'd say that," said Martha. "Come at six. Now I'm going back to sleep."

Polly looked at the clock. It was not quite ten. She would have to call Mary Rensberg. If she thought fast enough she could think up an excuse not to have lunch. Sickness, last-minute emergency. The telephone rang. It was Mary.

"Just calling to confirm," she said. "Come at one. The sign says CLOSED but just ring the bell. No one ever pays any attention to the sign, anyway."

Now that there was no way around lunch, Polly sat down to figure out what to bake. She decided on an apple tart and made a shopping list. This made her feel rather like a normal person, rather like the old Polly, who was, after all, a marvelous cook.

The day was full of clouds and intense, muted sunlight. Polly ambled around the neighborhood. She bought the paper and read it in a coffee shop. She prowled around the fruit and vegetable stand. It was just eleven o'clock. Her shopping was done, and there was nothing left to do.

The idea of going home was frightful—to be all alone with all those rooms. Polly did not have the temperament for meandering. She was made to achieve goals. Now she was forced to meander and it upset her. She wandered down a side street and stopped in front of a church. It was the Little Church of Saint Jude and the door was open. The darkness inside was velvety and inviting, lit by dozens of flickering devotional candles. Polly went in. The church was empty except for a young man who was praying in a back pew. The darkness, the coolness, the smell of wax and incense calmed her spirit. There were three small shrines: one to Saint Jude, one to the Blessed Virgin, and one to Saint Joseph, who, Polly knew from her Bible-as-literature class, was the father of Jesus.

What sweet security to believe you had a father and mother in heaven, as well as a sort of brother or cousin who, having done his stint as a human being before becoming God, understood how complicated life was. In that atmosphere, Polly thought how unremittingly unsentimental Judaism is. The Solo-Millers' synagogue—the Manhattan Synagogue—was one of the oldest in the country and decorated with non-representational Moorish designs. There were no pictures, no statues, no shrines, not one thing that made you think that God was other than a stupendous force, a huge idea too grand for the minds of men and women, no matter how observant.

In a synagogue there was no one to confess to, and if you could not forgive yourself you were lost. There was nothing to light a candle to, nothing that made you feel that a small wish might be granted or even asked for, only the stern, harsh law of the patriarchs, the hard, unrelenting law that did not give an inch.

The God of the Jews was not human or humane. He did not console and was as imperious as Polly's mother and father. Her mother and father on earth were not a source of consolation either.

Henry Demarest's sense of Jewishness was like the Solo-Millers'. It had to do with a sense of aristocracy. Anyone could be a Christian. Not anyone could be a Jew, and very few Jews were the sort of Jews the Demarests and the Solo-Millers were. It had been said of Grandfather Solo-Miller that he behaved as if he had chosen God, and not the other way around. The Demarests and the Solo-Millers went to synagogue on High Holy Days. This set a precedent for lesser mortals and reminded God that they had not forgotten Him.

In the darkness of the church, Polly wished that she had been a little Catholic girl; that she might go into the confessional, tell everything to a person she could not see, and be forgiven.

Jews do not kneel in prayer; they stand. But kneeling felt much more private, so Polly knelt. She had not prayed since she was a little girl. How thoughtful of the church to provide a padded knee rest, Polly thought. She said very softly, into her hands: "Oh, God, protect me so that I will not be so self-protective. Help me to be strong and to not be so upset or to know why I am so upset. I really try to do good. Is it so terrible of me to love Lincoln? Please help me understand what is happening in my life, and please help me make it all right again. Give me some courage. Make me not so frightened." She prayed this over and over again.

Her knees were stiff when she got up. At the shrine of Saint Jude she lit a candle and hoped God would understand what she was doing in a Catholic church. Over lunch, when she told Mary Rensberg that she had stopped at Saint Jude's, Mary said, "He's my favorite saint. I'm mad for him. He's the patron of people in desperate circumstances."

. . .

Outside, the light made her squint—hard early-spring light that showed up the flaws of everything. Traffic and pedestrians looked fierce and unavailing. A woman alone on a Saturday ought to be thinking about her children or her husband, Polly knew, but Polly was thinking about Lincoln. With him away her life did not feel normal to her. She looked down the straight road she thought was her future and saw only a divided heart, a person waking out of a bad dream against a wall hung with swords. She did not imagine she would ever feel her life to be all of a piece again. Polly missed the sound of his voice, his strong cold hands, the smell of his sweaters. He was always available, and always where he said he would be. The one time she had rung his bell and he was out, she had almost collapsed in tears. She had been fifteen minutes early, and Lincoln had gone to get a loaf of fresh bread for lunch. All her years of being trained by Henry's absences, his last-minute delays, his changes of plans had fallen away from her. What a luxury to be able to cry over some miscalculated time! That memory caused Polly's eyes to sting. Lincoln indulged her. He allowed her to fret. She had cried more in front of him than she had ever cried in her life. How could she live without him?

"I am just a mess," said Polly out loud. This startled her; she had never spoken out loud to herself on the street before.

Polly had sailed through adolescence. She had been at the top of her class and president of her school: a popular girl who never went through an awkward stage. Kind to younger children. Sweet to boys. A good dancer. She deferred to Paul, protected Henry, and was generally obedient to her parents. They gave her nothing to rebel against, since their values were wholeheartedly hers. She had not fallen in love in high school or college. Love, she knew, and all its trappings were for adult life. When you fell in love you did so to get married and have children and create a family. Instead, Polly had crushes that never lasted very long, and in fact she had never been in love until she met Henry Demarest, who was in all ways the right person for her to marry.

If you followed the straight path, why did you get into trouble? The street, as she looked around, was full of nice-looking matrons with young children, or baby carriages, or their teen-agers in tow. These women looked confident and settled. Not one of them could possibly be in love or trouble. Of course, Polly was confident-looking and *she* was in trouble. Perhaps, Polly thought, I ought to tap one of these women on the shoulder and ask for advice. But instead, one of these women bumped into Polly. It was Mary Rensberg.

The sight of her threw Polly. She did not want to be seen when she was so upset. It had been her plan to go home and compose herself before meeting Mary for lunch.

"Oh," said Mary, "what good luck to bump into you. I'm starving and I just brought us our little picnic to have at the shop. I can't stand going out to lunch in this neighborhood. I can brew us up a pot of coffee on my hot plate. I'm so glad we made this lunch date. It's nice to see you after so long."

Mary was beautiful. She had a small head, elegant bones, and real green eyes. Her silvery-gold hair was cut into an Eton crop and the clothes she favored were a stylish edition of what a girl who went to a French convent school might wear: a black cape, a gray jumper, and a starched white blouse. There were diamond earrings in her ears, and on her feet she wore a pair of suede brogues.

"Just follow me," said Mary, taking her arm. They walked down the street to Mary's shop, arm in arm like a pair of old-fashioned schoolgirls. Mary opened the door and ushered Polly to the back of the shop.

The front was lined with tables, Welsh cupboards, and

marble-topped washstands. The tables were all beautifully set —Mary sold Late Victorian china. At the back of the shop was Mary's worktable, and in the very back, a sink and a hot plate concealed from view by a Chinese screen. Mary took Polly's coat and hung it up, sat Polly down, and went off to make the coffee.

Suddenly Polly was overcome by shyness. She could not think of a single thing to say, and her distress lay upon her like a fever. She did not see how she could sit here for an hour and make actual conversation. This was not like lunch with Martha—this was social life.

In her shop, Mary looked so accomplished, so unapproachable. Everything she did she did stylishly. She had brought a picnic lunch to the shop in a small wicker hamper. She looked so unique, so good at things. Furthermore, she had triumphed over a bad time in her own life. Polly had thought it very brave of Mary to divorce Charlie Rensberg. She thought how hard it must be to share your children with a man you didn't like anymore, and yet Mary thrived. The Rensbergs were a big family, active in everything, with connections everywhere. That was quite a clan to leave, but Mary had left it. She had opened her shop and made a success of it, and could be seen on Sunday morning walking her daughters to the Episcopal church around the corner from the shop.

Mary reappeared from behind the screen carrying a pottery dish and a little espresso pot.

"Now," she said, taking four beautifully wrapped sandwiches out of the hamper. "Tell all about Paul and Beate. I introduced them, you know."

"I didn't know," Polly said.

"You didn't? How weird. I thought you all were very close."

"Paul never tells us anything," said Polly. "How did they meet?"

"My goodness," said Mary, "isn't it odd? I always thought Paul told you people everything and never had to tell anything to anyone else. Lean over and grab those two green-and-pink plates, and the cups, too. They're all clean. I just washed them. Beate is a customer of mine—a very good one. She likes fruitwood, very plain. I sold her the table she uses in her office for a desk, and a side table and a washstand—a really old one. I thought to myself: Paul would just adore her. And I was right."

"They seem very . . . unified," Polly said. "They're more like a pair of megaliths than a couple."

"They are," Mary said. "Pass me your cup. Now that they're married Paul only nods to me. They sent me an announcement but now it's clear that I am simply a tradesperson. I love these cups, don't you? I wish someone would buy this set. I don't suppose I could unload it on Beate after the Big Event."

"She seems very fond of green," Polly said. "But she also seems very anti-decoration." Polly passed her cup. She was very grateful to Mary for being so good at conversation.

"So clean, the Swiss," Mary said. "How did your mother take it?"

"Stunned at first," said Polly. "Now she's overwhelmed. They're having twins, you know. That's all she talks about anymore. She's waited for this quite a long time."

"Paula Peckham says your mama says Paul jilted me," Mary said. "It makes me very cross."

"She does think that," Polly said. "Every time she says it, I say the same thing: If *only* Mary had married Paul. How lucky we would have been. I always hoped you would marry Paul but I didn't think he'd ever be so fortunate."

"Marry Paul! What a ghastly thought. After those appalling Rensbergs. I can't tell you how loathsome they are. They travel in a flock or a pack, or a pride. Those awful sisters! The horrible mother! The actress cousin who's always in *Vogue* magazine showing off her perfect country house! Ugh! I don't know how my little angels turned out so well. Every time they come back from Charlie I examine them for horrible signs. I used to want to have their blood changed, to get the Rensberg out. I'm just a nice Protestant girl from Virginia. And you Solo-Millers! Besides," she said, lighting a cigarette, "I was never in love with Paul." She gave Polly a hard look. "Paul was my escort. I was his hostess when he gave a dinner party and we went to the symphony together. But he was my beard. I was in love with someone else." She blew a smoke ring and squinted. "I'm sure you don't approve."

"Oh, Mary," Polly said. A lump rose in her throat. "All the times I saw you, you looked so sparkly."

"I was quite miserable," said Mary, exhaling a plume of smoke. "Seeing you and Henry used to break my little old heart, to tell you the truth. In fact I once ran into you and Henry with my best beloved in tow, don't you remember? We were sneaking out to dinner and we smacked right into you on Park Avenue. It was two years ago, right around now."

"Oh, my," said Polly. "Tony Patton." Tony Patton was a partner of Henry's.

"It's just the tiniest little world," said Mary. "In point of poignant fact, my older sister went to college with his wife, Clover. So all those times you saw me looking so sparkly, I actually was thinking that I was about to die. Seeing you and Henry made me feel very small, I can tell you. I wouldn't say that I was jealous. I simply felt that either something had been left out of me, or something extra had been added to me. At any rate, I was not the kind of person who had things beautifully arranged. When I wanted to make myself really upset, I would lie in bed thinking about you and Henry and how lucky you were to be spared all that."

Polly drank her coffee slowly. If I do not tell Mary the truth, she said to herself, I will be exactly what Lincoln says my family is: put here on earth to make other people feel like hell. If I don't tell her how un-perfect my life is, I will make her feel exactly like my mother makes me feel. She put her cup down.

"I haven't been spared," she said. "Maybe this happens to everyone. My life has been turned upside down this year. For the first time in my life I got into trouble. You're not the only person who fell in love."

"Poor you," said Mary. She did not seem at all astonished. "Sometimes it gets your life in order, you know, but not always the order you expect. Are you fixing to leave Henry?"

"Oh, no," said Polly. "I love Henry. If I had wanted to leave him I would have picked someone I could leave him for. Instead I picked someone who likes to be alone as much as possible, is indifferent to children, and thinks most families are hell. He likes a very marginal life. That's just the opposite of what I want."

"Well," Mary said, "it just goes to show. I always forget that people never are what you think they are. I need more coffee. Finish your sandwich while I put the water on."

Polly ate her sandwich and listened to Mary rattling near the sink.

"My mother got me through that bloody mess," Mary said. "I must have been mortified at myself, because with the exception of my mother and sisters, I've never told another soul until now. I don't suppose you confide this sort of thing to Wendy, do you."

The idea of confiding her love affair to Wendy was so outlandish and dreadful it caused Polly to laugh. Having a mother to confide in sounded like the most exotic, unreachably liberated notion.

"I told a friend at my office," Polly said. "A wonderful kid, but if she hadn't been around, I think I could actually have held out and not told anyone."

"That's no good," Mary said.

"Sometimes I think I've gone for most of my life without telling anything to anyone," said Polly. "It's taken me years to talk to anyone, and I seem to have done it all in a year: my marginal chum, my office friend, and you."

Mary lit a cigarette and dropped the match into her pottery ashtray. It occurred to Polly that the company of a fellow sufferer was consoling. It was not that misery loved company; it *needed* company—the company and guidance of someone who had suffered the same misery.

Polly and Mary talked until late in the afternoon. From time to time the telephone rang and Mary fended off a customer. "Mrs. Rensberg is in Guatemala," she said. "They never know the difference," she said to Polly. "They just like to wave money around or bring their appraisers in." When someone came and rang the shop bell, she waved them away and pointed to the CLOSED sign.

When it was time for Polly to leave, they both stood up. They said good-bye with a sisterly embrace.

"Thank you, Mary," Polly said. "Thank you for telling me what you told me. Thank you for giving me lunch. You're the only person I know to talk to, except my chum at the office. She's wonderful, but she's single and she doesn't have children."

"That probably doesn't make any difference," Mary said. "Love is love and trouble is trouble."

"Not where I come from," Polly said. "Oh, Mary, you really make a person feel better."

"I'll tell you something," Mary said, opening the door. "If you love Henry, things will probably work themselves out.

People do drastic things to make things change and things do change."

"Sometimes it looks very bleak," Polly said.

"Buck up, kid," said Mary. "Come back and have lunch again. Nothing stays terrible forever. It only *seems* that way."

Polly walked home exhilarated, but by the time she reached her door she felt a terrible remorse. What have I done? she said to herself. She was mortified by her confession. She picked up the telephone.

"Rensberg Antiques."

"Mary, this is Polly."

"Oh, Polly, did you leave something behind?"

"No, Mary," said Polly. "It's just . . . I know I needn't say this, but . . ."

"Don't worry, kiddo," said Mary. "Your secret is safe with me, and mine is safe with you."

Twelve

Family life is deflective: it gives everybody something to do. It absorbs sadness and sops up loneliness. It provides work, company, and entertainment. It makes tasks for idle hands and allows an anxious spirit to hide in its capacious bosom.

With no one around her, Polly felt as if she had slipped out of earth orbit. She sat on the edge of the chaise in the bedroom. Her own room looked strange and sinister to her. She had absolutely nothing to do with the hour and a half she had until it was time to go to Martha's. If she had planned better she could have been baking a cake, but she had not planned. It was a small thing, but a sign of how Polly had let things get out of hand. Since she had not known how long she would be with Mary Rensberg, she had decided not to bake. She had bought an apricot tart on the way home, and now, when she felt so frightened and lonely, she was deprived of the diversion of measuring, sifting, rolling, baking, and timing.

A wave of longing for Lincoln broke over her. Not an hour went by that she did not look at her watch, calculate the time in Paris, and wonder what he was doing. She imagined his hotel room, him ambling down a street, him sitting at a cafe reading the *Herald Tribune*. She saw him standing in the empty gallery the way he stood in his studio when he was thinking out a problem: with his hands in his back pockets and his shoulders slightly hunched. Once in a while Lincoln worked while Polly was at the studio. It pained her how rarely she saw him paint. She loved to watch him.

She had helped him pack his paintings for shipping to France, and she wondered how he would hang them. She knew the date of his opening, and had checked out a news-stand near her office that carried foreign papers and journals. She knew that she would buy them all on her way to work and read them in her office to see whether he was reviewed. She knew that she could call his brother, Gus, and get the telephone number of his hotel. She knew that she could call him, and that for an hour she would feel better just for having heard his voice. But that was not fair to him, or to her.

Supposing in Paris he met someone and fell in love? Supposing Polly had given him a yearning to have someone in his life for good? Supposing he came home and brought this person with him? What did he need Polly for? She was married. She could not go to him even if he wanted her to. She could not even get to Paris for three days. It was better to leave him alone, to get out of his life, to let him think by himself.

It did not occur to her to call Henry. If he was not at a meeting, then he was in his hotel room preparing for a meeting, and her call would be a disturbance. It was not fair to ring up a busy, harried man just because you felt lonely and useless.

She could not wait to go to Martha's. Anxiety, she thought, was like a flock of birds on a telephone line. When people came around they flapped off, and when the people went away they hopped back on. The minutes dragged by. Polly was amazed at how long a quarter of an hour could be.

Wendy Solo-Miller believed in action. Inaction bred sloth and discontent. Messy lives were the product of weak wills. Polly had been trained with the notion that order cancels out sadness every time. A plan, an activity, a project, the idea of getting something done was the cure. Polly stood up. A shower would take between seven and ten minutes. Figuring out what to wear would take about two. Putting her clothes on would take five. She sat down again, picked up the telephone and called Martha.

"Would you mind if I was early?" she asked.

"Absolutely not," Martha said. "In fact, I'd love it. I laid out everything for dinner in the kitchen and every time I go in there I get scared. You can come and make your own dinner."

Polly picked up her handbag, threw on her coat, and rang for the elevator feeling that she had been saved.

If Polly had expected solace from Martha, she did not get it. Martha was in a tear.

"I cleaned up the house, and that's all I can do," she said. "I'm in a dangerous mood and Spud and I just had a fight on the telephone."

"I'm sorry to hear that," said Polly, taking off her coat. "What about?"

"About?" said Martha. "We don't fight about *things*. We just fight. I don't want to talk about this. It's too depressing. Come into the kitchen. I'm starving. Feed me."

She led Polly into the kitchen and then sat down. "I'm sorry," she said. "I invited you for dinner and now I just can't cope."

"It's fine with me," Polly said. "I'm feeling sort of awful myself, and cooking dinner will give me something to do."

"I love to see an upstanding person fallen low," Martha said morosely. "You have no idea what a comfort you are to me. If you would actually cook those lamb chops and figure out something to do with the string beans, I'd be very happy to listen quietly to your problems and give you the benefit of my many years of expensive psychotherapy. After all, it should be of some use to someone."

"I don't want to talk about my problems," said Polly, rolling up her sleeves. "Where I come from, we don't do that sort of thing."

"Well, it must be very dull where you come from," said Martha. "Where I come from we think that is the very stuff of life. What are you doing to those lamb chops? They cost me half my salary."

"I'm trimming them," said Polly, "and I'm sticking a little sliver of garlic right next to the bone."

"Gee, that's cute. I ought to learn how to do that, huh? Spud likes that sort of thing. Now what are you doing?" Martha had gotten up and was leaning over Polly.

"I'm topping and tailing the beans. For God's sake, Martha. You're breathing down my collar."

"You're my domestic role model," said Martha. "I have to watch your every move. Are you finished now?"

"No," said Polly. "I'll teach you how to make salad dressing and then we can sit down and you can tell me all your small, feeble problems."

"I'm too tired," Martha said. "I'll just open the wine and sit here without moving." She rooted around in a drawer for a corkscrew. "This is my basic kitchen skill—opening the wine. Also turning on the faucet and turning off the faucet. Talk to me. What did you do today?"

Polly accepted a glass of wine and told Martha about her lunch with Mary Rensberg.

"Isn't confession sweet?" Martha said. "Did you tell her who it was?"

"No," Polly said. "I didn't."

"Huh," said Martha. "Well, there you are. You know, telling me is really like telling a stranger in a saloon."

"It is not!"

"It is so. I don't run in your set. I don't go to your dinner parties. I'm in your office life but not your *real* life."

Polly turned back to the beans. What Martha said was perfectly true. Her life existed in neat little sections, like a grapefruit, but not so close to one another.

"Don't get in a flounce," Martha said. "Aren't you hungry? Shouldn't we start cooking?"

"The potatoes are boiling," Polly said. "Everything else takes two seconds." She sat down. "I hate the way I am," she said. "I don't have any courage and I'm a snob. Everything I was taught I swallowed whole because it was so easy. I can't even make a friend without insulting the friend. It was insulting to call Mary to make sure she would never tell, and it's insulting to you that you feel like a stranger in a saloon."

"Cook," Martha said. "Give me my dinner and I'll forgive you."

"I was being serious."

"So was I," said Martha. "Feed me."

While Polly washed the lettuce, Martha wondered out loud what being married was like if you were happily married.

"I mean before all this stuff with Lincoln happened," she said.

"Oh," Polly said. "It was everything I thought I wanted. I

wanted to be the steward of my household, and I wanted to be married to Henry. It feels so odd to tell you how much I love him when you know about Lincoln, but I do love him. He's big and wonderful. He has real nobility of character. He's eccentric and level at the same time. He's a really wonderful father, and when he's not so distracted he can be an inspired husband. I'm so used to not wanting to think about anything that isn't right. My mother used to tell me over and over: You have to concentrate on the best and leave what isn't best alone. It's a good motto for a lucky family. But I seem not to be able to do that anymore. When we were happy, we really were happy and things rolled right along."

"Even the not-best things," said Martha glumly.

"It's a lot easier that way," said Polly, "I can tell you."

"And then one day you found yourself in the arms of a handsome stranger."

"Try to shut up, Martha," Polly said.

"I'm just trying to figure out how these things go," Martha said. "You're all married. I'm all single. I don't know about this stuff, but I better learn because Spud nags me night and day and eventually something will have to happen, so I better be prepared. I hope the potatoes are done by now."

"The potatoes!" said Polly and she jumped up. "They're very mushy," she said. "We'll have to mash them. Give me your masher."

"Are you crazy? I don't have any such thing."

"Give me a strainer," said Polly.

"I'm not prepared for these emergencies. I don't think I have a strainer. Will a hairnet do? Oh, here's a strainer. This *is* a strainer, isn't it?"

She watched Polly push the mushy potatoes through a sieve.

"Now, if I could learn to do that," she said, "I'd have it all aced."

"Martha, be quiet and check the lamb chops. You have a great many things aced and you like to complain anyway."

"I *love* to complain. Look, I burned my hand."

"It serves you right," Polly said. "Dinner's ready."

When it was time to go home, Polly said: "It's very strange to be the age I am and have absolutely no experience with friends at all. This is the first time I've had dinner alone with a friend since I had Pete, and I almost never have lunch with a friend, especially not on a Saturday."

"So?"

"It ought to make me feel good," said Polly, "but it makes me feel strange."

And when she got home, she felt stranger. What would happen, she thought, if her home suddenly no longer felt like home, if there was no place on earth that she could be comfortable? How could she be comfortable if she did not feel like herself?

Pete and Dee-Dee were probably having a lovely time with their grandparents. Henry had his work, and Lincoln his show. Henry, Jr., had Andreya, and Paul had Beate. To put up with someone as moody as Martha, Spud must love her enormously. Mary Rensberg had her daughters, for whom she could take most of the credit.

Polly sat in her bedroom with her coat on, as if she were a guest about to leave. Nothing was going to get better, she thought. She had made her one false move. Others slipped and fell and made stupid plans, or plans that didn't work, or no plans at all. They got into terrible black moods and neglected their loved ones, and ordinary life went on. Polly did none of those things.

Why did a person for whom order and tranquillity were paramount suddenly find herself in the middle of a dark wood in which the things she had lived by and sworn allegiance to no longer fit her, in which correct answers were useless, in which feelings got out of hand and became not the means to an end but simply themselves: rampaging, clamoring, hungry?

The only person who had ever loved her for herself alone was Lincoln and she was going to have to give him up. Why didn't she simply go to the hospital and have her heart removed? He was her only comfort, the thing that kept her going. He pointed her out to herself. Without him the waters would close over her head and she would go back to being her old self—an empty edition of it—but functional. She would do what was expected of her, but her true heart would be forever closed to her family. No one would ever know her except Lincoln, and he would be as inaccessible to her as if he lived on another planet. In time, sorrow would leave her, and that would be a sort of death. Wasn't sorrow better than nothing? She would, of course, have her family, and as she had been told many times, family is the most important thing.

The next morning she was woken from a terrible sleep by the telephone. It was the children, calling from Maine. They had been to see Mrs. Dunaway, who had a new kind of chicken that laid light green eggs. Each child had been given an egg and had eaten it for breakfast. Dee-Dee had found a dead horseshoe crab on the beach and wanted to bring it home, but Pete said it smelled too disgusting. After these tidings, the telephone was taken away from the children and Wendy's voice came over the line. There was a tone of blithe hardness in her voice, a tone Polly knew well. Wendy was displeased. Polly supposed that she had forgotten something. She did not have to wait very long to be reminded what it was.

"Well, Polly, you haven't asked what time we're coming back," Wendy said.

"What time are you coming back?" said Polly, who was groggy.

"Do you realize that your children have their spring break this week?" Wendy said.

So that was it. Polly's stomach turned. She had forgotten the children's spring break.

"Did you have a plan for it?" Wendy asked.

"No," said Polly. She felt as if she had been kicked.

"If you had discussed this with me, you could have arranged to have them stay up here for a week," Wendy said.

"You could still do that, couldn't you?" said Polly. "Daddy said he has time off."

"That isn't the point," said Wendy. "Yes, we can take the time, but I do find this very worrying. You farm the children out. You get your Consuelo to give them their afternoon snack. You aren't there three days a week. Your mind is on your job. So much so that you forget their spring break. *You* were not brought up that way. It alarms me to see you neglecting your children."

Polly was silent.

"You and Henry have plenty of money," Wendy continued. "This job of yours is doubtless very enriching to you, but it takes you away from your children."

"What about all the volunteering you did when we were kids?" said Polly. "There were plenty of times when you weren't home. We had Mrs. Duffey when we were little, and Suzie when we were older, and you and Daddy went out a lot at night. It isn't so different."

"It's very different," Wendy said. "Your attitude is different."

"Mother, I forgot their spring break. I've never forgotten their spring break before. I've never forgotten anything before. If you can't keep them up at Priory, bring them home."

"And then what, Polly? Have them sit in the apartment every day with Consuelo while you go off to work?"

Polly put her hand over the telephone. She had begun to cry, and she felt it was dangerous to let her mother know.

"Is there something you'd like to tell me?" said Wendy. Her tone had changed. It was formal and demanding, as if to get a confession from a crook.

There was nothing Polly wanted to tell Wendy. Everything she had told Wendy for as long as she could remember was what Wendy wanted to know: I am class president. I have gotten excellent grades. I have won the Latin medal. I have been accepted to attend your old college. I am going to marry a very excellent man of whom you and Daddy will wholeheartedly approve. I am having a child. I am having another. I am taking my sister-in-law out to lunch. I am bringing you a chocolate cake.

Were there daughters anywhere who actually said to their mothers, "I'm having a terrible time. I'm having a love affair and need some advice."

"There's nothing to tell you," Polly said. "Put the children on a plane and I'll pick them up. You're my mother—you could help me out and keep the kids for a week. On the other hand, if you don't like the way I do things, perhaps you would rather not help me. I thought mothers were supposed to help —not make their daughters feel like criminals over some small mistake."

Polly had never made such a speech to her mother. She was amazed at herself. She was no longer tearful, but furious.

"All right," said Wendy, in a voice full of hurt. "I'll keep them here for the week."

"I'd rather you put them on the plane," Polly said. "I don't want them up with you listening to what a terrible and neglectful person their mother is."

"Polly, I did *not* say that."

"You did so," said Polly. "I'm a very good daughter to you. You have gotten years of useful service out of me. I spend my life being nice to you. You do nothing but criticize me—my job, my time, my house. If this is the only wrong thing I've ever done, you should count your blessings. A lot of people would be happy to have me as their daughter."

There was another long silence.

"I'm very sorry you feel this way, Polly," Wendy said. Her voice was a blend of the formal and the contrite. "I think you must be under some strain. I've never heard you sound this way before. I'll keep the children here, since they're having such a good time, and bring them home at the end of the week. But I do think you ought to take stock of yourself. I can't think why you're so angry and upset."

"Because I do one thing wrong out of thousands of right things and I get nailed—that's why," Polly said. "Thank you for keeping the children. I'm sorry about the mistake. Now I want to get off the telephone."

She hung up and sat looking out the window. She felt very free. She had never flown out at her mother, and she had never forgotten anything about the children before. She was that addled and distracted. It was sheer self-indulgence that had caused her to forget the children's school break. Polly had been rigorously trained to be virtuous, and deep inside she believed it was necessary that her character be constantly checked. Her real nature, without restraint, would get her into terrible trouble. And it had. It had led her into a love affair and she had forgotten her children's school holiday.

When her anger and remorse subsided, she was overwhelmed with tears. She missed Lincoln, plain and simple. She stood up and paced around the room.

"I am just in terrible trouble," she said out loud. "I am in an awful state. I didn't mean to fall in love. I never meant to."

Often she missed Lincoln so much that she could not breathe properly. She sat down on the chaise and stopped crying. She missed Lincoln more than she missed her husband or children and she missed him more than she was upset about her mother.

It was worse than grief or longing: she was marked for life. Nothing would ever change. She was condemned. She would always love Lincoln. This would prevent her from being happy with Henry. He would take the Solo-Miller side against her when the depth of her distress and distraction was revealed to him. He did not love her as she wished to be loved. Oh, the terrible, lonely, selfish longing to be loved in specific! She had set it up so that she would be caught between her faithful husband, who loved her generally, and a recluse who loved her specifically. Her future promised more of the same. The old Polly, Polly thought, would never have allowed this to happen. The new Polly was someone Polly didn't know—a yelping, roiling mass of needs, a person full of anger and desire. She did not see how she was going to stop loving Lincoln, and she did not see herself ever running off with him. Therefore she had condemned herself to a life of conflict and pain.

Her children would grow up very nicely all by themselves. But the thing about children was, they did not mitigate private grief, or compensate for private dread.

But Polly was not so much stoical as well behaved. She did not know much about behaving badly: she had really never done so. In bad times you organized your desk and paid your bills. You made lists of your priorities.

Polly sat down at her desk. The first thing, of course, was to say good-bye to Lincoln and mean it. It would be hard—

breaking any addiction is hard—but it was clearly the right thing to do. It was right for Polly and it was also right for Lincoln. Now that he had had a little more experience in love, Polly was holding him back from meeting someone else. Yes, Polly would let him go free, and he would find a girl who would answer him perfectly—another painter, who understood what solitude was all about. The idea of this perfect person caused tears to course down Polly's cheeks. She thought of Mary Rensberg and how lucky she was to have the sort of mother you can take trouble to. She tried to imagine going to Wendy. It was unthinkable.

Polly imagined going downtown and meeting her father at his law office, and setting out her problem before him. His noble, elevated features would turn rather dark. Daddy's Horizontal Flicker of Disapproval would dart across his face. He would be astonished, simply astonished, that a daughter of his, his reliable Polly, would be so childish, would put whim above responsibility, would jeopardize her household, was in fact capable of such action.

There was no one who would stand up for her. Her family would line up against her in shock, afraid that she was neglecting her children, that she might bring some sort of scandal to their door. No one would care that her feelings were real, or that she might be suffering. She was a producer of goods and services and image. None of these must be threatened, as all good tribe members know.

I should be doing some useful project, Polly said, but there was no useful project left to do. The only thing that was undone was an unanswered letter to Henry's sister, Eva, in London. Polly picked up the letter. It was opened, but unread, and it was now three weeks old. This was unlike Polly, who always answered a letter within two days of getting it.

Eva had been her best friend at college and would have continued to be her closest friend except that now they were sisters-in-law. It was no longer possible to talk with your best friend about boys and love when the boy you loved was your best friend's brother. It would hardly have done to complain about Henry to Eva: in that instance they were the blood and Polly was the water.

Eva had married an Englishman—a banker named Roger Forbes. They lived in London with their two daughters, Rosie and Theodora. In this letter, Eva recounted her recent happiness: she had done the illustrations for a children's book that would be published within the year. They had had the house redecorated. Rosie was still studying the violin and Theodora had started ballet lessons. Each year the family went to their country cottage for an American Thanksgiving, and Eva gathered every exiled American she knew. Before dinner everyone stood and sang "America the Beautiful"—her children sang this with English accents—and then they sat down to turkey, Indian pudding, and baked Brussels sprouts. A lavish description of this meal and its participants followed.

"It was very perfect," the letter read, "but it would have been even more perfect if you and Henry and the children had been with us. Still, life looks very sweet these days. I think one gets happier as one gets older—there is more to be happy about."

"Oh, go to hell," said Polly to the letter. She thought about the sort of letter she might write in reply: Dear Eva: The last six months have been the darkest of my life. Maybe someday you will feel this way. You will wake up one morning and stop chirping. This may not be possible for you, but it was for me. Everything is very difficult, it turns out. Your darling brother has not changed a whit. I just got defeated by the way he is—working too hard, away a lot, and absent often when present. So I on the other hand am having an adulterous love affair. I am in love, and for this reason I forgot to make proper arrangements for the children's school holiday. Next week I shall be brought before the family tribunal, where quite justifiably I will be tortured and then probably shot. Every day I cry at least once. I think one gets more unhappy as one gets older—there is more to be unhappy about.

She sat at her orderly desk. Being alone when you are at war with yourself is horrible. What was more useless than a childless mother, a husbandless wife, a lover without her beloved, a person with no friends? Henry was due back late in the afternoon. Why did this prospect fill her with dread?

It seemed to Polly that there were two Henrys, or maybe three. There was the Henry she loved, who was full of qualities, kind and tender, an ardent lover, good with children, a strong family presence, an unyielding intelligence, a man of character. There was the Henry she was frightened of. The other side of his good nature was very severe. Polly was just fine by him, but he was critical of almost everyone else. How lucky he had been to find such an excellent person to marry! Polly knew he felt this way, and it made her constantly terrified that she might slip and be found wanting. Henry liked things to go right. He believed that things should be done well. Polly often felt like an over-achieving child dragging the little red wagon of her struggle along with her. Why had she never realized that until now?

Henry had been brought up under the old order. It was not so much that his work came first as that it was pervasive. Polly was a perfect lawyer's wife. She came from a lawyer's family and Henry's work was familiar to her. Furthermore, it interested her; but even if it had not, she had been trained to be interested. Henry's work had been such an effective restraint that for years Polly had not noticed how repressive it was. If she was blue, or tired, or upset, and Henry was working, there was not much chance of getting to him. He made gestures. He brought her a cup of tea, or made the children scrambled eggs for their supper if she was sick, or he held her in his arms and comforted her if she was sad, but it was very clear that these gestures took him away from what was really on his mind. Henry could be short-tempered, moody, and snappish. This was not personal: it was the result of being pressed. His children did not take it personally, since their daddy instantly turned to them and hugged them to make up for any snappishness he dealt out. But Polly took it personally. How personally she had taken it she had not known until she had fallen in love with Lincoln.

But Henry embodied every quality Polly admired. He was fair; he stuck by his high standards; he did not pay lip service to anything he did not believe; he never toadied; and there was not one drop of artifice in him.

At home, Henry was most himself. He liked to wear very old clothes: a pair of blue jeans as soft as flannel and patched like a quilt, and an old cashmere sweater of his late uncle Alfred's that was peppered with tiny moth holes. Under this he wore a shirt that had no collar: the collar had frayed off. He had a battered hat, once white, now gray, that he had found floating in a lagoon in Maine. In this getup he liked to take the children out on a Saturday and come home with strange edibles—pig's feet, cheese that looked like braided string, boxes and jars of things with labels in foreign languages. Along with these were the ingredients for Henry's favorite drink, the root-beer float. This was made with coffee ice cream and root beer, a drink Polly found disgusting and her children adored.

In Maine he took the children fishing, or blueberry-picking, or bird-walking. He took pie-crust-making lessons from Polly and learned to make blueberry pie. At night he made up for Pete and Dee-Dee the silliest stories he could think of. When Henry was happy, and his work was going well, the household hummed along very happily. Suddenly it filled Polly with rage that when he was not happy the household was not happy. Who the hell did he think he was?

Who was he to have neglected her for so long? To call when he was away either so late at night that she was asleep or so early in the morning that she was barely awake? Who was he not to struggle under the same burden to be cheerful and kind and generous when things were not going well? Had he ever been really aware of anything that happened at Polly's office? He was interested in a mild way but Polly had never made him aware. This was not all Henry's fault. She had let him be the way he was. She had expected it.

Polly looked at the clock. She had been sitting at her desk for three hours without moving. She had not gone out to get the Sunday paper. Would Henry, who was methodical about these things, have bought the paper for his plane trip home, or would he expect it at home waiting for him? There was nothing to eat in the house. Henry had said they could go out to dinner, but a good wife—the Polly that used to be—would have had a chicken to be roasted, the makings of a green salad, and an orange cake to welcome a husband back from a week-long business trip.

She struggled up from her chair and changed her sweater. She had not washed her face or combed her hair. This was what happened when you slipped into your own misery: everything went to hell.

Polly had never been in a supermarket on a Sunday. She had her mother's prejudices about supermarkets. Wendy considered them a good place for harried people to buy paper items and cleaning products but not the proper place to buy food. Wendy dealt, and had dealt for more than thirty years, with a small, expensive grocery that delivered. She shopped by telephone, which seemed to her the way to do things. If you were an excellent customer, you got the best of everything. This eliminated the need for shopping, an activity Wendy found trying.

Polly had a friendly relationship with her butcher, and with the family of Koreans who ran the local vegetable stand. She liked to shop, and she was good at it. She never ran out, was never caught short at the last minute. She usually had the makings of a good meal in the house, and it frightened her not to. She and Henry could easily go around the corner for dinner when he got home, but the lack of the gesture—the idea of *not* making dinner—frightened her, too. One lapse could easily lead to another until there were no more gestures. To think that she might not care whether or not Henry was given a nice meal also scared her. What if she didn't care?

She grabbed a coat from the front hall closet and opened the door. There stood Henry Demarest, getting out of the elevator, looking tired.

The sight of him disoriented her. Then it made her furious. He was home early. He was never home early. Why couldn't he come home when he said he was coming home? Her anger confused her. She stood in the hallway gaping at him.

"Oh," she finally said. "I didn't expect you so early."

"Where are you off to?" Henry asked. He did not kiss her, or take her arm. The jig was up. The fact that she was angry and troubled was written all over her face. Henry, who counted on her good spirits, now saw that she was not of much use. It is one thing to be unhappy. It is another when the people you live with acknowledge it.

"I'm off to the supermarket," Polly said. "There's nothing in the house to eat. I'm going to get us something."

"We can go out, Polly," said Henry.

"No, no," said Polly. "You've been out all week. I'll just be a second. Don't you want to take a bath and stretch out?"

Polly had never greeted him thus. There was no waiting tray, no drink, no kiss hello, no Polly perched on the side of the bed waiting for Henry to tell her how things had gone. There was just Polly, rattled, overwrought, and dying to get out of the house.

"I'll just be a second," she said. "I'll just dash down to the supermarket and I'll see you in two seconds."

It was of course horrible to be horrified by the sight of your own husband. The idea of sitting down to dinner with him, of trying to make conversation, was frightful. What was she supposed to say?

In the supermarket, Polly harangued herself. People who shopped on Sunday were people who had let things get out of hand, who paid no attention to detail, who let themselves get lost. There were people who actually bought their *vegetables* at the supermarket—Polly did not believe that anything in a supermarket could be really fresh. These were people who did not calculate what meals would be served or who would eat them, who were not generous, thrifty, or composed enough to shop for contingencies. Shopping in a supermarket was a sign of bad housekeeping. How could these people bring themselves to admit their flaws publicly?

Only something very dire, like death or a love affair, ought to keep a person from doing things right. Polly looked around her. Were all these people with full shopping carts having love affairs?

But of course it *was* something dire that had preoccupied Polly, while other people simply lived. They ran out of milk, missed trains, did not have dinner waiting for their husbands, and even forgot to make plans for their children's school holiday, and some of these people were probably very nice, having a good time, and happily married.

Every anchor had slipped away from her. The fact was, she could not bear to go home. She did not want to be alone with

Henry. She wanted her children to come back and protect her, to make the interfering noises children make that get in the way of their parents' dialogue for better and for worse. Henry was clearly not very happy either, and neither of them had discussed it. They were like figures on an old-fashioned clock, bowing formally, ill at ease and far away from each other. And the truth was, or so Polly felt, that if they discussed anything at all, Henry would turn from her. Or did she mean that she would turn from him? In either case, she was perched right on the edge of failure. It was both their faults, but Polly should have been more aware of things. They had let each other down, and in the bleak, glaring light of the supermarket, their marriage looked to Polly hopeless and doomed.

She wandered down aisles full of soap, crackers, and canned vegetables. She had never bought a canned vegetable in her life. She thought of Lincoln, of the set of his shoulders. She thought of the times they had left his studio and meandered around the neighborhood. They always strolled arm in arm, but Polly often liked to hang back and watch Lincoln walk ahead. He had the ambling gait of a boy out of Mark Twain or Winslow Homer.

The image of Lincoln caused a physical sensation—a low blow. Longing, in its most concentrated form, was just like having the breath knocked out of you. Polly doubled over slightly.

She had never longed for Henry in that way because Henry was right in front of her. He had been hers to have. In the Solo-Miller family, love was intelligent and deep, and never unrequited. It was the basis of all good things and there was nothing secretive or covert about it. Love flourished in the sunshine, in public, in ceremony and ritual. It did not have to hide. It was the binding of life, the glue of families. The kind of love Polly felt for Lincoln was not the kind of which the

Solo-Millers ever could have approved. It was feckless, led to nothing, was productive of nothing, and didn't do anyone a bit of good. Love stood for ties and binds, for the things that made life work. The Solo-Millers were not against romantic feelings, but against romantic feelings improperly placed.

In front of her at the check-out counter were a young couple—a girl with curly red hair and a tall, sleepy-looking boy wearing a battered straw hat. The girl wore a big red coat, cowboy boots, and a wedding band. They were showing off.

"Kiss me, our Dan," said the girl. She stood on tiptoes. Our Dan leaned down and kissed her.

"All right, Dan," said the boy. "What is it we're making for dinner?"

"We, Dan?" said the girl. "I don't ever notice you rushing into the kitchen."

"Why, Dan," said the boy. "You said when we got married I wouldn't have to ever cook again."

"You lie," said the girl. "You misheard. Why, Dan, we're supposed to cook together."

"All right," the boy said. "What is it we're cooking?"

"Well," said the girl, "I thought chocolate pudding."

"Is that all?"

"Yes, Dan," said the girl.

"But why are there bananas in our shopping basket?" the boy said.

"Those are to put *on* the chocolate pudding," the girl said.

The checker, an impassive high-school girl, checked out their purchases: five bars of unsweetened chocolate, a bar of milk chocolate, a pound of sugar, four cakes of soap, and a bunch of bananas.

"Dan," said the boy, "you'd love me if I was ugly, wouldn't you?"

"No," said the girl. "I wouldn't."

"Ugly people can love, too."

"Yes," said the girl. "They can love and be loved, but not by me."

The checker packed their groceries in a bag and handed it to the boy. Dan and Dan exited, arm in arm.

Polly felt as if she had been pierced with knives, as if the boy and girl had been sent to rub her nose in the fact of young married love, full of silliness and improper meals, conducted by two people who shopped in the supermarket on Sunday and ate whatever they felt like eating.

Dan and Dan were standing in front of a bookstore sharing a bar of chocolate when Polly emerged. Even in her distress she had planned a balanced meal: spaghetti with butter and cheese, a cucumber salad, oranges and walnuts for dessert. Dan and Dan began to amble up the street. They knocked into each other as they walked, then separated, then knocked into each other again.

I'll just go up to them, Polly said to herself. I'll say: Dan and Dan, what is your secret for living? Have you ever felt so terrible that all the joy of life evaporated and even the most pleasurable things seemed to have no substance? Does death ever seem attractive to you? Have you ever gone through a long piece of time in which you cried every single day? Did you ever feel that there is no way out of your trouble? Do you ever feel that nothing straightforward, or easy, or uncorrupted will ever happen to you again? Do you ever feel that your life has been ruined?

Dan and Dan were now holding hands, and Polly could hear them laughing. They turned the corner and disappeared. Polly walked home as slowly as she could. When she got home she walked around the block three times slowly, and then, defeated by a brisk chill wind, she was forced to go in.

Thirteen

The house was quiet when Polly got back. She stood at the doorway listening for Henry. He could easily have packed up and left her, Polly thought. After all, what was less enchanting than an unhappy wife? Could it be pleasant to come home to someone who was upset, nervous, and devoid of cheer? Had she not let her side down? Why would Henry want to come home to her in her present state?

Henry harbored things—he always had. He brooded and reflected. In order to know what he was thinking, it was necessary to ask, and even then he did not always tell. In this way he was rather like Polly's father. Good manners can be a frightening thing, since one never knows what goes on underneath them. Henry could very well have been brooding and reflecting on the subject of Polly and harboring his feelings against her. It would not have surprised Polly to find Henry gone, and on her side of the bed a kindly note saying in the nicest possible way that he had left.

But of course he had not left. He had no place to go, and neither did Polly. They were both at home.

Henry had taken a shower, put on his old camel's-hair robe, and was taking a nap in the bedroom. Because he was a nearly perfect person he had folded down the Early American quilt, knowing that it was too fragile to be slept on. He had covered himself with the plaid car rug that was usually folded at the bottom of the chaise. The sight of him filled Polly with love and pain. When he was asleep he was just himself—not preoccupied, or tired, or angry. Sleep took all the tension from his face and left Polly looking at the handsome, winsome, manly boy she had married. How she loved him! How angry she was at herself for loving him so! That tender, sleeping man was not the fierce, Olympian, and remote person who often presented himself to Polly; the person it was often impossible to approach, who made it very clear that he wanted to be left alone.

Henry's nature was as dark and light as the two sides of the moon. When he was happy, he puttered around the house, letting his children climb all over him. In his happy mode he was a wonderful companion.

In sleep the frown was gone from his forehead. He looked young and hopeful and tired. His rich, brown hair was damp from the shower. In order not to get the pillow wet, he had folded a towel and put it under his head.

If a man does not want to talk to you much; if a man wants you around as a presence but not as a person; if you have to ask a man to kiss you hello or to take you into his arms; if he is abstracted and absorbed but still remembers to put a towel under his head to keep the pillow from getting wet, and remembers that the quilt is too fragile to be slept on and thus folds it up so neatly, what more of a demonstration of love is necessary?

Polly crept down the hall and began dinner. She set two

places at the dining-room table. The twilight made everything look harsh, hopeless, and dingy. No incandescent light properly dispelled this gloom.

As Polly was making the salad, Henry came into the kitchen.

"I don't want to eat in the dining room," he said. Polly jumped. She hadn't heard him come in. "Can't we just eat here?"

It had always been Polly's impression that Henry did not like to have his meals—except with the children—in the kitchen.

"I'm sorry," Polly said. "I didn't think you liked to eat in here, so I set the table in there. I'll change it."

"I'll change it, Polly. Don't get so upset."

A hot flush filled Polly's chest. "I'm not upset," she said. "I'm not upset."

The air was full of tension.

"All right, all right," said Henry. "Just calm down. I'll set the table in here. Don't be so hysterical."

"I'm not hysterical!" Polly shrieked. The look in Henry's eyes was terrible—the first acknowledgment of how terrible he thought things were between them. Was this what he had come home to? Polly sat down at the end of the table, covered her face with her hands, and cried uncontrollably. She was not safe. She was not anything more than an ordinary woman whose failure was staring at her. There was no old Polly, and no new Polly. She had no place to stand. This was not a fight: this was a symbol, a declaration. This was the sort of thing you never let happen. This was the one false move that ruined everything.

"Oh, my God, Polly," Henry said. He stood beside her. "What's wrong? What's wrong?" He stroked her shoulders. Polly sprang up.

"Leave me alone!" she cried, and when Henry flinched, she threw her arms around him and cried onto his robe. He smelled as sweet as cocoa butter.

"You've been unhappy for a long time," Henry said quietly.

"You never want to eat in the kitchen," Polly said.

Henry took her arms from around him. "Come on, Polly," he said. "We have to talk." Polly's heart froze. She was silent. They sat across from each other at the kitchen table.

"Talk to me," said Henry. "I'm your husband."

"I'm your wife and you don't talk to me," said Polly. "Sometimes I think that you're thinking of leaving me because I'm suddenly not what you bargained for." Light filled her head. Once she started, she could not stop. "You neglect me. You pay attention to the children because they don't require much. You decided I didn't require much and you never found out what I required. Your work is the only thing in this household that counts."

"I think you want to leave me," said Henry. "I've thought that for months."

"I don't want to leave you," said Polly, looking down at the placemat. "*I* don't require much. I want you to love me."

"I do love you," Henry said.

"I want you to show it."

"I do show it," Henry said.

"I want you to show it the way I want to see it." She looked up at Henry and suddenly they both smiled.

"That's a very universal wish," said Henry.

"It is not," Polly said. "You never ask about my work. You never ask how my day went. It doesn't matter to you how it went. Your work is all over this house. Your mood is dictated by work and then your work-dictated mood comes home and dictates the mood around here. I know you work hard but I think it's a shield. It keeps me exactly where you want me—

about a thousand miles away. You can be a fine father and a great lawyer and you look like a wonderful husband and you can make me feel as if I am running a four-star hotel. You don't pay any attention to me. How do you think it makes me feel that I have less effect on you than work?"

She stood up and looked at him. He had no particular expression on his face. This filled Polly with terror—the terror that he had been harboring a list of grievances against her, and now he was going to burst forth with it. Worse than Daddy's Horizontal Flicker of Disapproval was Henry's impassivity. She had spent her life being governed by one look or another. She pressed on.

"You look as if you're listening to a client," said Polly. "I'm not your client. I'm your wife and I'm supposed to be your sweetheart."

She sat down again. The floodgate had been opened. She looked at Henry, who now seemed worried, tender, and alarmed.

"I'm tired," she said. "I'm tired of feeling I have to be so good. I'm tired of working so hard to make sure every little thing is right. I'm sick of being the only person who behaves. I'm tired of thinking I have to work so hard to get anyone to love me. I'm tired of its being perfectly all right that Beate says things that hurt my feelings. For the first time in my life I made a mistake about the children—about spring break—and Mother comes after me as if I had done an ax murder. I stop being Little Mary Sunshine, I stop being so understanding about your work and your pressures, and you turn against me. I'm sick of having to be sensitive to everybody's quirks and needs, and I'm sick of soothing everyone's feelings. I behave and behave and behave and I don't get any credit for it. I want some praise. I want to be singled out. I'm tired of being considerate and asking everybody about their lives and their jobs when no one asks me one single thing." She had started crying, but now she stopped.

"Nobody asked for such perfection," said Henry.

"You did, too!" said Polly. "You like everything the way it is. You just don't know how hard I work to get it the way it is." Now Henry was silent.

"Speak to me," said Polly.

"What am I supposed to say?"

"What you feel."

"You sound ready to give me up," said Henry. "You sound as if you don't love me or anyone very much anymore."

"That's not what I sound like," said Polly. "Why do I have to be the unloving one? I'm right to be angry. For instance, you do neglect me. You expect me to understand it when you do."

"I'm scared of you," said Henry. "You know I love you. I do count on you. You're the best person that ever was. It's very hard to get to you, do you know that? I have a wall of work, and you have a wall of family. You make me afraid to ask what's troubling you. I'm afraid that even if you hated me, you would stay with me so as not to fail in front of your family. I wonder the same things you do. I wonder if you love me for myself or for the way I fit into things."

"I do love you for yourself," said Polly. "I'm so lonely. I'm so confused." When she put her hands on the table, Henry covered them with his.

This conversation, which both had been dreading and which neither had ever thought would be necessary, had rather knocked them out. No dire things had been said. They both felt slightly better, but winded.

"I'm sorry to have failed you," said Henry.

"Don't be so melodramatic," said Polly. "You haven't failed me. You've neglected me."

"I won't anymore."

"You probably will," said Polly. "But you're going to have to start apologizing for it."

She looked at Henry expectantly. One talk of this sort was not like a bracing shower. It did not wash everything away. She looked again at him appraisingly, as if he were a recent acquaintance.

"Do you want to talk more?" Henry said.

Polly did not want to talk more. She had heard in her own voice an imploring tone, pained and angry, and she was afraid. She was not used to this form of talk and did not know what it would bring. She and Henry were not like Spud and Martha, bickering amiably, working everything out by scrapping. This confrontation, which even Polly knew most other people would have found mild, disturbed her. She wanted things to normal down a bit so she could get her courage up.

"I want my dinner," she said. "Let's have a bottle of wine."

"All right," said Henry. "But let's eat in the kitchen and then have a horizontal evening."

Had Pete and Dee-Dee been home, they would have tropped into the bedroom and lain about like land tortoises. These days Pete and Dee-Dee were both learning how to knit. They both used big wooden needles, and the wool that had once been white was now gray. The sight of her children absorbed in knitting their dirty little squares was so comical and endearing to Polly that she could almost not bear to be in the same room with them. On cold nights the family crawled under the covers and Henry, if he was home, read to them from *Wild Animals I Have Known* by Ernest Thompson Seton.

Once upon a time it had filled Polly with delight to get into bed early of an evening after the children were asleep and read next to Henry. The sense of comfort, of domestic ease, of loving availability had filled her heart. But Polly knew in advance what their horizontal evening would be like. Henry would bring some papers to bed, or he would pick up a mystery and fall almost instantly to sleep, leaving Polly alone and wakeful, in the grip of the sort of physical desire you feel will claw you to death.

Polly and Henry sat down to dinner in the kitchen. It was like an uncomfortable second date: what an effort they were making!

"Lovely spaghetti, Polly," said Henry.

"I hope it's buttery enough," Polly said.

"It's perfect," Henry said. "Is there a little grated cheese?"

Polly leapt from the table. "I forgot. Isn't that silly? I left it out with the grater and I never grated it." She sat back down and handed Henry the grater and the cheese. Henry was looking at her with real concern. She realized that she was visibly frantic. It was very much not like her to forget the grated cheese. But she was so very upset. A cloud of misery and potential despair hung between herself and Henry. Talking to him had exhausted them. How was she supposed to talk to him more? Was it his fault that he was the way he was? Hadn't she spoon-fed him into the way he was? With all her blessings, did she deserve to be angry?

The idea of a dinner without dinner-table conversation was the end of the world to Polly. It meant that everything was irredeemably wrong, but she did not know what to begin to say. Henry thought a silent dinner was the end of the world, too.

"What does Wendy say is going on in Priory?" he said.

"Ronnie from Ronnie's Clam Box's wife left him," said Polly. "He was open when they got up. Dee-Dee found a horseshoe crab. That was about all. Then Mother and I had a fight about the children's spring break."

"So you said. But they're up in Maine for the week, aren't they?"

"I didn't arrange it," Polly said. "I forgot all about it. I packed them for a weekend and completely forgot about their break. I hadn't made any arrangements at all."

"Well, then," said Henry good-naturedly as he tossed the salad, "you'll understand when your mother sends the police over to arrest you."

"Don't tease me!" Polly cried. "You don't have to arrange their holidays and you don't get a lot of flak when you make a mistake. I do." Tears ran down her face. Henry got up, pulled his chair next to hers, and sat close to her. He took her hands in his.

"Oh, my poor Polly. Is everything making you so miserable?" He put her hands on his shoulders and pulled her close, but Polly broke away.

"I am miserable," she said.

"On the subject of your mother," Henry said, "I've told you a dozen times and you never listen. She's a lovable monster and she likes to make you feel bad."

"I do listen," said Polly. "But I have to put up with her. She's the only mother I've got."

"You're her only daughter," Henry said.

"I'd like to kill her," Polly said. "I'd like to strangle her. She doesn't hector Henry and Andreya. She wouldn't dare lay a glove on Paul. Why do I have to suffer?" She turned to Henry. "I know, I know. Because I make myself available to her. But why do I have to be reasonable and understand when I'd still like to strangle her."

"And me?" said Henry. He stood up, gathered the plates, and took them to the sink. "Do you want to strangle me, too?"

"Yes," said Polly. "I'm dying of loneliness. I know it's my fault. I should have stopped pretending everything was fine a long time ago. Now that I have, I feel that everyone is against me—you, too."

Henry stood in the middle of the kitchen. "Please, Polly," he said. "Come here to me."

"You come to me," said Polly.

Henry knelt by her chair. "Whatever it is, Polly, can it be fixed?" he said. "Do you not love me anymore? Please tell me."

"I don't want anyone to stop loving me," said Polly. "I'm so furious at everyone. Pretty soon everyone will start hating me."

"No one could ever hate you," said Henry. "You're the best there is."

"I don't want to be the best anymore," said Polly.

"You can't help it," Henry said. "It isn't something you do. It's something you are."

"That's what I mean," said Polly. "If I stop being that way, I'll lose you. I feel I have to be faultless, and the rest of you get to be loved in spite of your faults."

"This may come as a shock," Henry said, "but you aren't flawless."

"I try so hard!" cried Polly.

"Poor us," said Henry. "You want us to love you because you try to be good, and when you are good, you're angry because we love you for it. What is it you want?"

I am greedy and spoiled, Polly thought to herself. I want my husband and my love affair and my nice safe life. I want to stop feeling as if I were a stranger to myself. I want to be happy with Henry again.

She looked at Henry with a mixture of longing and dread. Even if you truly loved your mate, Polly thought, you were spared nothing.

"I just want to be myself," said Polly.

"You are yourself," Henry said.

"If I am, it's the first time I ever have been," said Polly. "I feel so awful. I feel as if I've been wearing clothes that don't fit me for the longest time, and now that I've taken them off, I feel worse."

"You don't trust anyone to love you any old way you are?" Henry said.

"No," said Polly, bursting into tears. "I don't."

"I do love you any old way," said Henry. "Now listen. Pour yourself a cup of coffee. You can drink it in bed with all the pillows fluffed up. You need to be more rested and less upset."

He walked her down the hallway, and while Polly put on her nightdress he turned back the bedclothes and fluffed up the pillows. When she got into bed, he arranged the covers over her.

"I'm going to spend five minutes going over some papers," Henry said. "For tomorrow. Then I'll be in."

Couldn't he love her enough to look at his papers in the morning? Polly thought. Did he think one talk was all she needed? Was he hiding from her in his work because he was frightened? Was it not a display of his true feelings that work came before love so prominently?

Lincoln's desire for her was unconditional. His life was arranged so that he could freely desire her, pure and simple. In marriage nothing was pure and simple, Polly thought. That she could not be purely angry at Henry, that she *believed* in his work problems, that she felt they had priority over her always, seemed to her the beginning, the middle, and the end of her unhappiness. It wore her down; it made her exhausted.

She was half asleep when Henry came in. He got carefully into bed and took Polly in his arms.

"Are you still upset?" he whispered.

"Yes," said Polly.

"About everything, or about us?"

"About you," said Polly.

"What about me?"

Polly slid from his arms. "Why couldn't you just come to bed and get up early to go over your papers? Don't I mean anything?"

"I'm very pressed," Henry said. "It's worse than ever."

Polly sat up. "I'd help you," she said. "I'd bring you trays and snacks, and rub your back and listen to you talk things out. I'd do all those things, if you'd only notice them. If they made any difference to you."

Henry reached up and pulled her down next to him. "I do notice," he said. "They do make a difference. I would die without you." He kissed her lips, her hair, her ears. She pressed herself close to him, and buried her face in his neck.

"Oh, Polly," he said. "You make my life so sweet."

He took her into his arms and they were together again.

PART FOUR

Fourteen

Suddenly, everyone was back. Pete and Dee-Dee blew into the house with pink-and-gold cheeks. Henry, Sr., and Wendy, not quite so golden, were home as well.

Henry had won his case on appeal, and the grueling part of his schedule came to an end. The cloud over his work lifted. He came home early for dinner and he turned the intensity of his focus from his work to his domestic life. With his attention concentrated on Polly, he was very hard to resist. He behaved like a man courting, but he was not so obvious as to bring home flowers. Instead he brought himself and his charm. The family ate dinner in the kitchen. They had horizontal evenings in the bedroom. Some nights, after the children were in bed, Henry and Polly took themselves off to the movies, where they sat holding hands.

Henry, when he wanted to be, was an indomitable force, and although Polly was generally grateful for the love she got, she was wary. She let herself be courted, and Henry's ardor was persuasive, but even though she was often quite melted away, there were also times when she felt that she was being made a project of.

"For goodness' sake, Polly," said Henry. "I *am* making a project of you. First you say I neglect you, then you say I pay too much court."

"I want love, not compensation," Polly said. "I don't want to get used to having you around and then have you snatched away by work."

"I can't control the pressure," Henry said.

"I want you to find some way not to be so distant," said Polly. "That's all I ask." She made herself confront Henry. The more they talked, the closer to him she felt.

She forced herself to say these things: it was not natural to her. It was traditional in the Demarest and Solo-Miller families to live things through. Mutual, silent understanding was their method, which seemed to Polly excellent when things were going well, but very bad when they were not. She made herself and Henry talk, and she steeled herself not to be afraid of squabbles or fights. More than anything else she wanted her old life restored to her. She wanted the weight lifted from her heart; she wanted never to feel despairing again. She wanted to be her old self: she thought she *was* her old self. She was so very glad to feel cheerful, to feel encouraged, to have Henry come home early, to have her children near her. She knew that the more good feeling you generated, the more good feeling prevailed. In her heart she was an old-fashioned do-gooder—surely if you did good, it came back to you. She gave herself wholeheartedly back to her family, who clustered around her, as if to show her how smooth life was when you were not having a love affair.

The one thing she did not want to think about was Lincoln. The thought of him made her remember how bleak and exhausted she had been, how very different her life had felt to her. She was used to him being gone, and now, he was finally receding. She no longer felt those sharp pains of missing him. Of course, she did not have time to miss him. She had Henry, the children, the printing of the spring report to supervise. What bliss it was to come home to a happy family supper, to an attentive husband, to a feeling that things were as they should be, that she was working hard to put her life on course once more and that the problems before her were only ordinary ones. Polly looked back on the winter and saw it as one low stormy afternoon with Lincoln next to her. Lincoln was the thorn in her path, the shadow in her golden light, the keeper of the secret of her fall from grace.

The days lightened. The late-afternoon sky was lilac, not gray. Of course, she was not quite her old self. She found herself reluctant to see her parents.

"Darling," said Wendy on the telephone, "where are you hiding? It's been ages since we've seen you. You can't be *that* busy."

"I am that busy," Polly said. "The spring report is at the printer's and I have to oversee it."

"Well, I'm having lunch with Beate tomorrow. She's going to have those babies any day and I feel we ought to be a little close to her. Why don't I book a table for three instead of two?"

"I can't go," Polly said. "I'll be in a meeting this morning and at the printer's this afternoon."

There was a long silence.

"Well, Polly," Wendy said, "I'm very disappointed in you. Beate is far away from her own family, and this is certainly more important than some report or meeting."

"Look," said Polly. "I've had quite enough of Beate and Paul. I've had lunch with her six times. I know she's far away but I will not sit back and let Beate tell me that *my* birth experience was improper, which she has told me over and over again, or that she knows more about having children than I do, and that since I am not as pure and high-minded as she is, Pete and Dee-Dee are going to turn out to be little war criminals and convicted felons. It hurts my feelings."

"She doesn't mean it," Wendy said. "It's just nerves."

"I had a first baby, too," Polly said. "And I wasn't that way. I'll be very happy to bring the little twins matching baby blankets but I'm not going to lunch and that's final. Beate has you and Paul. Furthermore, my meeting this morning is *very* important and if I am not at the printer's today the report will be delayed." A firm, clear voice—it amazed Polly to find it was her own—issued from her lips. She heard herself say, "And on the subject of children, Mother . . ." She could almost see Wendy flinch. This was not a tone of voice Wendy had ever heard from her before. She continued: "There are a few conversations I don't think we ought to have anymore about the children. I don't think you know how critical of me you are on this score. One subject is the school holidays. The other is my job and who I leave the children with. I take excellent care of Pete and Dee-Dee. Concita is a very fine, kind, and intelligent person. Nancy Jewell is a wonderful baby-sitter, and one of the nicest people on earth. Those children are arranged for and coddled and loved. I am almost always home at night. I don't want to be hectored on the subject of them anymore."

"I see," said Wendy. The tone in her voice was magisterial, but hurt.

Polly knew that some attempt would be made to make her feel awful on the subject of Beate, but she did not care. Beate and Paul especially rankled her. It made her furious that Beate was allowed to hurt her feelings. She would give Beate the fealty that was due a sister-in-law, but she was not inclined to like her. If in seventy or eighty years Beate softened up, perhaps, thought Polly, she would give her a second chance. As for the children, Wendy would temporarily maintain a hurt, chilly, hands-off posture. That was fine with Polly. But it made her angry that Beate's babies were more crucial than Polly's really important work, though Wendy was always hopeless when it came to Polly's job.

This policy statement accomplished, Polly bustled cheerfully around her household. Every day she felt stronger and clearer. With Henry near her she felt that life made sense. When she sat down to dinner she said a prayer of thanks that life had treated her so well.

It was only when she was alone that an alarm of panic rang through her. What was she going to do about Lincoln! He would eventually be home. What must be done was clear. Lincoln's presence in her life, she now saw, had compensated for Henry's neglect of her. It was as simple as that. Now that Henry had come back to her, now that they were together, Lincoln was a hindrance. She could not achieve her peaceful and loving domestic life with Lincoln scattered in her path like broken glass. It was too dangerous. In her heart Polly believed that the deed had already been done. She believed that she had given Lincoln up.

In the morning she walked the children to school. She saw women with fur coats over their arms walking toward the furrier's to put their coats in storage for the summer. In Polly's neighborhood, that was a sure sign of spring.

"Take my hand, Pete, please," said Polly as they crossed the street.

"I don't want to," said Pete. "I'm too old."

Polly regarded her son. In not so very long he would be taller than she. Would he go around breaking hearts? Would he be handsome and steady like his father, or would he be quirky and boyish in the manner of Lincoln?

"You can stop holding my hand when you're sixteen," said Polly. "And not before." She took his hand and held it. He was such a nice little boy that he gave her hand a squeeze. Dee-Dee, however, had to be held. She had entered a dreamy stage in which she had to be shaken out of her reveries and dragged away from her books, and her only two subjects of conversation were imaginary animals and her imaginary friend, Flower Bernstein.

"Ma, is a griffin real or imaginary?"

"Imaginary."

"Well, how do you know? Maybe a penguin is imaginary. Have you ever seen one?"

"In pictures."

"They might be just artists' paintings," Dee-Dee said, "or made-up photographs. Flower Bernstein's mother lets her keep a big red parrot in her bedroom."

"Darling, we can't discuss this and cross the street at the same time," Polly said. "When you cross the street, think of the street and the cars and the traffic, and when you're safely across, then you can think about griffins and penguins. Then you can go and live with your friend Flower and her parrot, but for now, please watch where you're going."

"I don't like to stop thinking about a thing," Dee-Dee said. "I like to concentrate."

Polly sighed. The life of the higher mind had struck at least one of her children. She kissed them good-bye and watched them walk up the steps of their school. My life has been saved, she said to herself. If I can keep up this steady pace, if I can keep my eye on these appropriate sparrows, I will be safe again.

At the office Martha Nathan said, "I liked the unhappy you better."

"Don't be so negative," Polly said.

"I hate you when you're chirpy," said Martha. "I liked your dark side."

"Be a little kinder to me, will you?" Polly said. "My dark side was terrible. It was my dark night of the soul. You don't wish that on a person, do you?"

"It was more interesting," said Martha, glumly. "Where's your friend Lincoln these days?"

"In Paris," Polly said.

"Still?" said Martha. "I thought he was back."

"He's coming back soon enough," Polly said. "But I don't think I'm going to see him."

"No? Why not?"

"Oh, Martha, you can't imagine what a lot of heartbreak this thing has been. I wasn't made for it. I was made for the bosom of my family. I can't go on like this."

"Huh," said Martha. "Lucky you."

"Don't be snide with me," Polly said.

"I'm not snide," said Martha. "I'm jealous. It's very enviable to be able to make decisions and have everything fall into place."

"Now, Martha, what's your problem? You sound rambunctious."

"Spud's in California," Martha said. "He's being interviewed for a junior professorship. Lots of money and prestige."

"And?"

"California, as we know, is full of first-rate medical schools," said Martha dismally. "I applied to two of them."

"I get the picture," Polly said. "If you get married I'll make you a wedding cake."

"Yes?" said Martha. "That doesn't seem fit compensation for a lifetime of horror."

"Try to shut up, Martha," Polly said.

"I just want an interesting life," said Martha.

"No, you don't," Polly said. "I've just been having one and you wouldn't wish it on a dog."

Each day brought Lincoln closer. Polly dreaded having to face him. She hated the idea of telling him that they could no longer see each other. Perhaps in some distant future they might be friends. Polly would be able to invite Lincoln for dinner. Then she and Lincoln might look across the dinner table with a secret look—the look of friends who have secretly been lovers. Life could be made to work, with the proper intention applied to things. To have a love affair when your husband is often away and, when home, is distracted is one thing. To conduct a love affair when you and your husband have rededicated yourselves to the success of your marriage is quite another.

After all, family life was the mortar that kept the bricks together; the pitch that made the basket watertight; the chinking that kept out the wind and the weather. It was life itself, without an inch to spare. A person immersed in the realities of family life did not stop to ponder the meaning of life: that person was *in* life, up to his or her neck and beyond. The family was the beginning, the future, and the past. It protected the weak and the strong. It brought the like-minded together and gave the unalike a common cause. It gave shelter and hope. What more, Polly wondered, could a sensible person possibly want?

Henry came home early from his office, got into his ratty house clothes, made himself a drink, and sat down on the floor with Pete and Dee-Dee. To amuse them he wore his battered fishing hat. At dinner they talked about Maine while Pete made threatening noises at his meal.

"Daddy," said Dee-Dee at the table, "tell Pete to stop mashing up all his food like that. It's disgusting."

"I have to mash it down and flatten it," Pete said. "I have to beat it down."

"It isn't going to bite you," Henry said.

"In its natural state it would bite me," Pete said.

"That's a lamb chop, silly," said Dee-Dee. "Lambs don't bite."

"They don't?" said Pete. "They kick, and when they grow up they bite. Think of it, Dee-Dee. That little chop was once part of a pretty woolly lamb."

Dee-Dee had her mother's forthright gray eyes. Pete's were hazel, and had the complicated look of his father's. Dee-Dee looked at her brother straightforwardly. She knew exactly what he was going to say. She yawned and regarded him abstractly. "Your dinner was once so sweet and woolly," said Pete, "so gentle and pretty." He looked at his sister, who was completely unflapped. Tears sprang into his own eyes at the thought of such a sweet little animal, and he was unable to finish his meal.

"When are we going up to Priory, Mommy?" Dee-Dee said.

"We're all going up Memorial Day to open the house," said Polly. "And then you and Pete and Nan and Papa are going up the second week in June for the whole summer. Then I will be up for the last two weeks in July and Daddy will join us for all of August."

Henry had promised Polly that the whole month of August would be hers. He would not spend it on the telephone to New York, or in his summer study working. Lying next to Polly at night, he told her how afraid he had been that she was going to leave him, how much she meant to him, how much he loved her. As a result of this persistent wooing, Polly fell in love all over again. Her natural breath returned to her. She was being saved from the arms of another man. For every move Henry made forward, Polly retreated from the idea of Lincoln. By the time he came back she would have nothing left for him, except residual gratitude.

After dinner the family sprawled on Henry and Polly's bed. Polly sewed all the loose buttons on Henry's and the children's winter clothes before sending them out to the cleaner to be mothproofed and stored. She made lists of things to take to Maine, of spring-cleaning chores to be done. The leaves were just beginning to be out on the trees, but winter seemed very long ago to Polly. She loved getting ready for the summer. As she sorted and stacked the coats and suits and sweaters, she felt as if the past were being stored along with the winter clothes. She felt as if she, too, had shed some protective clothing.

At her feet Dee-Dee read a book about colonial children. Pete did fractions. When he concentrated, he stuck out the tip of his tongue and knitted his brow. Henry and Polly leafed through the journals stacked up on their night tables, which they never had time to read. Spring rain slipped down the windows and muffled the sound of traffic below. From time to time they could hear the whistle of the doorman hailing a taxi. The banjo clock in the hallway ticked comfortingly and rang a sweet, tenor chime on the hour.

Polly put her journal down. Henry and Pete had fallen asleep. Dee-Dee was dreaming over her book. She had dropped her shoes over the side of the bed and was wiggling her toes.

It had been a long, terrible time, and the world had gotten horribly out of kilter, but now Polly was safe again. Propped up by pillows, with her family around her, Polly thought of how much anxiety is produced by living a double life, by that frantic planning to see Lincoln, by carving out time to see him. The office had spared her a great deal of sneaking, but she had not been spared that blind, jagged longing to be with him. Her life had been thrown up into the air like a deck of cards and it was only luck, she felt, that had caused those cards to land in such a graceful pattern.

The mornings were normal, too. Polly no longer crawled out of sleep distressed, or pulled herself out of bad dreams. Contentment, something Polly had not seen for a long time, appeared on Henry's features. He did not dash off into the shower but let the children crawl over him once or twice. Henry was like a volcano: you saw his manifestations, not his deep workings. He seemed happy and ardent, and looked at Polly as if he was afraid that she would melt away in front of him. He was on his best behavior, and his every gesture announced his awareness and his dedication.

In the kitchen Pete stood on a chair and stirred the oatmeal. Dee-Dee fetched the paper. Henry made the toast and Polly made the coffee. As soon as Henry and the children were gone, Polly cleared away the dishes, made a list for Concita, finished her coffee, and went off to work. How different these mornings were from those dark, bleak winter days.

On the first warm spring morning, Polly walked to work. She walked with a steady pace. Yes, she said to herself, my life has been spared. I can go for entire days and never think about Lincoln at all. I have been angry, I have been low, I have actually sinned, but my life is not going to explode. I am the woman I used to be. Thinking about Lincoln in this frame of mind was difficult and uncomfortable. What if he did not want to give her up? If he threatened to expose her? This frightened Polly so much that she did not stop to remember that this was Lincoln Bennett, her kind and excellent friend, who not so long ago had made life bloom for her. She conjured up a Lincoln who was angry and hurt, who wanted revenge and could easily get it. He knew thousands of things he could only have known through Polly. No one, and by no one Polly meant Henry, would ever believe that she had had a love affair, but she imagined Lincoln ruining her life by making Henry believe it. How else could he have come to know the minute details of her family life, or the names of Henry's brother-in-law's cousins? She imagined the stunned, incredulous look that would cross Henry's face. His faith in her would be entirely dashed. He would lose all respect and regard. He would be justifiably horrified at her ability to deceive. For months her sense of wrongness had been kept at bay like a wolf in a distant pen. Now it sprang free and pounced on her. Need was no justification for anything. It was just the lazy, self-obsessed person's reason for doing wrong.

Her mission was clear. She would have to see Lincoln and tell him she could never see him again. She would have to do it, and as she walked down the street it seemed easy enough. She had found reviews of his show in all the French art journals. It had been a great success. He would be very much sought after when he came back. If he wanted it to, his life could change for the better. This could be a crucial time for Lincoln. Polly could help him by leaving him alone. Everything had changed. How, Polly wailed inwardly, did I let myself get so weak? Was I so bereft that I would attach myself to someone so very opposite, who hates all the things I cherish?

As she walked into the office, Martha pounced on her.

"You look nice and gloomy," she said. "Just like in the old days."

"You look pretty gloomy yourself," Polly said. "What's up?"

They walked down the hall together.

"The wonderful job Spud was interviewed for—remember?" She sighed heavily. "He got it. We're going to California. I've been accepted at both medical schools, just so fate wouldn't let me slip through its net. I found out Saturday. Spud wants to get married."

"You don't have to," Polly said.

"I thought you were a walking sandwich board in favor of," Martha said. "Spud says this is it."

"Take a deep breath and the chloroform will put you right out," said Polly. "Where are you going to do it?"

"There," said Martha. "Both our families are there. How thrilled they'll be. Sold out at last. I never thought I would come to this."

"It's not so terrible," Polly said.

"Only sometimes," said Martha.

"This is making me very sad," Polly said. "I won't have you in the office anymore."

"Maybe I won't last long," Martha said. "I'll come running back."

"You won't," Polly said. "Sometimes I think you and Spud are doing things the way they should be done—struggling along, working everything out, and *then* getting married. I think you two will be married for life."

"Just like whales," Martha said. "That's what I'm afraid of."

"If Spud can find someone to perform the ceremony while you're unconscious, you're home free," said Polly. The telephone in Martha's office rang, and she ran to answer it. As she hung up her coat, Polly thought how strange her life would be without Lincoln or Martha in it. They were the first real friends of her adult life—an elusive painter and a neurotic genius. These were not the sort of friends Polly had ever thought she would make, but she had made them. Some part of herself had reached out and there they were. Some day she would visit Spud and Martha in California. Some day perhaps she and Lincoln might be friends—a long time from now, when things were as they should be.

On Polly's desk was a letter. She could see it from the doorway. It was in Lincoln's hand, and she trembled as she opened it. She did not stop to take her coat off. It said:

Dearest D.:
I will be back Tuesday and hope I will see you Wednesday. Don't call me. Just come down. Lunch will be waiting and if you don't come I will be forced to eat it all myself.

All yours, L.

The thought of Lincoln threw Polly into a panic. How was she going to tell him? The truth was very banal: things got better with Henry and it was no longer necessary for her to have a love affair. It was as simple as that. Her heart was beating hard. It was Tuesday. She would have to wait for twenty-four hours or more until she could unburden herself.

Order was metabolic. It was chemical. It was something you were born with a propensity for, and training refined your propensity. Polly's intentions were good—she wanted an orderly, productive life, cheer and contentment for those she loved, a safe haven, a gentle hearth, a sense of security and correctness. Lincoln was the mote in her eye, the thing out of place. She was desperate to make her life work once more, in the even, calm, and joy-producing way it once had. She wanted her life back.

On Wednesday she was full of dread. Not one thing slipped past her notice. She scolded herself for dressing so carefully but she did it anyway. She felt hot and flushed, and her hands were cold. Her legs felt watery. She tried to believe that she was getting sick, but she knew that she was not.

On the bus she was restless. At work she could not concentrate. Her papers swam in front of her eyes. The clock dragged its hands around slowly. At eleven-thirty she put her coat on. It had to be done. She was full of dread. She had never broken off a love affair, or any relationship, in her life. It was an enterprise that smacked of brutality, rejection, and sadness. In the taxi on the way to Lincoln's studio, Polly tried to study her heart, which she was sure was clean and new, dedicated and rededicated to her husband and family. The idea that Lincoln's love for her was now unrequited, that she did not long for him but was dreading seeing him, filled her with sadness.

At the head of his street she annoyed the taxi driver by dropping her wallet on the floor, scattering her change, and giving him the wrong amount. Then she overcompensated with a large tip and fled without properly closing the door. As she neared Lincoln's studio her feet dragged. Her heart lurched. Her hands, in her coat pockets, were damp. She felt like a child afraid to go to school. How awful it was to feel so awful about seeing someone she had loved so much! But then, everything had changed.

Fifteen

Nothing had changed. One look at Lincoln and Polly knew it. His big shoulders, his pouty mouth, the way he squinted, the way his hair fell across his forehead, the fact that he smelled of cigar smoke and lavender aftershave.

Lincoln saw what was on her face—she was always very clear to him—and he left her alone. He took her coat but didn't kiss her. He walked down the length of his studio and she followed as if she were a guest come to view his paintings. The table was set for lunch: the usual lunch of bread, cheese, grapes, and wine. Polly's throat choked up and her heart melted. She turned to Lincoln. Nothing, nothing had changed at all. She flung herself against him.

Lunch was still on the table. Polly had called her office to say she would be out for the rest of the day, and she had called Concita to say that she had been called away to a meeting, in the unlikely event Concita should call her at the office.

Polly and Lincoln lay in Lincoln's bed. It did not feel like sin to Polly. What she felt was not precisely romantic. It was a feeling of comradeship, as if she had come home to find an old, beloved friend.

"When you came in today I thought it was all over," Lincoln said. "It was written on your face. I thought my poor heart was going to explode."

"I thought it was all over, too," said Polly.

"If you're going to cry, Dottie, you might just want to press yourself against me. I don't mind being all slithery with tears."

Polly sat up and pulled the covers around her waist.

"It's quite a sight to see you sitting there half naked with your hands folded in your lap like a little child," said Lincoln, who was leaning on his elbow looking at her.

Polly looked not at Lincoln but straight ahead.

"I thought I had everything fixed," she said. "It was all so neat: you would get over whatever it is that makes you want to live like a hermit, and I would sort things out at home, and then we would wither away from each other. Oh, Lincoln, I know I oughtn't to talk about Henry, but he was so absent from me. He always had been. It was one of the unexamined things about our marriage. I wasn't unhappy with Henry. I was unhappy about the way things were—maybe that's the same thing, anyway. But while you were gone, we pulled together. I couldn't stand it anymore. He and I have talked and talked and talked. That's not something we ever really did. I guess we didn't feel we ever needed to. As a result I conned myself into thinking that everything I felt about you was the simple result of Henry's being so far away. And maybe it was, but after all, I fell in love with *you*, and now that Henry isn't far away, I'm stuck with my feelings. I still love you. You're the friend of my heart. I never expected my life to be complicated. I expected it to be a safe, straight line. I didn't expect it to be very different from my mother's life. I love Henry and I love you. I know I'm supposed to think it's wrong, but instead I think it's *mine*. It's my destiny, and my complication. I feel like a snake, Linky, as if I've shed my old skin. I'd rather be myself and have gone through all this misery than to be whatever it was I thought I was supposed to be." She turned and gave him a fierce look. "Now I've made this campaign speech, and I haven't asked you a thing about you. Maybe you want things to change. Maybe you met someone in Paris."

"Come down here, Dot," Lincoln said. He pulled her next to him and they lay side by side, leaning on their elbows, the tips of their noses almost touching.

"I thought about all this," he said. "I know the way I live is weird. For the moment, that's how I live. I like my solitude more than anything else besides you. If I can have you the way I have you, I want it to continue. It's pointless to wonder what will happen. We could both get very sick of this. Things could change. The fact is, I love you, and I want you around me."

"Oh, Lincoln," Polly said. "It isn't easy. No matter how I feel, no matter how I feel it's mine, I'm the one who has to live a double life, and I'm the one who has to betray Henry."

Lincoln was silent.

"I mean, obviously I *can* do this. Oh, Lincoln, I want you so much. I wanted you when I was unhappy and now that I'm happy, I still want you. I know I shouldn't say these things to you."

"Keep talking," Lincoln said.

"I feel I've come out of one unhappiness and into another. Nothing ever seemed very clear to me before—just relatively smooth sailing. I love Henry. I am so used to difficult people that I never realized how difficult he was to be married to. My father is difficult and my mother never uttered a word about it—of course, she's hardly easy herself. Well, I love Henry, and I know that I still have to be connected to you. I ask myself who I am that I deserve the love of two men. I think I'm spoiled and selfish and full of entitlement. Why do I think I can get away with betraying my husband? Why am I entitled to have a love affair?"

Now Lincoln sat up. He was furious.

"What about Henry's betrayal of you?"

"Henry hasn't betrayed me," said Polly.

"Oh, yes, he has," said Lincoln. "Your entire family betrays you. I'm not so stupid that I don't know a person who's starving for affection. You were a neglected and love-starved person when I met you, and your spirit has been starved by those loathsome people whose only triumph is that they produced you or were lucky enough to have you marry them." Lincoln looked at Polly bleakly. "You're going to end up hating me for saying these things."

"Keep talking," said Polly.

"I hate Paul. I think Beate is just plain unkind and insensitive. I'd hate your brother Henry, except he's such a dip. I think it's a good thing Andreya pretends not to speak English or else we might find out what a jerk she is. Why should a lovable person like you worry about being lovable? You fetch and carry and worry, and they get the good of it. Your parents want to keep you off balance, so that you will always be their perfect little Polly, ever striving to be kinder, better, and more repressed to make sure they'll all love you. What do these people do for you? Do they know you? They give you a little pat on the back and you think the doors of heaven have opened up."

Now Polly was silent. She looked at Lincoln with a kind of hunger. He was all hers—the first thing she had ever had of her own. He was her champion, the person who spoke against others in her behalf. The world Polly lived in was a made world. She had been born into most of her serious relationships. The one she had chosen—Henry Demarest—was a choice very close to home.

But Lincoln was her own. She had gone out and found him, all by herself. He was the first and only serious relationship she had ever had outside her family. He was her secret, her treasure, the thing she did not have to share. They had had to make up everything themselves. And so, as Lincoln said, Polly had been Bennettized, and he had been Solo-Millered. They knew each other from a private angle to which only they had access. There was no larger context for their friendship but friendship, which is the lot of strangers who fall in love. It was an entirely volitional relationship, and it lived outside the law.

Polly had never dreamed of a life like this. Her goals had been modest and in line with what she felt destined for: a husband, two children, a strong family, and a month's summer holiday in Maine. Once she was married, her life had been so accomplished that all she had to do was live it. But it turned out that life was not a straight path. You woke up on the wrong side of the law with the right set of feelings. How had she ever conned herself into thinking that she could give Lincoln up? She knew very well what her feelings were and they did not fit into her neat life. They did not incorporate with anything else. They made her life more difficult and often brought her terrible pain. But that came with the territory. She loved him.

She ate her lunch wearing only her slip. These slips endeared her ferociously to Lincoln. They were old-fashioned full slips made of cotton. Their soberness and the setting Lincoln saw them in were so poignant a combination that he often felt a little silly with love and found himself grinding his teeth. Now

Polly sat at his table, her hair mussed, looking like the model in the studio, the girl who came to have her portrait painted and then fell madly in love with the painter. They sat quietly. Lincoln was very happy to smoke a cigar and sketch Polly as she sat drinking her coffee contentedly.

It was surely not right to feel this happy, but it was also undeniable. The air outside was smoky with spring rain. The street was gray. The warehouses across the street were wet. Polly put down her cup. The pure feelings one had in adult life were complicated and mitigated, and they were dearly paid for, but worth everything they cost.

Late in the afternoon, when she was dressed to go home, Lincoln gave her the letters he had written to her in Paris but had not sent.

"I thought I was losing you," Lincoln said. "I had such a lonely little hotel room, but it would have been so cozy if you had been with me. It was an attic room with a square bed and a red comforter. It rained almost every day. I would come home at night tired out from hanging the show, or scared at the idea of the show, and I would lie in bed and think of you in your bed on your side of the Atlantic, reappraising us. I thought when I came home I might not find you."

"Here I am," said Polly.

"I brought you a little present," Lincoln said. "Put it on." It was a gold medallion of a cupid on a chain made of woven silk.

"I have something else to show you," Lincoln said. "It's your portrait."

He pulled it out from behind a stack of canvases. It was based on the drawings in his sketch book. There she was, in her gray skirt and sweater, standing in a doorway as if just about to enter the room. In the room was a flock of animals—

a lamb, a tiger, a mouse, a gray-and-white terrier, a long-haired tabby cat, an owl, and a fox. There was a large bowl of poppies next to a fireplace. Lincoln had added two babies with curly hair, sitting in a basket with their arms around each other. The light in the room was greenish yellow, like the light before a storm.

"I finished it a while ago," Lincoln said. "It's yours but I want to keep it here."

Tears sprang into Polly's eyes.

"I have nothing to give you," she said.

"You give me yourself," Lincoln said. "That's quite enough."

Sixteen

Early Sunday morning Wendy called, waking Polly to tell her that Beate had gone into labor.

"How lovely for her," Polly said sleepily.

"I'm all in a dither," said Wendy, whose usually firm, decided voice sounded rattled and uncertain.

"Calm down, Mum," yawned Polly. "You've had grandchildren before."

"Well, come to breakfast early," Wendy said. "I'm quite frazzled."

Polly sank back into the pillows. She had no intention of going early to her parents'. Although Wendy didn't say it, the fact was plain: Polly having a baby and Paul's wife having a baby were not the same thing at all. If I had sixty babies, Polly thought, and Paul had a baby the size of a walnut, his would be more sublime in every way.

She yawned again. Today she had actually set the morning aside for herself. Henry was in the kitchen making coffee and giving the children their pancakes. Polly was worn out. In addition to everything else—everything else being Lincoln and Henry—the spring report was now printed, bound, and had been presented to the Board of Education. It had been a considerable job, and, for the first time, Polly had made it known. The children had actually tiptoed around her when she worked at her desk, and Henry got out of bed every morning and made the coffee.

She sent Henry and the children on ahead to breakfast, reminding them to stop at the bakery for Henry, Sr.'s Swiss peasant bread and Wendy's *pain au chocolat*. For the first time in living memory, Polly was going to be late.

When she arrived the mood was official. The subject of birth was in the air, and Wendy was clearly displeased with Polly, whom she allowed to peck her cheek. Henry, Sr., seemed not fully present. He wore the expression of someone meditating on art, or justice, or freedom.

Wendy was telling the table at large at what time Beate had actually gone into labor.

"Do we have to talk about this?" Henry, Jr., said. "I think it's disgusting."

"It isn't disgusting, you silly ape," Polly said. "You saw me in the hospital after Pete and Dee-Dee. Did that look disgusting?"

"Those were *babies*," Henry, Jr., said. "I mean all the gore and blood and screaming before the babies."

"It isn't like that," Polly said. "Is it, Mum?"

"I'm afraid I don't remember," said Wendy. "I had you all in twilight sleep."

"What is twilight sleep?" Andreya asked.

"Oh, a lovely sort of half haze they used to put you in," Wendy said. "It was the fashion at the time. It made everything look rather bluish. Perhaps that was the color of the delivery room. All I can remember from each of your births was that heavenly Dr. Marshammer smiling at me."

"Dr. Faulhaber," Polly said.

"Now how do you remember that?" Wendy said.

"Because his granddaughter Linda is our pediatrician," Polly said.

"Is she? I never put the two together, since I always thought of him as Dr. Marshammer and her as Dr. Faulhaber," Wendy said. "The birth itself, Andreya dear, seemed rather unworldly in twilight sleep, not like all this natural childbirth, which always seems to me so rugged."

"It's wonderful," said Polly.

"I thought it was wonderful, too," Henry Demarest said. "I saw the whole thing."

"Geez, that's really disgusting," said Henry, Jr.

"When my brother was born at home," Andreya said, "the nurse brought the *Nachgeburt*—this is the afterbirth—in on a white porcelain dish."

"Can't we talk about something else?" Henry, Jr., said.

"If you can't stand it, go into the library and wait for Pete and Dee-Dee to come and play with you," Polly said.

"I don't think certain things are *quite* table talk," Wendy said.

"Nachgeburt," said Henry, Jr.

"I *am* worried. I hope all that placid Swiss birth-environment thing they feel so strongly about works out," said Wendy.

"Oh, for goodness' sake," said Polly. "Having babies in the ordinary way is good enough for most people."

"Polly," said Wendy, "be more patient."

"Mother, I don't think you know how often and how persistently the subject of this placid-birth nonsense comes up. This whole thing has the effect of trying to make me think I had my babies all wrong. And you go along with it!"

"Darling," said Wendy, "she's much older."

"So what?" said Polly. "The night before Pete was born we

had ten people for dinner, and the day before Dee-Dee was born I went to help you go shopping, for upholstery fabric, remember?"

Pete and Dee-Dee, meanwhile, had begun to fidget, and were excused from the table.

"You can tell they never had a placid birth environment," said Henry Demarest.

"I think it's snooty of Beate and Paul not to come to dinner, and not to go with us to a restaurant, for fear of poisoning their little twins. I think they're pious and preachy and very silly," Polly said.

"I didn't know you felt that way, Polly," said Wendy.

"Yes, you did," Polly said. "We talked about this once before. You know exactly how I feel."

"Aw, come on, Pol," said Henry, Jr.

"Listen, Henry," said Polly. "You probably won't even be required to go to the hospital to visit. You won't have to show up with an expensive baby blanket. You don't have to do anything, but I will have to sit around and listen to Paul and Beate tell me how superior the birth of their children was to the sloppy, noisy, incorrect birth of mine. I'll have to hear how the champagne I drank while I was pregnant will turn Pete into a bank robber or Dee-Dee into an unwed mother. You don't have to put up with this and you aren't expected to, but I am, and I'm awfully tired of it."

The horizonal look of disapproval flickered through Henry, Sr.'s eyes. He did not approve of bickering at the table. He did not approve of dissension of any sort.

"I'm sure you'll do what's proper to do," he intoned.

"I'm not so sure I will," said Polly, building a sandwich. "Somebody pass me the capers."

Nothing more was said, but Polly knew what was to come. Wendy would be icy cold for several days, and then Polly would receive a lecture. Wendy did not believe in sibling rivalry or favoritism, for all she practiced it. If Polly did not knuckle under, she would be asked out to lunch by her father, who would further lecture her. The family would be in a minor uproar. The idea of these lectures and this commotion had kept Polly nicely in line. Now she did not seem to care. She had no intention of listening to anyone's lectures, and she was not going to buy an expensive pair of baby blankets. She would doubtless end up baking a cake or taking a covered dish to Paul and Beate—that was the proper thing to do—but at the first mention of birth environments, she was going home.

As they sat drinking coffee, the telephone rang. It was Paul to announce that the Solo-Miller twins had been born, a boy and a girl. They would be called Matilda Zoë and Paul Heinrich. The little girl would be called Zoë and the boy Henry so as not to have two Pauls in one household.

At this news Wendy touched her eyes with her napkin. "Oh, dear. Oh, dear," she said, and seemed quite overcome with emotion.

Polly thought of Pete and Dee-Dee upstairs. Their grandparents doted upon them, but they had not doted upon Polly for producing such fine children. Whereas Paul—well, Paul had provided them with a priceless treasure. After all, daughters are expected to provide their parents with grandchildren. And Paul had always been so odd and unmarried that it made the event twice as wonderful. Polly looked at her mother. There was nothing you could do with Wendy, Polly realized, but she did not have to honor Wendy's feelings, especially when they hurt *her* feelings.

"Oh, come on, Mum," she said. "It's just another pair of grandchildren. Besides, another Henry will give us all a lot of confusion to cope with."

Wendy wiped her eyes. "I'm afraid I'm overwhelmed by the idea of having a grandchild called Zoë," she said. "I don't like an exotic name."

Meanwhile, Henry, Sr., reported, Paul had given specific orders. To ensure continuance of the placid birth environment, Beate would not see visitors at the hospital, nor would she see them for the first two weeks at home.

"According to their Dr. Ping," said Henry, Sr., "the babies must be kept in a softly lit room, with soft music, and wrapped in soft cotton blankets, I think Paul said."

"Maybe they should keep them in the fridge," said Henry, Jr.

"I think it sounds very intelligent," said Henry, Sr., who thought Paul was a normal person.

"I think it sounds very boring for the babies," said Henry Demarest.

Polly had stopped thinking about Beate's placid birth. She was thinking about Lincoln. They had arranged not to see each other on Sundays, since it put too much of a strain on Polly, who was running out of reading seminars.

She looked around the table. She smiled at Henry Demarest and realized that to marry her he had had to take his place at the family table, and he had done so graciously and generously. Perhaps that wall of Solo-Millers had been oppressive to him, yet he had fitted in.

This was her family, her tribe, her flesh. She felt not forced to love them, or condemned to be angry at them, but as if she were merely seeing them. Her place at this table was optional —she did not have to be there if she did not want to. But she did want to. Martha Nathan believed that strife got you from one part of your life to the next. Polly was not sure what her strife had produced. Her heart did not feel light, but free. If you were forced to experience the terrible things in life—loneliness, deprivation, anxiety, the fear that everything is going to be taken away from you—it left you tempered like steel and strong enough to feel anything. She was not going to be her old self and she was going to live with a certain amount of certain discomfort. If you were going to have a love affair you had to endure the fears and trials that went with the job—like a coal miner or a lion tamer.

She felt some new self emerging out of her terrible sorrow, and she did not know what it would be like, but it would be idiosyncratically hers. Her family did not know the secrets of her innermost heart and there was no reason to tell them. Furthermore, they did not deserve to know. If she changed, they would have to change. She was not their old Polly anymore, and never would be again.

It had been arranged that Henry, Jr., and Andreya would take the children kite-flying. Squeals from the study upstairs reminded everyone that breakfast was over, and that it was time to go to the park. Pete and Dee-Dee came bounding down the stairs.

"It's all that champagne you drank during pregnancy," Henry Demarest said to Polly.

"I'm sure it was the lobster Newburg," said Polly. "Pete and Dee-Dee. Listen to this. You have two new cousins. Beate and Uncle Paul have had their twins. They're called Zoë and Paul, but Paul will be called Henry."

"Zoë," said Pete. "What a dumb name."

The children did not find this news thrilling. They would have been much more enthralled if Polly had told them that a beagle puppy was coming to live with them.

The children were helped on with their jackets. It was spring, but there was still a slight chill in the air. Off they went—Henry, Jr., and Andreya, Polly and Henry Demarest and the children—to the park.

Henry, Jr., liked a plain, ordinary kite. He bought them at the toy store and made them more aerodynamic at home. He had loaned Henry Demarest his second-best kite—an old army weather kite. Andreya had made herself a box kite out of pink linen, and for each of the children she and Henry, Jr., had bought a Japanese kite—Pete's in the shape of a dragon, and Dee-Dee's in the shape of a fish.

Polly stood on a little rise and watched. I am a fallen woman, she said. I am wearing my husband's grandmother's wedding ring as well as a medallion of a cupid given to me by my illicit lover. She could not help it, but her heart was full of love—for Henry, for Lincoln, for her brother and sister-in-law and parents and for her children.

All the kites went right up. Henry, Jr.'s, being more aerodynamic than the others, went higher. Henry Demarest's sailed up magisterially. Andreya's bobbled up, and then hung sweetly in the sky. Polly thought of Lincoln's kite, which hung on the wall of his studio, black and silver in the shape of a sting ray, with the two mean little red eyes Lincoln had painted on it.

The children's kites zigzagged. The dragon's green tail rattled in the wind and the fish wriggled. At the sight of these jaunty, ornamental kites, Polly's eyes filled with tears. The dragon had been made so that it would swoop, and when it did, Polly felt her heart break open to love and pain, and to the complexity of things.

No kite, of course, had been given to her to fly, but she felt as excited and grateful as if it had.